THE
FASCINATION

Money, Power, Greed, Sex, Fear, Addiction

BOB RENTERSON

authorHOUSE®

AuthorHouse™ UK
1663 Liberty Drive
Bloomington, IN 47403 USA
www.authorhouse.co.uk
Phone: 0800 047 8203 (Domestic TFN)
*   +44 1908 723714 (International)*

Published by AuthorHouse 02/27/2020

ISBN: 978-1-7283-8721-5 (sc)
ISBN: 978-1-7283-8722-2 (e)

*To my family, Alex and the Market
Tavern, Sandbach, thank you.*

Contents

Sergey—Moscow

The bodyguard lifted his tattooed left arm and squinted down at the luminous dial on his old Russian army-issue watch, his blue eyes flashing in the dimly lit corridor, in the labyrinth that sat beneath Sergey's lap-dancing lounge in Moscow. The hands pointed out 10:35 in the evening, and Yuri, the wearer, was keen on another nicotine intake.

Yuri glanced over at his colleague and put two fingers to his mouth as he headed for the rear door. He grimaced as he walked past Sergey's office, where the black leather studded door was slightly ajar, drawing a stream of diagonal light across the darker corridor. He caught one of the two girls in the room panting out, "Oh yes, oh yes, oh yes. I'm coming. Don't stop."

Yuri pulled on a heavy brown overcoat and drew back a thick-lined curtain as he opened the door into the backyard area of the club.

The bitter cold air filled his lungs and took his breath away. Snowflakes whirled around in the air, dancing like wood shavings in a timber factory, jostling about until they joined the white carpet beneath. He lit up his cigarette and took a deep draw down into his lungs, exhaling some ten seconds later.

Sergey stood, black jeans straddled around his ankles as he clasped the white buttocks of the naked twenty-year-old Latvian girl who was bent like a hairpin, hands clasping the edge of his large oak desk. Sergey was rocking in and out of her as she gasped, insincerely, for more. He pulled out and beckoned her onto the table and took her doggy style as another girl leaned in behind them to lick his balls and anus.

Sweat dripped from Sergey's temple, sliding past the bulging veins on his forehead and down into the crack of her beautifully formed arse. As he pounded away, he licked his index finger and slipped it into the girl's bleached starfish. She squealed, this time quite sincerely. He swung out and round, exploding into the other girl's expectant and open mouth.

Yuri looked up into the whale-coloured sky, flicked his butt end into the white, and re-entered. His earpiece buzzed.

"Yuri, the banker is here to see Sergey."

"What the fuck is he doing here again?" Yuri replied in his dry rasp.

"Fuck knows. He wants to see Sergey," the doorman replied.

"Send him down."

Yuri draped the overcoat back onto the wall hook and headed towards the strip of light.

"Sergey?" he shouted into the room.

The door swung open, and the two girls stepped out and disappeared into the greyness.

"Yes, Yuri?" came an almost breathless response.

"The banker is here again and wants to speak with you," said Yuri.

Sergey raised his eyebrows. "Why?"

"He says he will only speak with you."

Another guard had escorted the banker down into the basement. Yuri stopped them and frisked the banker, who was a lean six-footer dressed in a dark suit, white shirt, and red tie.

"Send him in," said Sergey.

The banker, eyes half-closed to the brighter lights of the office, walked into Sergey's command centre. The walls were concrete slabs decorated with a number of oil paintings of nude women. The ceiling was black, with eight spotlights pointed towards the scarlet carpet. The desk took centre stage, a large black executive chair behind it. Two black-leather sofas lined the walls to the left and right. At the rear of the room was another desk, decked out with a bank of computer screens flickering through CCTV images of the club, naked dancers, and the swirling snow outside. To either side of this were black metal filing cabinets. The main desktop was clear, bar a small white-lace G-string waiting for its owner. A large cast-iron radiator was to the left of the door.

Sergey smiled with a flash of exceptionally white teeth as he readjusted his crotch with his hand. He nodded to Yuri, who left the room.

Several minutes had passed. Shouting erupted from the room, and then two shots rang out. Yuri and another guard drew guns and tentatively shoved the door open, swinging their extended gun-carrying arms, looking for a target. Sergey was sitting on the edge of his desk, gun in hand, shaking his head, a sick grin across his face. The banker was on the sofa to the right, his neck twisted back towards the wall and half of his head missing, blood draining down his shirt, making his tie indistinguishable.

3

The guards lowered their weapons.

"Fucker wanted more money. We'll need another banker for laundering. Stupid fuck. Tidy this mess, pack him up, and take him to the meat factory," Sergey ordered.

You didn't change deals with Sergey, Yuri thought. This wasn't the first time and wouldn't be the last that someone met their demise in this room. The concrete walls had been suitably sealed, so cleaning the splatter wouldn't take long. Yuri was pleased when Sergey had invested in a meat factory. Lugging bodies down to the river, heads and hands missing, or trying to dig graves in frozen ground had never been to Yuri's liking. The meat factory was neat, simple, and quick.

Sergey was wiping the CCTV history—not that the police would ever bother him.

Hans—South Africa

Hans awoke to the morning sun and the gurgling of his fifth son, who was soon to be searching out the nipples of Hans's beautiful wife, Sabrina.

Hans gently eased himself up onto his left elbow and gazed down at Sabrina. Her long black hair glimmered in the sunlight as the rays danced through the floor-to-ceiling windows, which made up one complete wall of the bedroom. How lucky he felt.

The cool breeze of the air conditioning drifted across the satin bed sheets, and under the sheets, Hans could see his wife's nipples rise like small erupting cupcakes in an oven.

Sabrina began to stir as the child's murmurs became louder. Hans reached out to cradle Carl, less than a month old but with the same jet-black hair as his spouse.

"Good morning, my love," he said as Sabrina's brilliant green eyes set upon him and lit up. Carl immediately let out a spirited yelp, and Hans passed him to Sabrina for yet another feed. He watched intently at this miracle, without speaking, a wide smile across his face showing no teeth.

Sabrina was just thirty-five years of age and had met Hans when she worked as a chemist at his father's company.

Back then, she was twenty-four, and Hans had been thirty-one. She had narrowly missed running Hans over, or so she thought, in the office car park as she reversed without really paying any attention. He had feigned injury, flailing over the trunk of her car like a wounded animal. She was really shaken and even more so when he burst into laughter at her tears. When he saw that she was getting very annoyed, he began apologising profusely.

Sabrina had no idea who this very handsome and athletic-looking man might be, but she remained incensed.

When she returned to the car park that evening, there was a white rose pinned under one of her windscreen wipers, with a note that reiterated how truly sorry he was for playing the fool. She smiled, having realised that she could have easily knocked him over and hurt him.

The next morning, Hans was walking just in front of Sabrina as they went to enter the company building. He kindly swung round and held the door for her. She wondered if he knew she was there the entire time. He smiled, and she thanked him for the rose. Hans asked whether she would risk a drink with him one evening.

Sabrina thought long and hard and said, "Perhaps. Call me. Here is my number."

Hans called later that afternoon, and they arranged to go out the following evening. He took her to a smart, but not ostentatious, local restaurant. She found out that he had started work at the plant about eighteen months ago but had been on a number of external courses. He was single and had served in the military. "Having been a bit of a handful," as he put it, in his younger years, his father had insisted he remain after National Service until he had calmed down.

There was no love lost between him and his father, and he felt that his father's decision was more to hurt his wife, Hans's mother. Hans was now training in sales management in the executive office above the plant.

Sabrina felt like she had known Hans for years. He listened intently to what she had to say and spoke confidently about life. The night had been so easy-going, and they seemed to have many things in common. Hans was very knowledgeable about the work that she did and also had a good affinity with horses; she was a keen rider and eventer. Riding was one of Sabrina's favourite pastimes, and she did it most weekends. Hans also rode and occasionally played polo.

The evening finished on a high, and they shared a passionate kiss and embrace on the doorstep of her home as he dropped her off.

She saw him later the following day, walking along the main hallway and peering into her lab, making funny faces through the glass partition when no one was looking. As he moved on, Sabrina overheard some of the other technicians mention that he was the owner's son. She blushed and suddenly felt very uncomfortable.

They had arranged to meet that evening, and Hans apologised for not mentioning it. *So sincere*, she had thought. But he, too, felt uncomfortable about being the boss's son. Sabrina said she needed some time to think things through, but after a couple of days, she realised she wanted to see how things progressed with this lovely man.

· · · · · · · · ● · · · · · · · · ·

Sabrina reached out with her bronzed arm and held Hans's hand. "Hi, baby, did you sleep well?"

Hans smiled an even broader smile, with a flash of white teeth, and nodded. He kissed Sabrina fully on the lips. As he rose from the bed, his tanned six-pack rippled, and his biceps looked like small rugby balls as they pushed his immaculate frame upwards. He was six feet two inches, with cropped blond hair and blue eyes, small long nose, and a broad, dimpled chin that was clean-shaven across soft, smooth skin. There wasn't an ounce of fat on his body. He dressed in blue shorts and a white tee shirt.

"I'll get Hannah to boil some eggs, with some toast," he said, disappearing down the spiral staircase, and as he did, he heard his other sons stirring with shouts of "Mummy, Daddy, where are you? Time to get up!" He and Sabrina had been busy; the other four boys were two, five, seven, and ten, all blond and green eyed, eyes from Sabrina, the hair from Hans; all were tall for their age, especially David, the eldest. He grabbed the two-year-old and hurtled down the main staircase to the kitchen, with the other three in hot pursuit.

Sabrina finished off with Carl and placed him back into his cot as she headed off for a quick shower before breakfast arrived.

Hannah, the maid, was already preparing the variety of breakfasts for each member of the family. Hans placed George into his high chair. Michael at age five, Sean at seven, and David raced their father to the pool, where Titus, Hannah's husband and general house butler, was waiting to ensure that all went well.

The house, with white-washed walls shimmering in the sun and grey tiled roofing, stood in manicured emerald lawns surrounded by palm trees, overlooking the coast on the Eastern Cape of South Africa, some sixty miles south of Durban. The pool straddled the back of the property, its curves following that of the house, which bowed out from its French windows which led to the short walk to the pool's white steps, which arced out into the bright blue water.

Hans felt the warm morning sun on his torso and dived into the pool, relishing the water riding over his body. The three young boys plunged into the warm water and wrestled with Hans. Titus joined them, and as had become customary, Hans swirled round to start his twenty-five-lap marathon.

After the pool came breakfast; Hannah made sure the boys put on dry shorts, and then they all sat down on the cushioned seats at the counter and ate a varying combination of cereals, with George looking on, all smiles. Sabrina would catnap for some of the morning, given the nightly feeds.

It was now seven thirty in the morning. Hans showered and dressed in a blue suit and white short-sleeved shirt; he had business meetings most of the day, and casual would not do, although the shirt would help to keep him cool.

Sabrina drew him in, and their tongues played the fandango; he snuggled into her, and as Carl snoozed, he slid his tongue down her still extended tummy and belly button until he found a small cusp of hair and dug deeper into her now very wet mound. It had been some time, and she came quickly.

Hans knew Sabrina had no appetite for women; he disappeared to wash his face and returned kneeling down onto the bed and kissed Sabrina's now dozing forehead and then Carl's, who was now cushioned up against Sabrina's breast. He placed a white rose from their garden on the pillow next to her.

The drive to the office from the large estate was thirty-five minutes; the air conditioning was cool on Hans's face as his chauffeur, Simon, headed along the almost empty freeway.

Simon had been employed by the company for twenty-seven years and did all of the running about that was needed. He picked Hans up each morning and drove him back in the evenings and to any meetings during the day and night.

Simon was in his sixties; Hans hadn't sought to find out his age exactly. and it had never been volunteered, but they usually had good and frequent chats about world events in general, cricket, rugby, and any other sport that South Africa was excelling in at the time.

The chemicals company was handed down when his father had died in an accident some seven years before; the company had grown large over the years and had given Hans and his family a tremendous lifestyle, even more than Sabrina could have imagined, given that profits didn't seem to be that large.

The dark metallic blue Mercedes S class pulled up to the security gate, and Hans showed his face, with a smile and hearty "Good morning," to two of the security guards at the gate.

"Good morning, sir" came the immediate stereo response, as his car was waved through the rising barrier.

Hans strode through the reception, his leather soles sliding along on the black marbled floor as he passed the maple wood reception, greeting all on his way to the block of elevators that would whisk him to his top-floor office suite and boardroom. It was going to be a busy day, and Helen, his personal assistant, met him as he exited the elevator, tipped off by reception that he was on his way. Helen was a tall, leggy twenty-eight-year-old blonde, with green eyes and a penchant for short skirts and tight blouses; Hans used this weapon to warm up his suppliers at meetings.

Coffee, juice, and iced water were in place in his office, as usual.

He looked went over his diary first off and then went into his first meeting as the day cascaded forth.

Hans finished the afternoon in the office; as always, he took an untraceable cell phone from his drawer. The cell phone SIM card was replaced by Hans every two weeks. The new number would then be sent to his contact list, under an access code.

There was a coded message from one of his agents in the United States; he was needed on business. This was urgent. As Hans placed the phone back into the drawer and locked it, a wave of excitement and anticipation came over him, just like a poker player who's been dealt a royal flush.

Hans's heart rate increased significantly, and he had a rush of butterflies in his midsection; then he felt the trepidation and fear—overwhelmed again by the excitement. His mind could not focus on anything else now; he needed the details, the information that would follow. Planning had to start immediately.

He would be sent an encoded file to an encrypted email address; this would disappear from existence once he got the information. The file was nothing but numbers. He would translate them with a code that was maintained on his laptop. The code was changed after every assignment.

This software interpreted the core details of people, towns, cities, itineraries, and updates which would flow throughout his new assignment. Less delicate information would flow normally.

Hans now had a rough outline of where and when he would be required. He made out a quick note of dates and listed a number of suppliers he would like to meet when in the UK, Belgium, and the US. He also wanted to stop off via Switzerland on his way back to South Africa, and appended this to the note for Helen to handle the following morning.

The drive back home was unhindered, and Hans was back in time for a swim with the family before dinner. All of the boys gathered around Carl's cot for the family bedtime story. David and George would then have one from Hans, whilst Sabrina read a further story to Mike and Sean.

After story time was over and the kids were all in bed, Hans sat down with Sabrina on the veranda and muttered a few things about his day; he asked how the boys had been. The summer holidays were ending, and they had had a great time just messing around the pool today.

"I'll need to visit a few suppliers later in October," he said to Sabrina, "a few days in Europe and then the States, fourteen to twenty-five days at the most."

"I thought you had finished your business trips for the rest of the year," Sabrina replied. "You do work so hard, Hans."

"I'll hurry back, so keep it warm for me," Hans said, chuckling.

"I am beginning to feel a little better, and I'm sure you can warm me up before you go," Sabrina retorted.

The next day, was arranged for Hans's trip in October: first to Heathrow, then the hotel, the Connaught, to acclimatise. How lovely, he thought. A meeting in London, and the next two days in Brussels, then back for more meetings in London if possible, and a flight out the next day to New York; he was booked into the Peninsula and then onto the Beverley Hills Hotel in Los Angeles. LA to New York then to South Africa and home via Switzerland.

His day at the office had been without incident, and the next day was Saturday; he was taking David and Sean out for a day trip in the morning. Sabrina was going to spend her day with their other sons.

Joe—New York

Joe Scattini looked down the length of Wall Street, a sneer of disdain across his face. In this small stretch of concrete, a seventh of a mile long, rested the hopes and wealth of the greatest country in the world, individuals with incomes greater than the gross domestic product (GDP) of many countries. He sneered down on the passing ants on their way home for the weekend; it was only four forty-five, umbrellas raised against the teaming rain, jousting along like two black lava flows sliding against each other on the sidewalk. He could see the spire of Trinity through the grey and sorry weather.

His office was on the penultimate floor of the bank's New York headquarters, the penthouse floor housing the bank's opulent dining and meeting rooms, decorated with gold leaf wallpaper, plush carpets, antiques, and works of art. Joe had been told that each meeting room had cost over one hundred thousand dollars. This had been Joe's home for the last sixteen years. The leather-topped desk had belonged to his father, a relic shipped in from Italy, that was positioned diagonally in the corner, so Joe could see the door and also take in the view through the office windows.

Joe was the first generation of his Italian family to be born in America; the rest of the room was furnished around this well-worn piece of history: a few glass-topped mahogany wall tables, a green leather Chesterfield sofa with two matching chairs, and an antique bookcase, housing several first editions and many other leather-bound literary masterpieces (not that Joe had read any of them).

Joe thought back to those early days down in Little Italy, where his parents had run a bakery and restaurant, bringing up seven kids, six boys and one daughter. There had been Joseph Junior, the oldest, who had died when he was seventeen; next the daughter, Maria, just over a year younger; Giuseppe was the youngest at seven, then Joe (technically another Joseph but shortened for clarity). Junior had been killed by some Irish hoodlums when Joe was ten.

His mother never recovered from this and died when Joe was just thirteen. This had been devastating on the whole family but particularly so on their father, having lost his eldest son and then the wife he doted on.

However, somehow, they clubbed together and made things work.

Maria and the three other brothers, Tony, a year older than Joe, Alonzo, three years senior to Joe, and Emilio, now the oldest boy, a year younger than Maria, continued to run several restaurants and the bakery business, which had grown into a large commercial concern supplying hotels and restaurants around the city. Joseph Senior lived in an apartment above the bakery; he was eighty-four years of age but still keen to be helping out in the early hours of the morning, baking bread.

Giuseppe had left the family business but worked closely with Joe; he set up an investment group, which ran a spider web of businesses, many of which had benefited from Joe's patronage.

The loss of their brother, followed by their mother, who had become an empty walking shell of her previous self, probably ensured that the family remained close over so many years, always looking out for one another.

Joe had always looked up to Joseph Jnr, his hero and mentor, in those early years. The Irish hoodlums were no more; Joe had seen to that. Joe had maintained a deep-seated loathing of the Irish and ensured none progressed in his employ.

Joseph Snr had met Mary, Joe's mother, on the boat from Italy into New York; both were seventeen. Mary was travelling to join members of her family in the States and Joseph to find his fortune, as Italy was in disarray after the war. It was an immediate mutual attraction, Joseph had a confident swagger; he was six feet tall and had dark brown eyes, which danced in the light and gave the hint of fun as he smiled. Mary had long black hair, framing a perfect olive complexion and green/blue eyes. She was petite at about five feet two inches tall and very slim. Joseph sported a mass of dark brown hair, swept back and glistening in the sun's dancing reflection bouncing off the ocean.

The two gradually got to know each other. Mary was captivated by Joseph's drive and enthusiasm. They would speak for hours on end about what New York would be like, the skyscrapers, the opportunity, the bustle of it all, then the bakeries and restaurants that Joseph was hoping to open. His father had run a busy bakery in Naples, supplying all of the finest restaurants and hotels; the bakery had a small cafe attached to it, serving many kinds of pastry.

His father had died in the war, and the business had been left for his mother, Sophia, and the three sons to run during this very difficult period. Joseph was the eldest of the three and had taken on the mantle of man of the house and protector. The end of the war had brought a lot of relief, but life would never be the same. Sophia was quite a beauty and had caught the eye of an American Army sergeant. This had caused some discord amongst the boys, as they felt this was disrespectful to their late father, but he had been a heavy drinker with a nasty temper, so although they welcomed the fact that he would not be back, they also had difficulty grasping how their mother could fraternise with the enemy.

Joseph also felt that the situation usurped his position as the family head, but at the same time, ahead in years of maturity, he realised that his mother was happy. Frank, the American, was a warm and charismatic man who had been a baker in the States. He always played the student with Joseph, always complimenting his work, rather than the teacher. He integrated well with the younger boys, both of whom were under ten, but treated Joseph as a man, an equal.

This relationship had also given Joseph the chance of heading to the United States and Frank's extended family, and both men felt this separation would be good, as Sophia's emotions were always torn between the two of them in very different ways.

Before leaving the ship on Ellis Island, Mary and Joseph exchanged addresses, and the rest is very much history, a large family, successful bakeries, and now several restaurants. Trips to the homeland had become an annual event from the eighties onwards, and the Naples clan had grown into quite a dynasty, with Joseph's two brothers having fathered eleven children between them and now were grandfathers and great-grandfathers to twenty-four children. Family gatherings were a spectacular yet intimate affairs; most of the members got on tremendously well, and summer weekends in the hills, where the family had invested in a large hunting lodge surrounded by olive groves, were always a busy affair with constant visitors.

Early life in New York was hard, but the family supported each other as best as they could; Maria took on the motherly role, Emilio went out to work, and their father came back from some distant place in his own mind to reengage.

Joe had always been bright and was doted on by his sister; Maria had instilled a confidence in Joe that he was untouchable. Maria had nothing but compliments for Joe, and he proudly strutted around. This coupled with his ability to engage with girls on an emotional level made him a big hit. He was also hard as nails and would never give ground in any fight or conflict. No one crossed him, because they knew they may win a battle, but a war would ensue that would probably mean someone had to die.

Joe never stood down, and people knew about the Irishmen that were no more.

Joe was fifty-nine now, with crystal clear black pools, with a tinge of green, for eyes, which could drop a rhino at fifty yards. There was a depth of sadness in his handsome face, which was difficult to fathom, but possibly emanated from an overall frowning expression. He had a full head of silver-streaked black hair, swept back with a right-of-centre parting. Joe had always been quite small and was just less than five feet seven inches tall; he made up for this in bark and, as all who knew him, with bite, as well.

Joe turned and placed his hands on the top of the leather executive chair as Frank entered the room. Joe exploded into expletives, peering out of the windows, now heavily speckled with rain droplets, neck extended like a buzzard, and addressed the world as a whole:

"Fuck this ongoing recession, fuck the Russians, fuck the Asians, fuck the politicians, and fuck the spineless shareholders of corporate America, fuck everybody."

Frank knew not to interject and just stood there, a statue, waiting for the eruption to finish. This little man on his pedestal, seeking to tell the rest of the world how to behave.

As divisional president of corporate finance and lending, Joe had turned the fortunes of the bank around, following the debacle of the last recession and the heavy provisioning that had been required in capital markets. "Those traders were just two-a-penny and plain fucking useless," Joe would say, "all pumped up making money when my dog could do the same during the good times. At least my fucking dog could see a recession looming."

Now a continuing credit squeeze and the bureaucrats up top had decided to sell his division, his company, the division that had over the last decade become 35 per cent of the bank's overall profit generation, a division that had the best income-to-overhead ratio in the financial world (well, in New York, anyway), a division that had given all of those greedy bastards huge annual bonuses.

Credit decisions on new and established lending were becoming unbearable, and the business was slowly being strangled, as his bank and others starved the corporate world of cash. These were usually good times for Joe, as he would be in a position to swallow up the competition like a shark during a feeding frenzy and, at the same time, hide so much in the purchase price accounting, as well as lending to stressed businesses hungry for cash, then forcing them into default and taking them over for a pittance, but now he was on the block.

He needed an aggressive purchaser, a firm that had the cash to push the company on, but with more mindless headmen who didn't have a clue about what he did or how he made his money, but would be blinded by the bonuses, by the sheer smell of money.

The lean and mean would survive, an irony in that humankind had systematically exterminated widespread plague and death, where only the strongest survive, but still allowed this cyclical death knell to continue in corporations that shed thousands of jobs and destroyed small-town America. During this time, he had to make sure his division continued record profit growth so that he banked the bonus he had been promised for selling the company.

Frank was Joe's number two, a balding lamppost of a man who would have been the perfect role model for Bram Stoker's book, had the two ever met. Frank was head of credit at the division and kept a close eye on all of the firm's lending.

"I'm sorry, Joe, but we've problems with AASA. Rick was in a car accident, and he ain't going to last," Frank said; he knew to get straight to the point. Anything else would be seen as weak.

Rick was the chief executive officer and major shareholder of AASA, a client of the bank, with overall borrowing of $27 million, down from $35 million a year ago. Joe and Frank had been working closely with Rick over the last twelve months to reduce AASA's borrowing, which had blown out of control after horrific losses. Main management had left in droves, and Rick was holding it all together.

"Our latest reports on the company show that we've got a week before it folds and loss estimates are circa three million dollars; all of Rick's other assets have been ploughed into the business, and his house has long been in the wife's name," Frank continued.

Joe sat there and said nothing, his brain ticking over on the information flow; he was agitated and snapped a pencil he had been twirling through his fingers.

"We believe there's some life insurance coverage and other small property assets that may be in the background, according to our investigations," said Frank.

Joe grimaced, his dark eyes boring into Frank's. "Get Tony down to the bedside and see what fucking coverage that bastard has. I don't care what fucking time it is."

That was it; the order had been given, and the intent implied. Joe wasn't one for conversation; in the fifteen years they had known each other, Joe had never once asked what Frank did in his personal life. It was work and work only, but Frank had become very wealthy working for Joe. There was an unspoken bond, not one of friendship, but one of mutual benefit, a need to coexist.

Frank was also fifty-nine now and had been in finance all of his working days; he had been married for thirty-five years and had three boys, all now graduated, two working in banking and one as a dentist. All three boys were married;

one of the bankers was going through a divorce at the moment (luckily, no kids in that marriage). The dentist had two girls, and the other banker one boy, so Frank was Grandpapa to three.

Frank had been at Joe's side through thick and thin; things had been pretty good for the last eight or nine years, as Joe had moved up the pecking order, with Frank right behind. With seniority came the ability to make decisions and commitments without anyone else's approval. This had given Joe effectively an open chequebook to buy other businesses and lend money to whoever he liked, which he did on a regular basis.

Frank's family had been in the States for several generations; Joe had made sure that there was no Irish ancestry and had discovered that there was a Prussian family tree somewhere in the background, probably where Frank got his meticulous discipline from.

This team of Joe, Frank, and Peter, the division's chief financial officer, had been exceptionally solid over the years.

Frank and Joe rarely socialised; there was an annual gathering at Joe's for his senior management, but Frank's wife, Marjorie, never attended. She hated Joe and found him overbearing and arrogant, as well as running roughshod over Frank on a regular basis. She never gave Frank a hard time over it; she appreciated the money that came with the territory but didn't see why she should have to put up with Joe's company. Joe had never said a word; he didn't really care if Marjorie was involved or not.

Frank was in the inner circle and knew about all the skeletons concerning clients and how Joe operated, but as he was to later discover, he knew little Joe's darker side, not that he chose to ponder on the subject.

Joe's team had been hiding things for years.

Yes, there were regular audits from both the bank's internal auditors and the Fed, the banking regulator, but these were so well managed and orchestrated by Joe to ensure nothing untoward was ever found.

The internal audit team was always welcomed by Joe, Peter, and Frank and had always been given a brief by the bank's overall CEO that this was a critical part of the bank and it made significant profits, so do a good job but be accommodating. The audit team had stopped their unannounced visits some time ago. They always provided a list of the client files they wanted to review, which always looked at deals where losses or provision for future losses had been made, the top ten largest clients by loan size, large expenses, and then two to three random file requests, a systematic approach that could be anticipated and manipulated.

No one else in the office interacted with the audit team; all files were vetted and vetted again to make sure they were immaculate. Loans that Joe and Frank supported beyond good lending practise were never earmarked for provision; all discussions and decisions were never formally documented, leaving no audit trail. The trio had an answer for anything and everything, all well-rehearsed but never to the degree that caused suspicion; the three monkeys.

Large movements of money, in cash form, were always hidden away in separate books and reconciled as bona fide electronic transactions or cash deposits from restaurants and clubs to make sure everything balanced.

The Fed audits were exactly the same, with the three being the only ones allowed to meet with them to discuss their deals and processes.

Audit reports were always exceptional; Joe and his team ran a tight ship as far as the outside world was concerned.

Joe dismissed Frank. He tapped Linda's extension and said, "A bad close to the day."

Linda immediately stepped out of her seat and sidled into Joe's office; she locked his door. The two headed to his en-suite, where he pushed her to her knees as he sprung his cock from his trousers and stabbed this into her mouth. After a few short minutes, he felt the weight of the world lift from his shoulders and the pressure behind his eyes fade.

David—New York

At thirty-one, David Kettner was the youngest of the bank's vice presidents. He worked hard and partied even harder. Promoted through the ranks, his department produced astonishing profits, and colleagues referred to him as the guy with the golden touch (others used less generous terms, replacing "touch" with another word).

David was at his office desk in downtown New York.

His staggering good looks were no doubt from his Swedish model mother; he had blond hair and deep blue eyes. Robert Redford's Sundance Kid immediately came to the mind of anyone glimpsing David at one of New York's trendy nightspots.

David's parents had ensured he attended the best schools both in Europe and the States, coupled with significant worldwide travel. He finally graduated from Harvard, and this education and global experience was another factor in his blistering career rise.

However, the shallowness of his upbringing, where lack of parenting was supplemented by money, had given him a taste for an expensive lifestyle that his millionaire father had accommodated, but with all the insecurities and need for adulation that now came with it.

His parents went through an acrimonious divorce, and his father had moved to San Diego with a new wife twenty-five years his junior; his mother went back to Scandinavia, and communication was really just email catch-ups, rather than any regular get-togethers.

His three hundred -thousand-dollar salary just wasn't sufficient for his lifestyle, with dating models and aspiring film stars, plus the gambling, but so long as the bonuses kept rolling in, he could just about hold it together.

Luckily, the bonuses and some money laundering commissions had continued to do just that, but David was also working on other plans.

He had started life in Boston; his father had headed a private equity firm there and married a Swedish model, some twelve years his junior. His general feeling was that he had a been a fashion accessory for his mother as a baby, but a total nuisance to both of their international lifestyles from three onwards, constantly criticised by his mother for changing her shape, so much so that jobs dried up. From five, he was shuttled off to boarding school and rarely saw his parents. Their careers dictated many of his homes. Father was buying businesses across the world and would spend considerable time on-site nurturing these companies. He boarded in Boston, England, and Sweden.

He was naturally bright, and studying came easy to him, but there again, he had little else to do. In one school in England, he was the only boarder who stayed weekends.

The education had positioned him well in life to get a good job, but he had no substance, no understanding of family life. In his own mind, he had become a free spirit, but to his friends, he was a spirit with no home. David hurtled through life with no boundaries and had been taken in by all the devil had to offer him: drugs, alcohol, sex, gambling and fast living, fuck the consequences. He had been out with more than a thousand women but had no real friends, just hangers-on sucking up to his wallet. But at least he was known and welcomed by the doormen of every hip club in the city.

David needed this continuum of hype; neither of his parents had ever said, "Well done, David," and at the schools he attended, doing well was a way of life. So every smiling face, at the trendiest nightspots, welcoming David was just the tonic he needed, no matter how shallow the orchestrated gestures were. He had a wardrobe full of designer-labelled clothes and shoes; he drove a Lamborghini Gallardo, but deep down, he was always on edge, waiting for an Armageddon of some kind. David also loved watches and collected them when he had the money. The laundering contact had given him an eighteen carat yellow gold Breitling as a special thank you. He wore this on most nights out, as in New York a $50,000 watch meant a lot to the girls who were hunting partners in many of the bars David frequented.

The guys loved him; he was living their dream. The girls loved the persona, but there just wasn't any warmth or depth in any of his relationships.

However, life had changed recently; David's latest squeeze, Melissa, was a nightclub singer, and this was the real thing, something David had never experienced before. One-night stands and short-term relationships had been consigned to history. This girlfriend had settled his inner demons; he wanted to embrace life with this new partner.

But he needed to get out of a financial mire; he had been playing hard and gambling heavily.

In order to cancel several gambling markers, David had agreed to do a few money-laundering transactions for the mob; these had progressed into larger and larger asks. It seemed that these people already had several other inroads into the bank but needed more guys from the branch network; there was complicity higher up in the bank. He acquiesced; he had to.

All in all, it was quite easy to cover this new influx of capital, as the bank's systems were lax, and strangely, even the internal credit guys had not picked up on anything during routine audit visits, which proved he had covered his tracks very well. The deal had apparently been ratified, overseen, and set up by some high-ranking official in the bank, who was obviously very well placed. All David needed to do was to get the cash into the systems at his branch level. He had no idea who it was and really had just been pleased that his life could go on, unchecked.

So he was now a part of a team within the bank that orchestrated the laundering of significant amounts of illegal money. David just assumed that others in this team had been sucked in the same way he had been.

Money flowed in from across the globe but mostly from South America; sometimes, it was cash, arriving in armoured cars from the bank's Mexican subsidiaries.

These transactions increased over the last couple of years and accounted for major earnings at the bank, which took a 10 per cent commission, as David termed it, for losing the money in the system and repatriating the funds into bona-fide accounts held by mob businesses. Fifty million dollars a month was passing through the false accounts, many of them restaurants and clubs that obviously would bank a lot of cash. David felt sure more commission was being made elsewhere, but he never sought to discuss this with the people who came in and managed the accounts. He was happier now that his gambling was paid off, although he continued to lose heavily. He was given a regular allowance at casinos and clubs of fifteen thousand dollars a month but rarely ended up with credit at the end of the month, and any change to this arrangement was always met with a firm no, as the powers that be did not want David flashing any unexplained cash around. He was a pawn that could easily be sacrificed, which he understood all too well.

The cocaine-fuelled nights had also been taking their toll; his mood swings were renowned.

Joe—New York

Tony, the account manager, was at Rick's bedside within the hour; he found out that life insurance policies and smaller assets totalling some $5 million were in existence, with payment to be made to his wife and three children.

Tony had made it very clear that the bank and Joe personally would hound Rick's wife and children, particularly the children, "who wouldn't get a fucking job for as long as Joe had breath in his body," unless the loans were repaid in full. Joe would of course keep his fees to a minimum so the family would get some of the cash.

The assignment of the insurance policies and assets was done there and then; lawyers were brought in to finalise the necessary paperwork; they knew they had to put the hours in for Joe. Rick died four days later. AASA went bust, the bank got their money, and the wife and kids received $1.5 million after collection fees of half a million dollars.

After the pay-out, Joe said, "I nearly lost a fucking night's sleep over that idiot; half a million dollars should cover that."

The bank's share price had made it vulnerable in the dog-eat-dog consolidation games that was seeing more and more banks and insurance companies devour each other to buy market share, create volume, and cut overhead (i.e., slash jobs), but problems in the credit markets were always in the backdrop.

The bank was now to sell Joe's division, enabling it to buy back shares, return to core fee-earning activities, and ease its borrowing needs.

Joe's share options would vest (so he would make a lot of money earlier than originally planned), as would many of the other directors and senior managers; several would be become multimillionaires overnight. Joe had been there for years; he craved more and more money, but it was the power that kept him there. Profits had to be maintained, and this was proving difficult, as many of Joe's clients were struggling. He and Frank had been hiding things for years; amazing what a few creative acquisitions can do to keep loans going to underperforming companies.

Joe's life revolved around himself; he had no great interest in anything that didn't make money, help him get one over on a competitor/peer/client, or give him the prospect of great sex. He did have a couple of stepdaughters who went to boarding school and had a seven-year-old son with Monica, his second wife, another Joe Junior the Second; he doted on his son.

Joe left the office at five in the evening; he took the elevator down to his waiting limo and whisked off to the Hamptons, where he was to play Joe Jnr at tennis. The car smoothed through Manhattan and headed out to the Hamptons. Monica was out at a Women's Institute Fundraiser committee meeting and wouldn't be back until later.

Martha, the nanny, let Joe in through the imposing double oak doors, which led into a black and white chessboard of a marbled floor, fifty feet by fifty feet. The double staircase of the main hall faced the entrance, splaying out in an arc like lava spewing from a volcano. Joe grunted a good evening and headed off to his study, once again through two double doors to the right of the main hall.

The study had a plush wool carpet, and the walls were panelled with dark walnut, with large bookcases holding hundreds of leather-bound volumes, once again many first edition works of the great novelists of our time. Joe threw his tailored suit jacket over the back of one of two leather chairs facing a red leather-topped desk. For a moment, he peered at the wall of CCTV screens; Joe Jnr was already warming up on the court with his tennis coach. *Cheeky fucker,* Joe thought, but he still wouldn't beat him.

Joe quickly fired up one of the three computer screens on his desk, checked the world's stock markets, viewed his brokerage account, and made a quick transfer of funds between his accounts. After completing a few follow-up emails, he spun out of the chair, strode up the stairs to his dressing room, threw off the rest of his clothes, and climbed into his white tennis gear. He bounded down the stairs and out through the back of the house into the grounds and down past the white marble pillars of the pool house to the AstroTurf tennis court, where his son was smashing an impressive shot across the net, which the instructor scrambled to get to.

There had been a light shower, and the smell of the freshly cut grass filled Joe's nostrils; he felt great and took a few deep breaths as he stepped onto the court, giving Joe Jnr a high five whilst acknowledging the coach.

"I see you've warmed up and are ready to do battle," Joe said, grinning. "Let's knock a few balls about and let me limber up."

Joe felt the blood pump through his veins; no matter the circumstances, he hated to lose.

Joe Jnr was a solid player, but at seven, he just couldn't fight against the sheer aggressive onslaught of powerful volleys from the net. The games didn't last long.

The coach stayed to watch the destruction for fifteen minutes, shook his head, and strode off to his parked car at the side of the enormous house.

Joe and his son played for an hour. It was Friday, and after the game, Joe Jnr would take a shower in his en-suite and head down for dinner, already prepared by Martha. Tonight was Italian spaghetti and meatballs in a tomato sauce, rich with garlic. The two would eat together and then catch up with the Simpsons before Joe Junior the Second was whisked off to bed by Martha. He may catch a glimpse of his mother when she came back from her meeting.

Joe had changed into cream tracksuit bottoms and was at the counter waiting for the meal to be dished up. Joe Jnr came down dressed in cotton Spiderman pyjamas.

At this age, he worshipped his father, who was great at everything and the best tennis player. He didn't see defeat as humiliating, and it just made him try harder to emulate his dad.

"You played a great game, Junior," Joe said.

"You are just so good, Dad," he replied.

"So how was your day?" Joe asked.

"Yeah, pretty cool. I got 100 per cent in my maths exam," he said, beaming.

"Wow, great. Can't wait until you can come and work with me," Joe came back.

Martha dished out the meatballs, and the two ate heartily; they were good meatballs. Conversation ceased; Joe struggled to engage with a seven-year-old. The weekend would once again consist of tennis on both Saturday and Sunday; Saturday evening had been set aside for yet another black-tie dinner, where Joe would be holding court over three tables of guests.

Joe returned to his study and fell back into the large, red leather swivel chair. He flicked his screen on, input the password, and accessed his trading accounts and stock holdings.

Life had been good, certainly over the last fifteen years or so. Joe had studied hard as a boy and joined a commercial finance company after college. From there, he set about working his way up and through the career ladder; he was excellent in networking, arse-kissing, and brown-nosing the right people at the right time. He had a natural flair for dealing with people, understood how to manipulate them, and grasped how businesses ticked; he learned a lot from his father and on the streets of his childhood. All the while, he maintained his own carefully thought-out agenda of climbing to the top of the ladder, money, power and he didn't care whom he used or stood on to get there. Gradually, he had been taken under the wing of one of the high-flying vice presidents at the company. As his mentor, Gary, was promoted, so was Joe.

The company became quite profitable and began to acquire smaller businesses. As the firm became a large fish in a diminishing pond, some of the large commercial banks started to take notice. Joe was now on the executive board and was building a solid reputation as a deal-maker. He had been given his own underwriting authority and was able to lend businesses up to $25 million at that time, without further reference.

He now headed up the commercial lending arm of what was now a multifaceted finance and insurance group, with Gary as the ultimate chief executive officer. This was when many of his Italian friends had taken a keen interest in Joe's progression through the finance markets. They introduced a lot of new business to Joe and were able to open doors to much larger banks and institutions.

Joe had started to lend to many interrelated businesses; several of them had Mafia links, but fees were good, and he was also looked after personally with cash and benefits. If there were ever any difficulties with business, Joe's friends would always step in to ensure repayments were made or the companies were taken over and integrated into their existing organisation.

One such introduction was at a dinner arranged by one of the multimillionaire Italians who had taken a particular interest in Joe and his future. This is where Joe was introduced to Federico, the vice chairman of a large bank; they bonded exceptionally well. In the early stages, this new friend would introduce deals that were too small for his own bank or could be shared between his institution and Joe's company.

It wasn't long before Federico became chairman and began to orchestrate an acquisition of Joe's flourishing company. Joe was made the chief executive of the new subsidiary and became very wealthy due to the shares and options he held, which paid out when the acquisition went ahead. Gary stayed on and continued to run the remainder of the group, having banked a large bonus for selling Joe's division, as Joe had done so himself.

Federico stepped down as chairman four months ago, and his deputy had replaced him, John O'Callaghan, a bloody Irish descendant who had never got on with Joe. John wanted a significant change at the bank and wanted Joe and his division gone.

There was a knock at the study door, and Martha came in with a tray of home-baked cookies and a diet soda for Joe.

Joe thanked her; he opened the drink and slugged a few mouthfuls back, waiting for the gas kickback, before taking a few bites out of the peanut and milk chocolate delights that Martha had prepared that day.

After supper, he moved on upstairs, said goodnight to Joe Jnr, and then stepped out on to the long landing overlooking the main hall entrance. Monica was still out, but Joe was comfortable in his own company. He still had his tennis pumps on and walked to the far end to the master bedroom, opened the large oak door, and flipped off his pumps as he walked into his own wardrobe and dressing area.

In the main bedroom was an enormous four-poster bed; Joe felt like he had to literally jump to get on to the mattress, it was that high off the sky-blue carpet. There were large ornate, floor-to-ceiling mirrors, surrounded by gold frames of paintings that Joe had bought from a valuation firm that had seized them from a wealthy stockbroker, who had defaulted on his dealings. Joe had given the valuation firm an exclusive contract with his bank to undertake a number of very lucrative assignments, paid for by the bank's clients, for which he received an exceptional but defendable price on the works of art. The valuation firm had said if the transaction was questioned, they would say their instruction was to sell quickly in a quirky market to immediate cash buyers; no one could fault the process, but the 70 per cent discount to market value worked for Joe. Nothing was ever questioned; they were professionals doing a job, and of course they wouldn't sell things at under value.

In a cabinet beneath a fifty-inch plasma screen were a thousand DVDs, regularly updated with the latest releases, supplied courtesy of the film distribution company Joe's bank financed. There were hundreds of kids' movies in Jnr's TV room, as well as one hundred and twenty-five of the latest gaming DVDs, once again supplied without cost every time another one of Joe's clients released a new game.

The walls were covered in a blue and cream flowered silk covering, which was like touching the walls of a padded cell, only softer.

The room curved round to a large bay window, which had a French renaissance circular table and six chairs surrounding it, and beyond to terrace doors that opened out onto a large balcony that overlooked the rear of the mansion and the glass-topped pool house to the left and the tennis court in the distance. There were a number of large teak sun loungers on the balcony and a central oval teak table and four chairs.

Joe shed his tracksuit, socks, white V-neck tennis sweater, and shirt. He looked himself up and down in one of the mirrors in the walk-in wardrobe; he looked fit and well, no overhang or fat anywhere to be seen.

To the centre of the wardrobe was a glass topped counter with row upon row of designer silk ties; he was particularly fond of the Paul Smith ties Monica had bought in London for him; with their dotted designs across a range of similar colours, they were always a good talking point, when things had been on warmer terms. To the right was a wall of shoes, and to the left of the archway leading to his shower room was shelf after shelf of every designer aftershave known to man, stacked three deep.

Spectacular bottle designs, liquid colours, Kilian, Joop, Polo, Hermes, Paco Rabanne, Lacoste, Millionaire, YSL, Gucci, Dior and the list continued on and on; he was particularly fond of Esencia from Loewe.

Joe stepped into the charcoal grey slated shower room and turned on the body jets.

After the shower, he changed into casual clothing, slacks, tee shirt, sweater, loafers, and took a large Cuban cigar from the automated humidor to the other end of his wardrobe. He snipped the end into a bin and took one of the forty or so cigar lighters that were all neatly stacked to the left of the cabinet.

His wife was not yet back, so he strode out to the back of the house and down to the ornamental lake that was home to a magnificent collection of koi carp. The lake was crossed by a curving wooden bridge that flowed from one side to the other. He turned the one-inch flame jet to the cigar and drew in deep puffs, blowing the smoke into the cooling air.

The lake had an electric canopy that would automatically cover the water if the temperature dropped to a dangerous level for the fish.

It was open now, and Joe could make out the fish silhouetted by the underwater lighting.

The rear security lights clicked on; Monica was back from the meeting she had been attending. She stepped out onto the terrace and waved; Martha had obviously informed her where Joe was. She immediately went up to Joe Jnr, who had been waiting for her, and read him several pages from his latest Harry Potter book.

Hans—South Africa

Hans awoke at six in the morning and followed the normal morning routine; the boys were quite animated and looking forward to the day, and Sabrina had joined them with Carl. After they finished breakfast, George and Michael were taken off by the nanny to get ready for a pool day. The two other boys, David and Sean, kissed Sabrina goodbye. Hans leant in for a hug; Carl was now dozing in his small carry-cot pram.

"Have a great day, my boys," Sabrina said.

Hans said, "Let's get to it then, boys," with a big grin.

The three strode out, the two boys mimicking their father all in a rigid and disciplined line, across the manicured lawns to the waiting five-seat helicopter, which straddled a large white H in its own paddock, near the stables.

The two boys, followed by Hans, jumped into the baking cockpit of the Bell 206, B-3; they simultaneously strapped themselves in and put on headphones and slipped their sunglasses back on. Hans went through the checks again (he had already gone through these earlier in the morning) and started the engine. He gradually brought the rotor speeds up and lifted the aircraft into the air, then with a sharp dip of the nose, the helicopter lurched forward with gleeful shouts from the boys as they headed out along the beautiful yellow-sanded, rocky coastline and then inland to look for wild game.

The chopper zigzagged over the cracked, terracotta, and green landscape, chasing herds of antelope and zebras. The sun shone bright and hot against the cockpit, and Hans could feel the sheer heat on his face, which although cooled by the air con, reddened his brow and cheeks. With one movement, he pulled the chopper up and to the left in a graceful arc as the craft fell onto its left side like a dolphin springing from the waves. Hans then stabilised the chopper and brought it down in a wide clearing, the blades whirring up dust like an almighty desert storm.

Hans shut down the engines and surveyed the area carefully as the dust settled; he slid the door open and stepped onto the hard-baked mud. Within seconds, sweat was pouring down his back.

"Come on, you two, get the guns and the ammo," Hans said.

The boys scrambled around in the back of the craft and brought out two high-powered rifles, Thirties, with telescopic sights, and Sean's Twenty Bore shotgun. Hans strapped a utility belt around his waist (it had a large hunting knife in its sheath) and then slid a forty-five handgun into the holster. He surveyed the area through his German twelve times magnification binoculars. The herds had moved off some miles into the distance; he could see a pride of lions a mile or so away under a tree, mostly asleep and completely unperturbed by the previous racket of the chopper. He motioned to the boys to move off as he closed the chopper doors.

Some of the groundsmen employed by Hans had tracked a warthog to a nearby waterhole. This was their target for this trip and proposed barbeque on Sunday.

They were positioned to be downwind of the waterhole, where they hoped to track the warthog. They planned on walking a good mile and taking position on a hilltop overlooking the water. This was a regular event for the boys, and they really enjoyed themselves, from the dressing up in their individual safari suits, hats, and water flasks, to spending time with their father and stalking game. Hans had often drummed into them the importance of proper gun control, shotguns always broken when not in use, guns always on safety and always pointing up or down to the ground, never aiming at anybody. Given the dynamic nature of the area, they did keep shells in the broken shotgun and in the chamber of their rifles. The rifles with the boys would be on safety, but Hans kept his safety off and allowed David to do the same if Hans wasn't close by.

They were very aware of all of the potential dangers in the wild and were always very vigilant. David led the troop through the bush; the lions had not moved at all; in this heat, they would stay under their tree, surveying the area like women window shopping when stores are closed, not missing a thing.

Hans saw a glint of light reflected from something in the bush; he beckoned the boys on and said nothing other than that David was now in charge and they would rendezvous at the hilltop now some half a mile away.

"David, take your safety off," Hans said, "but remember your gun is a lethal weapon. Just be prepared."

Hans slipped into the undergrowth and was gone. The boys thought this was just all part of their ongoing training; Dad had left them alone from time to time and would then meet them farther along the trail, no doubt tracking their every move.

There was another flicker of light from the same location as Hans tracked around to flank the position. As he drew nearer, he could make out the soles of two pairs of shoes, their owners lying prostrate, face down, in a cluster of bushes. Beyond was a small herd of elephants.

He was now on his stomach, crawling closer on his elbows and knees, through long bleached grass, to the target. His heart was pumping, not with fear but sheer excitement, gleeful even, as he approached his new prey. One pair of the soles shuffled slightly, but they didn't go to get up; the two men were blissfully unaware of what was coming up behind them.

Hans drew his large hunting knife as he lunged into the bushes, cracking one of the men in the forehead with the butt of the knife. The other man struggled to rise, pulling his ancient-looking rifle up towards Hans's torso. Hans now knew that he had a couple of poachers in front of him; he hated these men, killing for no reason other than tusks from defenceless elephants or rhinos (an irony, given Hans's history).

The rifle pulled further up in the direction of Hans, but he quickly grabbed the barrel, twisting and wrenching it from the poacher's grasp. At the same time, he shot forward, slicing through the perpetrator's neck with his knife. Blood splattered up Hans's bare arm as the man slumped, clutching the blood-pumping gash in his neck, nothing but gurgling noises.

The other poacher, initially stunned, went for his own knife, but Hans anticipated this; he spun round and drove the palm of his hand up into the other man's nose, pushing the bone into his brain and killing him instantly. Both now lay motionless in the undergrowth.

Hans took the hand of the slit throat man and pushed his palm into the other's broken nose; he placed the fallen knife back into the other's hand, having slid this through the neck wound blood, which was now at a dribble. Hans brushed gently over his own boot prints, which made the scene look like a scuffle had taken place between the two men.

He walked backwards from the bush, brushing away his own footprints but carefully leaving where the two poachers had entered intact. *Why bother?* he thought; the animals would be done with any evidence before dawn, and even if the bodies were discovered, the police would be pleased to see the back of two poachers and wouldn't look much further than the assumption that they had killed each other.

Hans then backtracked and ran to catch the boys. He washed the blood from his arm with water from his flask before he caught them, where they were laid out, surveying the area from the hilltop.

"Hi, guys," Hans said with a big smile.

"Hi, Dad; you took your time," they chimed in unison. "And you're sweating an awful lot."

Hans felt very pleased with himself, a broad smile rising across his face.

Just at that moment, they saw the warthog; David raised his rifle, released the safety, and took aim through the telescopic sights. The warthog looked up towards them; his front legs collapsed, hit dead centre between his eyes. The noise of the shot reverberated around the plain; birds took flight from the water and bushes alike; gazelles launched themselves away from the explosive bang; and the lions blinked in their direction but stayed where they were.

"Great shot, excellent," Hans and Sean said.

The boys cut a staff and tied the hog's legs to it; Hans and David perched this on their shoulders. Sean took it in turn to lift the pressure off David's shoulders as he switched from time to time to alleviate the weight, and they all began the walk back to the chopper.

Joe—New York

Joe was up early on Saturday and played tennis with his son; another drubbing. He caught up with his wife for thirty minutes or so before he caught up with some colleagues at his club in the Hamptons. This evening, he was at a sportsman's dinner with bank clients.

Sunday was much the same, but Monica was the one who was out most of the day.

Joe was Monica's second husband; she had married young and drifted apart from her previous ex. After a blissful start, life with Joe had from become one of clinical forbearance. Joe had little time for Monica's emotional needs, and after a very expressive and communicative first year of dating and marriage, the two rarely spoke about anything other than ensuring formal engagements where both were to be in attendance were appropriately noted and diarised. Joe confided nothing with Monica, asked for no opinion, and took no judgement.

Monica had thrown herself into charity work and had gradually weaned herself away from the other shallow wives of the millionaires who surrounded their lives.

Joe—New York, Monday

The weekend had been busy, but Joe was showered and dressed and ready for breakfast at five forty-five this Monday morning. Breakfast consisted of a mix of fresh fruits and yoghurt prepared by Martha and chilled mineral water. He checked the computer screens in his study to review world events, but there was nothing of consequence. *There wouldn't be,* he thought; *New York hadn't opened yet.*

Doug, his chauffeur, was on the drive; there was a light mist and drizzle, clinging, penetrating water ensconced in the mist in an enveloping bath of moisture that would penetrate even the best overcoats. Doug idled the engine and listened to the radio, waiting for Joe and the early morning grunts that would follow before he settled down to reading credit files.

At least the morning journeys didn't entail Joe puffing away on a large Cuban cigar, which was a regular occurrence on the evening return and necessitated Doug putting his suit out to air on the small fire escape railings outside of his apartment window, weather permitting.

Doug was at Joe's beck and call and had been for the last four years, three months, twenty-one days, twenty-three hours, forty-six minutes and counting.

Joe peered through the study's double-glazed windows at the swirling mist outside as the car's double exhausts added to the melee.

Mondays were credit committee days, where the bank's offices would have submitted deals for lending or other sanctions by close of play Thursday of the previous week, for discussion by Joe's main credit sanctioning board. Transactions would be presented by the manager responsible for the submission, together with his line manager and underwriter. This for local and larger deals would be done by the visiting entourage being called into the boardroom of fourteen tired-looking faces that made up the board, with Joe at the helm of the table facing the large double doors that led into the den. Regional offices would be allotted times to discuss smaller deals and minor changes to be debated; they were dialled in to present by conference phone.

Joe read many of the files on the journey to and from the office but also set aside a few hours every weekend to do the same, slumped on the leather sofa in his home study. Notes and opinions were scribbled on the front of each credit pack, each being at least thirty-five pages in length. Joe insisted that the credit files had a wealth of validating information, unlike other banks that trusted their team, who submitted three- or four-page executive summaries of their submissions. The presenters were then mercilessly attacked, ensuring that they knew all the facts, presented every issue, and assessed dangers in every deal.

The other thirteen members would seek to gauge the direction Joe was taking the attack; just for kicks, he often played a game and changed tack mid-discussion, and would sit like a Roman at the gladiator games to see what would be given the thumbs up or down.

Joe left his study with a light Mac on his arm; there were umbrellas in the car and plenty of people to carry them, he thought, smiling to himself. He caught a glimpse of Martha leaving the kitchen to wake Joe Jnr for school.

He stepped out onto the sandstone terrace, surrounded by large Greek-style pillars supporting a large ornate canopy over the massive wooden double doors.

Doug was waiting on the gravel to usher Joe into the rear seat; no umbrella was needed, but Doug held one in his right hand just in case Joe should experience the discomfort of water dripping onto his suit jacket or perfectly coiffured hair.

Joe grunted a thank you as he slid into the rear seat. Doug had taken Joe's briefcase and placed it on the other rear passenger seat.

Joe slipped his jacket off and hung it on the back of the driver's seat; he spun round to engage his seat belt and grabbed a chilled bottle of still mineral water from the central console.

Doug disengaged the main brake, placed the automatic gearbox into drive, and delicately tapped his foot across the accelerator pedal; he knew Joe would be listening and watching to ensure the gravel was not spewed across his drive. He turned the car down the long drive to the electric gates.

Sagaponack was some ninety miles from the office, and Doug had the route carefully planned, with alternatives should traffic problems dictate. Generally, it took two and a half hours, and Joe could get a lot of reading done.

The journey to the office was sedate, but Doug always ensured good speed if he was able; the sun was stabbing through more and more the closer they got to the city centre. It would be a pleasant day, weather-wise, at least.

Doug pulled the limo up outside the Wall Street office. Joe had slipped his jacket on; the sun was up, and he told Doug that he would leave his Mac in the back. All the credit files had been read, marked up, and filed back in his briefcase. Doug opened the door, and Joe stepped out onto the sidewalk and stretched, his eyes squinting with the impact of the morning sun. Doug leant across and grabbed the case, handing it to Joe, who grunted a thank you and headed off towards the magnificent entrance to the bank building.

It was 8.26 a.m. Joe swiped his card at the turnstiles and headed for the eight-strong elevator bank; there were four ranks, so thirty-two elevators serviced the building. Joe would take the executive elevator, thus avoiding many of the floors and staff on his way to his office. There were a few "Good mornings," but no attempt at prolonged or meaningful conversation.

Joe stepped out of the elevator and turned left towards the staff entrance, the opposite end to the general reception at the right of the corridor, and once again swiped his card for access. He swung right to take in the wide and long corridor. The smell of cooking, ham, eggs, and pancakes hung in the air as he passed the staff restaurant on his left; there were twelve people stuffing their faces with the subsidised food, downing coffee or sodas and filling up with carbs for the morning session.

He pushed the door open at the corridor end; his eyes swept the main office like an eagle, to see who was already at their desk. Joe always kept a note of who was in and who was late. He had sacked many over the years for turning up late; staff members were well aware that physical presence was critical, no matter how well they were performing. Joe enjoyed the adulation, a mix of fear and respect, of his staff and never considered that anyone was ever worthy of critical note for their contribution; after all, this was his business, and he alone was the reason for the success of the division.

His office was situated in the far-left corner, and Linda, one of his personal assistants, was at her desk that fronted the mahogany door outside his office and personal bathroom suite.

"Hi, Linda," he said, smiling. "All good with you?" Out of sight of other staff, he winked as he strolled up to her desk and placed his case beside it.

"Hi, Joe," she said, smiling broadly, flashing a perfect set of bleached white teeth (paid for by Joe). "No doubt you had a great weekend?"

"Yes, pretty good," he replied. "Some tennis, and another boring dinner, same old."

"Poor you; let's hope the week kicks off well. Your coffee tray is brewing away in your office; shall I join you for a debrief now?" Linda asked.

"Give me ten minutes, and then come in; thanks," Joe said and marched off into his room.

At nine thirty, the credit board would assemble in the boardroom to discuss the credit submissions. This would be an all-day event; they had nine deals in for review, and each one could easily take an hour or more. As they came closer to five o'clock, the room would become more intense to move things on. At two thirty in the afternoon, Joe could guarantee that at least two members would have nodded off and be experiencing a "dream of a transaction."

This was all a part of the circus that Joe enjoyed, the power, the acrid fear in the room, the brown-nosing, the adulation, and the underlying but undisplayed contempt that festered within his ageing team; they felt this was the only way to earn the bonuses and head towards retirement.

Joe was the conductor, the maestro at the table, and he loved every second. He had thirteen senior executives at his behest all day, waiting for the sacrificial lambs to bring in their lending requests, that they had sweated days and weeks on, building relationships, expectations, promises, and the main sell was always going to be internally.

Linda came into see Joe at nine and took notes on the week and cascaded any messages. Joe would be required in LA at the end of the week, a perfume retailer pleading for more concessions and funding. The local office felt they needed the CEO on-site.

LA was a pain in the arse for Joe, given the three-hour time difference, but it would mean good fees, and he would make sure his costs were charged to the client. He had known the client for a number of years; initially, things had gone well, big growth, and Joe had been looked after very well by JJ Henderson, the owner and CEO.

Joe was more than pissed that the meeting was a morning one in LA, so that meant an overnight, with no hope of the client paying for his entertainment. That said, he had other suitable clients locally, and it would make sense to arrange an early dinner the night before to meet and greet the local team and then take in the local delicacies, of which there were many budding yet unemployed actresses.

Joe would also take Frank and Peter with him.

Nine thirty came around quickly. He and Linda finished up, and Joe clutched up his files, like a hawk taking prey in its talons, and headed for the boardroom.

David—New York, Monday

David sat at his desk; his mind was wandering, and nothing could keep his attention.

Further funds were due in from South America soon, but they had to be off to Russia via the Caribbean immediately; this was the chance David was looking for, a new life with Melissa in Europe, together and away from it all.

David had been planning for some time, and he started diverting the money immediately it had arrived. This would be through a complex web of many banks across the globe, some taking large commissions for passing the funds through without questions, but he would still be left with a life-changing sum.

In his dealings, tracking down defaulting clients, David met several private detectives and specialist agencies and had sought their advice on getting new identities and passports. He had sourced a new identity nearly a year ago, just in case he needed to get away quickly.

Over time, he had set up bank accounts in European cities. On his last visit, two months ago, he had rented an apartment in Copenhagen, bought a car, and signed up for a Danish language course to start in the New Year, all in his new identity.

Hans—London, Monday

Hans arrived at London Heathrow following an uneventful flight in from South Africa. His business class seat ensured he could get off the aircraft relatively quickly, but this was all defeated by the long queues at Immigration. Hans stood in the Non-European Union queue as patiently as he could be, although his mind was working overtime. Forty minutes later, he was ushered to a window.

The stone-faced officer went through his standard questions, looking intently at the computer screen and then comparing Hans's face to the passport photograph. "Purpose of visit?" he asked.

"Business," Hans responded pragmatically.

"What business are you in?"

"Industrial chemicals," Hans responded.

"How long are you here for?"

"A few days, then off to the States and back to South Africa."

"Where are you staying?"

"The Connaught."

"May I see your hotel reservation and return tickets?" the uniform asked.

Hans was prepared and handed the documents over, having removed them from his travel wallet.

"Thank you," the clerk said. "Enjoy London." He waved Hans on and passed back the documents.

Hans picked up his suitcase from the carousel and headed for the green, nothing-to-declare channel. He walked through unchallenged and headed for the Heathrow Express Train, direct to London Paddington in fifteen minutes. He enjoyed the anonymity of public transport; no detailed record of his movements. Once at Paddington, he jumped into a black cab and asked for the Connaught; it was early evening in London, and the weather was dry but chilly.

Hans looked out at the bustling rush hour streets and then across the wide expanse of Hyde Park as he was ferried to the doors of the Connaught. The cab door was opened for him by the hotel doorman in resplendent top hat, and his suitcase whisked away by the bellboy. Hans tipped five pounds and paced off in the direction of the check-in desk.

"Welcome back, Mr Van Rensburg," the young girl at the check-in desk said. "We trust you have had a pleasant journey."

"Yes, thank you," Hans said.

"We have upgraded you to the Brook Penthouse Suite, Mr Van Rensburg. May I take a credit card, please?"

"Thank you, very kind," he replied, handing over his titanium Black Amex card.

"Would you like me to reserve a table in our restaurant tonight, sir?" she asked.

"Yes," Hans said. "Eight forty-five, please, just for one."

"Very good, sir. That's booked in. The bellman will show you to your room, Mr Van Rensburg."

Hans walked through his spectacular suite and ambled onto the balcony, taking in the views. He unpacked his bags and distributed his toiletries in the large bathroom.

He lay down on the bed and dabbed in his home number; it would be later in the evening there now, and the boys would be in bed. Sabrina answered, knowing it would be Hans.

"Hello darling," she purred. "How was your journey?"

"All good, baby," Hans said. "How's everything at home?"

"Everything has been fine," she responded.

They chatted about the boys, the day, business meetings, and Hans said he would call again tomorrow and chat with the boys.

There was just a few hours' time difference between England and South Africa, and Hans felt good, given the exertions of the journey. He changed into gym gear and headed to the gym for a forty-five-minute workout.

After the gym, Hans showered in his room and dressed in tan trousers, white shirt, and a bronze sports jacket; he slipped into dark brown suede shoes and headed to the bar.

He sauntered over to one of the large armchairs in the corner of the bar. The bar was small but closeted its occupants in Old World charm; low lighting and candles added to this in a way that dismissed all the city's ills.

"Hello, Mr Van Rensburg," acknowledged the waiter. "What can I get you?"

"A dirty vodka martini, please," said Hans.

Hans relaxed back into the chair and took in the surroundings, which hadn't changed in decades. The clientele was a mix of businessmen, Middle Eastern, Asian, and Indian, moneyed middle-aged women, and middle-aged men with young nieces in tow. Practically all female eyes in the room had shot a quick glance (or in some cases, a long stare) at this fine specimen of a man. Hans held the stare of one particularly beautiful brunette, who was with a couple of her girlfriends, and smiles were exchanged.

Hans checked his emails and sipped on the vodka.

Dinner consisted of wild sea bass and steamed vegetables. Hans headed off to the suite, opened up his iPad, and logged into a secure email account to check that nothing had changed.

James—London, Tuesday

James Buchanan was forty-one and could've been in better shape, which had deteriorated rapidly following a messy divorce four years ago. His frame was slight, but the fast food, business lunches, and the booze had added a pot belly you could rest a glass on and brought his weight to near two hundred and forty pounds. His face was not unattractive, albeit the double chin did nothing to help; this also aged him, perhaps into late forties, early fifties. In this round mass were piercing blue eyes (even more so following a night on the ale), Roman nose, and full lips. His hair had seen better days, and what was left was now speckled with grey. He sported a goatee beard of various colourings; some of his office joked (not to his face but amongst themselves) that the rainbow beard was probably a mix of leftovers from various curry nights and saved for a later serving.

It was now early October, with autumn in full throw and winter fast approaching. However, the clocks had yet to be reversed, and although dusk was eating into the perfect blue sky, it had been a crisp, crystal clear day, which made James feel good to be alive.

James had awoken early, feeling a little liverish from the beers from yesterday evening, but nonetheless shifted himself into jeans and pullover. He could hear the dog's tail thumping against the kitchen floor, in expectation of the morning greeting, food, and a quick walk.

The black Labrador, Betsy, jumped up onto James's chest as the door opened; he shouted, "Down, Betsy; get down. Oh, for God's sake, get *down*!"

James pulled an oilskin jacket off a hook in the hallway and strode out onto the gravelled drive, crunching underfoot and into the fields opposite. A brisk walk had both expelling significant amounts of vapour into the air, James like a smoker coughing up his last breaths. The dog was chomping on the lead, and James was swinging pooh bags from his other hand.

"Just what I need after last night," he mumbled to himself, but Betsy was pleased to see him. He recollected a joke from yesterday evening, which was quite poignant, given his relationship with the ex-wife was a little more than strained.

"Who loves you more, the wife or the dog?" was the question posed by one of James's accountant chums to the crowd of ten drunken men.

No answer was forthcoming, but the accountant carried on:

"Try locking the wife and the dog in the trunk of your car and leave them an hour; open the trunk, and who's still pleased to see you?" This caused riotous laugher and ensured another round of drinks.

James's mind was racing, and for some reason, he went back to thinking about the earlier days with Helen, his ex.

James had met Helen through work some fifteen years ago. He was a young investment banker working all hours and binge-drinking over the weekend. On a Thursday night after work, James and his partners in crime from the bank had escaped to a pub in the city. Long gone were the days when city pubs closed at nine in the evening.

They descended on the Lamb Public House in Leadenhall Market, a pub James would frequent many times in later years for long boozy lunches, where the intake of beer was interrupted by hot roast beef, carved in front of you, stuffed into a large chunk of French bread and smothered, in James's case, with hot English mustard or horseradish sauce.

Leadenhall is a restored covered market of high arching iron and opaque glass roof construction; it was home to several pubs and restaurants along its cobblestone streets.

Next to the pub was Lloyds of London, then and still, the beauty in the eye of the beholder metal, tubular designed building with elevators transcending on the edge of the construction, like Sherpas scaling mountainsides. Beneath these was a good vantage point for spotting young women in short skirts, although the angle wasn't enough to get anyone arrested, trundling up and down between office floors.

There were eight lads in their mid-twenties who had been joined by three secretaries who supported their report writing. The girls all came from Essex, a county neighbouring London which seemed to have bred a tremendous variety of beautiful women as well as hard-nosed market traders, which made the city banks vast profits by betting on the movements in currencies, commodities, stocks, literally anything that had a buyer/seller capability. Thursdays was the big night out in town, and the Essex women came out in droves, looking for a wealthy husband to bag. For some reason, they all seemed to wear enough make-up to cover the San Francisco Bridge, which James had experienced by literally scraping off the residue from his white office shirts and pillows in his apartment bed. In those days, they also tended to wear tight blouses, miniskirts, and white shoes. Many of the Essex men adorned white socks covered by their Loake leather brogues (or, even worse, slip-ons) and expensive, tailored suits with extraordinarily coloured silk linings of gold, pink, red, and royal blue.

James was chatting to Kay, or to the plaster of make-up, false eyelashes, and red lipstick, whilst sneaking peaks down the grand-canyon between her uplifted breasts, about not a lot at all.

John, one of his colleagues, tapped him on the back and positioned two fingers to his own lips: "Cigarette time." Back then, it was still perfectly legal and acceptable to smoke in the pub, but the lads wanted to weigh up who was shagging which of the girls tonight, so they headed outside for some fresh air in between half-hearted puffs of their cigarettes.

Under the Lloyds building was a wine bar, and as James and John strolled to and fro and chatted, they espied a group of giggling girls, eight of them, all sitting at an outside table, which was stacked with wine bottles.

James had immediately determined that the long-haired brunette was his and pushed John's jaw back into place, as he had playfully dropped his as he too surveyed the opportunities.

The brunette had cigarettes out and had literally dived into a very capacious shoulder handbag, obviously seeking the long-lost lighter or matches. James reacted quickly and was at her side, lighter in hand.

"Would you like a light?" he asked.

Their eyes connected, and her deep blue eyes clenched like a fist, ready to strike a huge blow, squinting menacingly in his direction.

"Table service? Why, thank you," she said, putting her cigarette into those lovely lips and proffering the tip to the lighter.

"Hi, I'm James," he began, but before he could finish, the brunette had said, "I'm sure you are," and leant back into her group of friends.

John had joined the group on the other side of the table and was making good headway with a very drunk blonde from South Africa, who was laughing at anything he had to say.

The girls were on a birthday celebration for Sarah, a remarkably unattractive, mousy-haired girl with a big nose from Surrey, who had been eyeing up James. John bought a couple of bottles of wine and was now on touching terms with the South African. James said he would head back to the team next door.

All were still ensconced at the bar, just under the spiral staircase that dominated the wooden floor. Kay was now hand in hand with George, and James was history there. "Ho hum," he said to himself as he was prompted to buy more drinks. "Your round."

James shouted back, "Yes, I know I'm round; I'm on a diet."

As James sunk a pint of Guinness, a group of rowdy girls entered the bar. John was in the melee; he had brought the group from next door.

James and the brunette were at a stand-off; who would crack first? Kay and George were swopping spit in the corner of the bar, leered at by some of the older voyeurs, nursing their pints at the bar. The other two secretaries looked on in horror at the entourage now invading their territory, and their long, red false claws were curled, ready for battle.

John was doing well with Charlotte, the blonde, who was an underwriter at Lloyds, as were several of the other girls. The brunette, called Helen, as James had gleaned, was an associate at Allen and Overy, a law firm.

John called Charlotte over and introduced her to James; she slurred a "Hi, nice to meet you," and wobbled to the right, like a yacht caught off guard by a gale, but managed to bring herself back to the vertical before nuzzling into John's shoulder.

Helen joined the trio and said, "Hello, James, long time no see."

"Why, hello, Helen," James replied. "Yes, who are you again?"

The other lads had now deserted the secretaries and were in animated chat with the other girls, having realised that they were all the worse for wear and game on.

A few bottles of wine arrived at the bar, and the girls spilt more than they managed to pour into their glasses. Apparently, John had plied them with a few Sambuca shots next door.

This had certainly mellowed Helen, and she and James were now getting on well.

George and Kay stumbled out into the covered market and headed off in search of a cab to take them back to George's flat. Some of the birthday party girls left, and there was now an even girl-and-boy match.

John and Charlotte suggested heading to the West End for a spot of clubbing, and Helen asked James if he was up for it.

The evening finished at 4.30 a.m., well, the next morning, with a quick drunken fumble outside of the club before they exchanged numbers and disappeared in opposite directions.

James called the next morning at just before noon; they had both been at their desks at 8 a.m., although large coffees and regular trips to the restroom had been the order of the morning. James had suggested meeting after work. Helen feigned another date with a girlfriend; she felt too rough to go out. James was quite relieved, although he would still go out with the lads; he wouldn't have to be on his best behaviour. So they arranged to meet on Saturday night for dinner.

James was living in Clerkenwell and Helen in Cartwright Gardens, near to Kings Cross. James suggested meeting at Uppers, a trendy restaurant on Upper Street, in Islington.

So their romance began, and Helen moved into James's apartment after six weeks.

Both were fiercely competitive, which flared irregularly in their earlier days, but they ignored the early warning signs and ended up married.

Hans—London, Tuesday

The next morning, Hans awoke to his alarm, devoured a fruit juice from the minibar, and changed once again into gym gear for a thirty-minute workout.

Breakfast had been arranged at the hotel; he was meeting a large supplier client and then had a late lunch at Le Pont De La Tour on the south bank near Tower Bridge.

James—Home, London, Tuesday

James was back at the house for a shave and a quick shower and was ready to face another day in the city.

James was an executive vice president for an American firm's banking division in corporate lending. His boss was Joe.

He heard the cab pull up onto the drive for the trip to the train station. He headed out looking smart in one of his tailored navy-blue suits with yellow gold lining, crisp white shirt (courtesy of the cleaners near to the office, allowing significant gut room), yellow silk tie, and black belt, socks, and brogues.

"Morning," James said to the driver. "How are you doing?" He always got fifteen minutes of update in what was the dynamic life story that was Carl the cabbie. Today was no different; Carl's mother had had a stroke, his girlfriend had just been diagnosed with MS, some idiot had shunted the car from behind, and his dog had a cataract. James oooed, arrred, empathised, and sympathised all in the correct places.

Then, as usual, Carl asked, "Any share tips I should be looking at?"

"Not much on at the moment," James said. "The city and world still in a downturn."

They pulled into the station cab rank. James said his goodbyes and confirmed with Carl he would give the necessary sixty-minute warning of his return this evening; he had an account with Carl's cab company.

The station platform was busy as usual, but the suits were all happy to queue in lines, knowing exactly where the train doors would come to a halt. There were a few nods of acknowledgement and grunts of good morning, but beyond that, the journey into London was usually silent, apart from the rustling of the morning broadsheets, the warble of some idiot's unwelcome mobile phone (they had forgotten to switch the phone to vibrate only), and a few whispered conversations into mobile handsets.

James had picked up *The Telegraph* and would read the *Financial Times* in the office and catch up on other news via the internet.

Evening journeys back were a little more raucous, given many of the riders would have had liquid lunches, mainly the brokers who headed to the pub for the afternoon and had a couple of sharpeners at one of the city pubs after work.

James was little different from the homogenous mass of city workers, avoiding eye contact in the mornings, even though some travellers had been making the same journey for nearly a decade. There was the usual disappearance of retirees, additional new recruits, and more recently lay-offs no longer in the mix.

The sky was clear blue, with little sign of anything wet coming their way as the train ground north towards its destination. The journey would be about fifty minutes, subject to no inconsiderate bastard jumping in front of a train, cows on the line, fallen leaves on the tracks, lack of staff, train in front broken down, kids on the tracks, signal failure, landslide, terrorist alert, or fire.

He would end up at Cannon Street, London City's station serving the South East, on the north side of the Thames and within easy walking distance of the banking district.

James had arrived at his City of London office opposite the Bank of England in Threadneedle Street. He walked from the train station; the morning had remained crisp, clean, and freshly reinvigorating, although he wasn't sure if he needed a coffee or another beer. He sought out a straight black coffee from Costa, never Starbucks (following their tax investigation). He nodded at the desk security as he aimed towards the bank of elevators, using his pass card to enter the office suite. He grunted at some of the junior analysts (some of whom had been at their desks for some hours) and entered his own office, ditching his jacket onto the coat stand and sliding into his high back chair. He swung his legs under the desk and switched on the two computer screens. Charlotte, his PA wouldn't be in until nine thirty, but he was off to a breakfast meeting at 8.15.

The coffee had cooled enough for a few large swigs as he read the *Financial Times* headlines; he checked emails and took a quick look at the news and markets before he was back in his suit jacket and off to his first meeting.

He had a breakfast meeting with clients at One Lombard Street, a usual morning meeting place and good selection of breakfast treats. James was looking forward to a large cholesterol and protein fix of eggs, bacon, hash browns, toast, tomatoes, and sausages.

There would be a couple of larger chubbies at the table to help him out.

One of these was Jeffery, a larger-than-life character, well over two hundred and seventy pounds of wobbling seal fat, who enjoyed food and drink to the full. Jeffery was a FTSE 250 chairman and charming company, the lard was well packaged in tailored Savile Row suits. Jeffery's company had been a bank client for nearly five years, and breakfast was a regular update meeting with him and the chief executive officer also in attendance.

James chuckled to himself as he said his hellos to Jeffery and the other lard arse, Roger, the chief financial officer, and shook hands; when he was first introduced to Jeffery, he had asked his boss what he needed to know about the client. His boss had looked him straight in the eye and said, "Don't leave your hands on the table or anywhere close to Jeffery's plate."

Sure enough, as that initial dinner ensued, he could see that Jeffery could have easily mistaken a hand as a spare rib to gorge on.

Breakfast progressed well; they had known each other for some time and never had any problems. The clients had asked for a few changes to the existing facility, and James had requested additional information so he could submit a credit application to the credit board. Shouldn't be a problem, but there were of course the fees to be charged for change.

James, suitably restored with food and fruit juice, said his goodbyes and headed back to the office, where he would meet with his personal assistant for a fifteen-minute update and planning meeting. He made a few notes on the client request from breakfast and sent them a follow-up email about the additional information needed.

Charlotte was some fifteen years his junior; "fit as a butcher's dog" was how she was commonly described. She was from Essex, a county renowned for its sexuality, surgically enhanced women, and swaggering men. Charlotte had adapted to city work life and dressed a little more conservatively than the usual Essex girl, usually seen in anything tight and revealing, orange fake-tan, bright red lipstick on pout-enhanced lips, and tottering around in white stilettos (strange how little had changed in fifteen years), in a black sleeveless dress, and dyed blonde hair. The legs were always tanned, and there was a small ankle tattoo and ankle chain. She was thin and about five feet six inches tall.

There had been a few drunken office nights out recently and a few fumblings between the two of them, not unnoticed by some of the other staff; their relationship had become a lot more casual since then. Charlotte saw a successful banker, who was scorned by his wife; he was a good provider and someone she respected and admired. He listened to her, and she felt safe with him. Age and love handles didn't come into it, and she knew she would get her man.

After the flirtatious start to his office day, there were a few credit applications to read, prepared by his team, a few calls to make, and a lunch meeting with a couple of partners from KPMG; like most of the large accountancy firms, they referred new business opportunities into the bank and also courted the bank to undertake due diligence work and insolvencies.

Lunch was to be at his favourite retreat, the Sweetings Fish Restaurant, where he dined almost daily with accountants, bankers, and clients, the staff canteen, as it were. He felt the fish was much better for him, but adding a few pints of Guinness and fries didn't seem to register that these were not so healthy.

Sweetings is a bastion of old school city, only open for lunch; it took no bookings, and people sat at school-like long tables of eight, whether they are with your party or not. Although no one ever seemed to listen to other guests' conversations, it was always wise to be coded in discussions and not mention any names.

James arrived at twelve forty-five, on time. As he entered, he saw the fish and shellfish display to his right, spread out in the window for passing trade to see. It was like the window of a fresh fish shop, ice chunks and white marble displaying the wares. To the left, the bar was full; city gents sat on stalls tucking into crab sandwiches, Guinness, and wine.

The manager said hello and shook James's hand whilst taking his coat back to the little cloak area behind the small desk.

"Good to see you again, Mr Buchanan," the manager said. "How many of you today?"

"There are three of us today," James said as he motioned towards the top of the small set of stairs and looked into the bar to ascertain if his guests had arrived.

"I'm first," he said and headed to the bar area.

One of the white jacketed waiters scurried over. "Good to see you again," Angelo said.

"There's three of us today, Angelo, and I am first to arrive," James said. "I'll get a drink at the bar."

"Okay, okay," the waiter said in his heavy accent, which had never left him since he left his native Spain many decades ago. "I'll make sure you get a table in the back." Angelo had a full head of grey hair; his real name was actually Angel, but he felt more comfortable with Angelo and had been at Sweetings since sometime dated BC.

Once again, there were bars on all sides where people were eating and chatting, with staff behind each of the counters looking after their clientele. In the middle of the room was a melee of diners waiting to be seated, mainly clutching metal tankards of Guinness, speckled with some glasses of wine. Several of the staff mouthed or nodded their hellos in James's direction. Angel came from the back-room restaurant five minutes later, making sure James was looked after.

"Are you ready yet?" he asked.

"My two guests have not arrived yet," James said, "but it's good to have a few pints first; this is my second."

Angel spun around and returned to the back room.

James headed across the black-and-white mosaic tiled floor, which must have been there since the beginning of time, to the drinks bar and ordered in three pints of Guinness (he knew already what his guests would have). The pints were each served in metal tankards, topped to three-quarters full, allowed to settle, and then topped to the brim.

James saw his two guests arrive at the top of the stairs, and he ushered them down, shook hands, and passed out the tankards.

"Excellent timing, guys," James said. It was just past one.

"Purrrrfect," said Allan, the senior partner.

The three caught up on the latest gossip; Allan and Colin made significant inroads into their pints in minutes. *Ouch*, James thought; *this was going to be a session.*

Angel popped over again and beckoned James and his colleagues into the backroom restaurant area. Three more tankards of Guinness were deposited on the table as the they sat down and joined another four guys, who were on their main courses.

James, feeling hungry again, grabbed a slice of buttered brown bread, ladled on some of the home-made tartar sauce, and devoured it.

Angel was back. "Wine?" he asked.

James was now feeling a little bloated, what with breakfast, Guinness, and bread; the wine sounded a good idea. His KPMG guests nodded in agreement.

"Bottle of the Chablis Cru and a bottle of still mineral water," James said, and Angel was gone.

In the corner were a number of photographs of Angel, in his younger years with a selection of attractive young women; one of them was a young Grace Jones.

"So what are we eating today?" Angel asked when he returned with the wine.

James looked across at Allan.

"Prawn cocktail to start, followed by the grilled halibut," Allan said, taking the cue.

"Roe on toast, skate, please," Colin followed.

"Crab cocktail and Dover sole, thanks," responded James.

"Great, selection of chips and vegetables, sole off the bone?" Angel asked.

James confirmed in the affirmative to all. Guinness finished and a glass of wine down, the food arrived.

James tucked into the delectable crab salad cocktail, followed on with off-the-bone grilled Dover sole, spinach, and fries, washed down with the dry white wine.

Today, the two accountants with him were discussing the potential of financing a large multimillion-pound transaction; at £100 million, it would mean big underwriting fees. James saw this as a deal he could then share with three other banks at, say, twenty-five quid (city bankers will usually say twenty-five pounds or quid and omit the millions, to avoid alerting eavesdroppers of large amounts of money being discussed); they in turn would sell the asset to other banks and institutions, making a commission all the way through the process.

Colin had just returned from holiday in the South of France with his wife and four kids. Colin owned a ten-bedroom villa in Provence on an eight-acre site of gardens and woods, overlooking ploughed fields and woodland. He was churning on and on about the cost of upkeep and how the pool filtering system wasn't working properly and how the French didn't seem to care about getting things fixed in a timely manner. James and Allan had started to listen intently but now both were losing the will to live.

James began to swish his wine from side to side in its glass, and his mind began to wander onto all the things that needed doing at his house that he never got around to anymore, as he continued to nod in acknowledgement of the droning conversation from his lunch companion.

Lunch finished on a handshake and an agreed way forward on the deal. All in all, a good day, in a poor market.

Joe—New York, Tuesday

Joe was having a relatively normal day in the office, making decisions with Frank on transactions, flitting in and out of the finance screens, and barking down the phone at some unsuspecting junior members of staff.

He looked down to check the time on his diamond-encrusted gold Rolex.

"Ah, midday," he muttered to himself. "Not long before lunch with Linda."

Linda had joined the company six months earlier, as an addition to Joe's existing PA. Linda was a nineteen-year-old Puerto Rican, and Joe had taken her under his wing. The affair had started one month in, and Linda and her twenty-one-month-old baby boy were now living in a rented apartment paid for by Joe (or the bank; that part seemed a little blurred).

Linda was a beauty; all the office lotharios had been warned off. She was five feet four inches tall, and Joe insisted she wear flat shoes. She was slim, a size two, as he had found out buying her some of the best designer label clothes; she had small feet, long legs, small muscular arse, and large breasts, with a young-looking J-Lo face. He just fell into those dark brown eyes the moment he was introduced to her.

Linda had never experienced such attention and charm. The father of her son, another teenager, had disappeared from the scene after he found out about the pregnancy. Linda's life had been a tough one; her father had left when she was two, leaving her mother to work two jobs as an office cleaner; Joe related to the hard upbringing.

Joe decided on one of his favourite Italian restaurants for lunch; he often used it for business, as it had discreet dining booths where the occupants were out of sight from other guests.

A few more papers were signed and out of the way. Then he punched the intercom button for Doug, his limo driver, and told him to get the car ready downstairs. A few moments later, he punched Linda's button and said, "Ready in five minutes outside; the car is waiting."

"Okay," she replied. "See you there."

Linda wasn't too sure how this had all started, but looking back, Joe had time for her, unlike other people in her life; he was charming and attentive. He had taken her along on some business meetings, and she was in awe of the way he could deal with people and make decisions so quickly. Then one business meeting left them alone in the restaurant after lunch, and that had turned into an afternoon together, and the rest was history.

Linda knew that they would have a good lunch; Joe was excellent company, and they would be back to the office in good time.

Joe used lunch to chat through the sale of the division.

"We are down to the last six bidders for the business," he said. "They have another two weeks to revise their bids, on the back of the additional information we have given them."

"What happens then?" Linda asked, but a lot of what Joe talked about was way over her head.

The waiter interrupted to say, "Ah, Mr Scattini, it is marvellous to see you again, and looking so well."

Joe smiled; he was enjoying the attention.

Joe said, "Hi, Ciro, good to see you too; can we have some still water and an iced tea for the lady?"

"Of course, Mr Scattini, immediately." Ciro smiled in turn to Joe and then Linda, and he was gone again.

Joe went straight back to business.

"Well, we either get down to the best three and let them battle it out, or we go with one, if their offer is substantially better than the others.

"There are some good bidders; some have little idea what they are doing in this business, looking to diversify. Always stick to your knitting, I say, and don't dabble in things you really cannot understand, but good for us, as we will get left alone."

Linda smiled and asked, "Do you want to come round this evening?"

Joe felt his blood pressure rise, amongst other things, and grinned. Linda loved that this man, so powerful and the scourge of the business world, would melt into a smile over her, a smile no one in the office had ever seen before.

The waiter returned with the drinks. "And for lunch, Mr Scattini?"

Joe ordered for the two of them. "Two grilled monkfish, no sauce, and a fresh green salad."

Joe had had a heart scare five years ago and had changed his lifestyle dramatically; the beta blockers were doing a good job, and his doctor was pleased with his progress.

The waiter disappeared again.

"Let's get together at four forty, and we'll go straight to your apartment. You can wear that great little black satin outfit for me."

Sex with Joe was always a bit of a rush; he was rather selfish in bed and did have to get back to his wife. There had been a few nights when he had stayed over on business, and these had been more fulfilling. Linda at least felt appreciated, something she had not experienced before.

The food was fresh and well cooked. They finished up, and he dropped Linda on the corner near the office. She would have to walk the rest of the way, whilst Joe was whisked up to the front doors. Didn't want the staff complaining, although he didn't really care.

Hans—London, Tuesday 1

Hans had taken a black cab from his hotel out of Mayfair and was now on Regent Street, heading down to Piccadilly Circus. They passed the statue of Eros as they carried on through London's smaller imitation of Times Square.

The cabbie was chatty, and once he realised he had a foreigner on board, he pointed out some of the interesting sites and history on their way. They followed down through Haymarket and Trafalgar Square, the home to Nelson's column, England's most famous admiral.

They headed down towards the Embankment, where the cabbie pointed out the Millennium Wheel on the south bank and suggested that Hans spin round to see the Houses of Parliament at Westminster, the UK's seat of government, dominated by Big Ben.

There were several boat restaurants and pubs on the river as they headed east towards Tower Bridge.

They stopped at traffic lights just before Tower Bridge; Hans looked to his right to take in the Tower of London, where many had lost their heads to the axe man: Anne Boleyn and Catherine Howard, two of the six Queens of Henry VIII, probably the most famous. Many traitors had historically been chained and drowned with the rising Thames tide at Traitors' Gate.

The cabbie had told Hans the Tower had been opened in 1078, nearly a thousand years ago, and also housed the magnificent collection of the Crown Jewels.

Tower Bridge was finished in 1894 as a suspension bridge lifting its centre daily to allow larger boats and ships through.

The cab crossed over to the south side of the river and turned left into an area known as Shad Thames, a mass of warehouse conversions overlooking the river and served by cobbled streets. He once again pulled left and dropped Hans at the end of LeFone Street for a short walk along the cobbles to his restaurant.

Bill—London, Tuesday

Bill was a fit-looking forty-two-year-old, being in relatively good shape due to his sporting past rather than a healthy active lifestyle now. He drank too much and ate too little at the wrong time of the day. Bill, for once, had crystal-clear blue eyes with thick brown hair greying at the sides. He was carrying the remnants of a tan earned two weeks ago on a trip to Turkey.

He was an accountant by training and now worked as a freelance insurance investigator, a role he had taken up with some large insurance companies because of the travel element, particularly between the UK, where he lived, and America, where his ex-wife and two daughters resided. Although considered one of the best in the business, his drinking had got the better of him on occasions with top management, hence now the freelance element to his career.

Currently, he sat in a London pub near St Paul's Cathedral and the wobbly Millennium Bridge. The Samuel Pepys pub overlooked the River Thames, the aforementioned bridge, and the Tate Modern Gallery. There was a small balcony perched on the side of the building looking down at the mud below, as the tide was currently out. Bill himself was perched on one of the stools, leaning on one of the high tables on said balcony as he sucked in the remnants of a cigarette. The sun was high in the sky on this October day, and it was jacket-warm. It was two o'clock in the afternoon, and the newly constructed Shard building dominated the skyline. Bill was three pints of Peroni in and catching up on emails on his iPad.

Bill had slept in till eleven this morning, following a boozy networking evening with insurance, accountancy, and banking contacts in the city, and he had been in serious need of a hair of the dog but was now feeling back in the zone. He had always been a big drinker but rarely drunk, in the eyes of anybody in his company, and able to operate coherently after drinks that would normally incapacitate mere mortals.

Last night had kicked off with a drinks-reception in the crypt of St Paul's Cathedral and following the champagne, canapés, and the all-important networking a small group of the nine most serious drinkers had sidled off into the night and headed to Dion, a wine bar Bill knew near St Paul's station. They had a live R&B band on, which were superb. Bill and the group had managed to annex a table at the far end of the bar and ordered bottled beers and champagne. The nine men were on good form, many catching up on the mundane things guys chat about: sport, jokes, office trysts, cars; no depth, no sharing of emotional turmoil. Bill probably had twelve hundred or more jokes floating around in his grey matter, always waiting for an opportunity to push some plausible-sounding situation into whatever conversation was ongoing at the time.

Phil, a balding in-house lawyer in the group, had mentioned a car accident that his wife had had in his new company car; luckily, no one was hurt. This immediately sparked the possibility of a few jokes in Bill's agile mind.

There were five involved in this latest train of conversation, and given an opportunity to speak, Bill mentioned that another mate's wife had also been in a recent accident, which had left her in a coma. The chatter and joviality drained from the atmosphere as the guys leant in to hear more about this sorry tale of events.

Bill carried on, knowing he had hooked the audience, straight-faced.

"Shocking, she was on the way to pick the kids up from school, slid on oil into oncoming traffic. Dave my chum has been going to the hospital every day for the last three weeks, been on compassionate leave from the office, the kids being looked after by the outlaws," Bill went on.

"Wow, shocking, devastating, sickening" were shared amongst the incredulous listeners.

Bill then explained, "Yeah, the doctors had suggested reading to her, playing her favourite music, recording the kids playing and replaying this, getting their dogs to bark, and do the same, anything that might get through."

Then in for the kill: "One of the doctors suggested some touching, even sexual contact," Bill said.

The guys weren't too sure where this was going, but there wasn't a smile amongst them; some were nodding that they had heard that this therapy worked, and each was thinking about the agony of this situation.

"Well, the doctor suggested some oral sex, and when left alone, Dave obliged. Fucking hell, she flatlined there and then!" Gasps from the men listening.

"The crash trolley rolled in, and the doctor asked what happened."

"'She must have choked,' said Dave." Bill grinning from ear to ear as all realised that they had been sucked in, literally.

The group erupted into laughter and backslapping; this caught the attention of the others, and the joke was summarised for their benefit by the audience.

The drinking carried on in earnest, another opportunity with a different group of drinkers; there had been a girl reported missing on the news, and this passed through the chatter without further comment. Bill mentioned that his friend's wife had been missing now for three weeks. He said that he had a call that very evening from Dave, who was wailing loudly down the phone. He had their attention, wide-eyed and awash with booze; could this be true?

"He was crying so badly, he told me that the police had been round and told him to prepare for the worst." Bill thought one of the guys might have a tear in his eye, nah, not possible surely. He carried on, "Dave was so shocked by this news from the police and was gutted that he would have to go back to the local charity shop to get all of his wife's clothes back."

Once again, there were belly laughs and acknowledgement that the joke had been taken in the listeners.

There were plenty more to come, but Bill kept everybody on their toes.

There had been a few touchy-feely situations with the guys and some of the attractive young women in the bar, but lap dancing seemed to be on their wayward minds. The immediate options, given the time, were Secrets at Tower

Bridge, Holborn, or Stringfellows, either Covent Garden or Oxford Street. Given his past escapades, Bill had a card at Stringys, which entitled no entrance fee for his entourage (a £180 saving). He had met Peter, the owner, a number of times, and his resounding memory, even though alcohol-fuelled on each occasion, was that the guy had the softest hands he had ever felt (having shaken hands with him one drunken evening), man and girl alike.

He preferred the more established Covent Garden venue, and this was decided as the next destination. St Paul's is not the greatest place for black cabs at one in the morning, so Addison Lee contract cabs was called on someone's office account to pick the guys up from Dion.

Fifteen minutes later, the two black people carriers were whisking the sodden passengers across town, east to west. Away from Bill's hotel, but sod it, he thought.

They were at Stringfellows within twenty minutes, and all grouped together outside the club's red-roped entrance. The bouncers recognised Bill, who dropped them ten pounds each as the entourage stumbled forward and were let through into the upstairs bar area. A few lost their overcoats and bags at the cloakroom on the right. Several exited left to the toilets. Bill suggested that they grab a beer at the bar and leant across to kiss the resident head barmaid, Karen, a svelte forty-plus-year-old blonde, who had apparently been a part of the furniture for many years. Beers were ordered with more champagne as the girls descended upon the group of men, like great whites in a feeding frenzy.

"Hi, who, where, why, do you want a private dance, shall we get a table, I'd love a drink" were part of the chorus going on in everybody's ears.

Three girls were in different states of undress on a podium opposite the bar; one eye was always on these and one on the three or four girls all vying for the attention of each of the men.

Bill caught the eye of one of the managers, and they were escorted downstairs to the main auditorium and a private, curtained-off area. The girls from both upstairs and downstairs crowd around the area, pleading with their eyes, "Let me in." All in all, twelve girls joined the team, and a couple dozen more slumped back into the red velvet seats to drink more, whilst taking in the naked sights that were now prevalent amongst them.

Romanian, Russian, Polish, Austrian, the list went on and on.

Bill stumbled out at four in the morning with two of the guys and headed over the road to a cafe and ordered a full breakfast of eggs, sausages, bacon, toast, beans, and tomato, with a large glass of orange juice.

The three bleary-eyed and sometimes incoherent men continued to reiterate what a great night before realisation that a working day awaited, following the questioning eyes of loved ones when they arrived home. Nothing so bad for Bill; he needed a cab to take him back to his St Paul's hotel. No questions, no agonising, just sleep and an empty itinerary tomorrow, empty full stop.

He headed to the Pepys at lunchtime the following day.

Email traffic from his kids and indeed his wife had picked up over the last three to four months, and for the first time in many years, Bill felt that he was getting his shit back together. He still had the occasional relapses, just like last night and what would follow on today.

Bill waved back at the waving tourists on one of the pleasure boats traversing the Thames; cameras flashing, he gave his best side.

He had met Monica, the ex-wife, in Amsterdam nineteen years ago, he on a friend's stag party sampling the delights of the red-light district, which brings a different meaning to window shopping.

Monica was with friends from her university exchange year in Paris, where she was studying architecture, experiencing the open drug environment, smoking spliffs and eating drug-infused cakes. Monica was a classy American from Long Island, twenty-one, long blonde hair, a flawless complexion, stunning hazel eyes, and a smile that lit up a park, not just a room.

They had literally staggered into one another beside the canal; her figure, with a lithe firm butt and small but perfect breasts, immediately made Bill start panting like a little puppy dog.

Bill was then a thrusting young accountant with Price Waterhouse Mergers and Acquisitions; without hesitation, he had blurted out, "You're the most beautiful girl I have seen this afternoon; may I be allowed to buy you diamonds and scatter rose petals at your feet until the day I die." Monica had blushed and immediately fell in love with his English public-school accent and the stare of his sparkling blue eyes.

Both had been drinking, Bill quite heavily, and Monica was also a little high.

Monica's friends had started to giggle and pulled at her hand to move on, and Bill's friends had started to mock him over his doey eyes. Bill told them to "shut it, I'm in love," and they retorted that he was "just looking for a deep meaningful overnight relationship."

Bill and Monica seemed oblivious to what was going on around them, and indeed, Bill's friends had started to realise that Monica's group were not that unattractive, either. The two groups began chattering and moved on to some of the bars and clubs for the rest of the day. The two had a great time and followed up in the coming months with weekends in Paris, London, and sometimes Bruges, and this became life for Monica and Bill. They could not take their eyes off each other, and the lovemaking was the most glorious and intense, sometimes lasting not hours but days.

They married within a year of meeting, in Bruges, the glorious Belgium city that both had fallen in love with. The beautiful architecture, the canals, the lovely people, and the restaurants and bars in the main square. Family and friends flew in from the United States and the UK.

Monica finished her education in London, and Bill bought an apartment in South Kensington, close to the great museums and a short walk to Harrods and Harvey Nichols. Life was superb, but after a time, Monica had begun to miss the States, home, family, and friends. Bill had promised her that he would move to America with her within two years, but after promotion after promotion, the years began to move out, and the next big job was always to be the last before they moved.

Life remained good, but Monica still craved the United States that she had left behind and the emotional support of close family and friends. Two baby girls, twins, arrived, called Madison and Chelsea, one for the US and one for the UK, and with Bill working away so much now, the relationship began to come under strain. Monica felt that she had little support from anybody, let alone Bill, and the emotional strength she craved was three and a half thousand miles away. Bill's family were quite disparate, and none lived close.

The years drifted by with promise after promise broken, until one late evening, he arrived back at their house in Kensington after a drink with work colleagues and found the house empty. A letter on the mantelpiece explained very bluntly that she and the girls had left for the States. He collapsed to the floor and wept.

He tried everything to make contact and to trace them, but all led to dead ends, and her family closed ranks. Bill turned to solace in the booze bottle and a string of soul-destroying one-night stands and short-lived relationships. He was incapable of opening up to love and began to pity himself on what he had let slip through his fingers.

At first, he was angry that he had been deserted in such a way. Then came the realisation that he had missed so many opportunities to make things work as a family, but no, he had always known best. Work and the resulting money were key to making sure all could be happy, in his mind, but he was never a part of the life and lives that he supported. All the time he had spent with the wasters in the market, the sad fuckers just like him who wasted their time drinking and covering the same conversations time and time again.

Bill had begun to resent these friends, and although he lurched from sober to drunk days for a long period, he sought to avoid these erstwhile chums with a vengeance. Ironically, cutting this networking out made little difference to the deals referred to him, so he had, like a shot to the head, realised what a waste much of his life had been at the expense of his family. A family that loved him for him, not because of his ability to drink and tell jokes and be the last to leave, but just simply him.

Monica had needed emotional support, which he should have been there to give, and with no family or real friends on the doorstep to take up the slack, the marriage had drifted to a tether end that had eventually snapped.

He blamed everyone and no one, but at the end of it, he realised that he had just blown it. A near-perfect partner, lovely kids, home life that could have been great and the envy of all of his shallow mates, but it was all too late.

Six months moved on, Bill lost his illustrious job in forensic accounting, the drunken binges and the envious, malicious enemies he had made soon took the opportunity to stab his unprotected back. Bill pulled himself together and secured a consulting role at one of the world's largest insurance companies in corporate markets, an ex-client contact, primarily concentrating on forensic accounting and fraud, which meant he had the opportunity to travel to the US to further his search for Monica and the girls. He kept in contact with her family and received a break when Monica finally agreed to meet him in New York. She was friendly on the phone, explaining her need for time and space. She was living in Manhattan and had reignited her plans to become an architect.

They arranged to meet up in New York; she explained her deep frustrations and felt that she needed more time to sort herself out. The girls were great, and Monica's family were taking care of all of the bills and school fees, but she felt Bill should contribute as well, for the time being. Monica went on to explain that she needed Bill to be a guarantor for the apartment she wanted to rent. Daddy was being funny about it, as he wanted Monica and his granddaughters to live at the family residence in the Hamptons. Bill had always been conscious of the father-in-law's need to be in control, and hoping to start building a bridge to return, he signed the guarantor form immediately, with witnesses.

Unwittingly, on doing so, he acknowledged under US law that he was the benefactor for the family, and Monica ensured Bill would contribute via the US courts in the divorce that ensued, which were a lot more aggressive than the UK. He forgave Monica because at least he got to see his daughters every three months, and the need to see his girls and pay his way kept him relatively clean.

Life continued on this basis for some time, until Monica met a wealthy financier, introduced by her father at a house party on Long Island, and was to marry him. Contact dropped off from Monica, but he managed to see his daughters on a regular basis.

Bill ordered another beer and, although tempted by the pizza menu, decided against it. He had caught up on the email traffic and followed up with some of the people he had met last night. A few of them were due to join him for more beers here at four thirty. "Oh, dear," he said to himself aloud and lit up another Marlboro, as a six-foot two-inch, black-haired man joined him on the balcony, clutching a pint of Guinness.

Hans—London, Tuesday

After lunch, Hans decided to walk along the Embankment towards Tower Bridge and onwards past the Mayor of London's offices, then past HMS *Belfast*, a World War II battle cruiser, now a museum. Hans called home and spoke to the boys and his beloved wife; he said that the battery on his mobile was low and as he finished the call, he switched the phone off.

He walked over the Millennium Bridge towards St Paul's, which rose majestically right-up in front of him. To the right of the bridge, Hans saw a small balcony jutting from the wall of a pub—a pub he had passed in the cab on the way to Shad Thames.

A lone man sat on a stool watching the world go by whilst puffing away on a cigarette. Hans took the steps down to the right of the bridge onto the embankment and walked past a restaurant called Northbank, which had a small terrace overlooking the river. "Must be great in the summer," Hans mused, as he swung left and up onto Lower Thames Street towards the pub. He saw the sign for the Samuel Pepys and strolled down the alley back towards the Thames. He strode up the stairs, and when he reached the top, he swung right to the restroom.

In the restroom, he turned his navy-blue jacket inside out to reveal a double-sided colour of light blue, removed the collar from his shirt, pulled on a black wig, and put in brown contact lenses and black eyebrows. He was able to exit at this level back to the entrance; there were no cameras, and now disguised, he strode back up the stairs and ordered a pint of Guinness at the bar, to kill some time. He toyed with this for a while at the bar before walking out onto the balcony where the same guy he had seen from the bridge was lighting up another cigarette, in between gulps of Peroni. They nodded at each other by way of acknowledgement, and Hans took in the Shard building towering into the sky.

Hans's pay-as-you-go shuddered in his pocket. His target was on the move, earlier than anticipated.

He left most of his pint and left the pub. He had noticed a footbridge crossing the road up onto Queen Victoria Street, and he took a right to walk down past Mansion House and onto Cannon Street Station, where he paid cash for a return ticket and boarded a train. He passed through the first-class carriage, where two men were engaged in conversation, one much older than the other and a little worse for wear.

He was holding out his iPhone, which was receiving a tracking signal from another cell on this train.

James—London, Tuesday

James decided to escape the drudgery of the rush hour and take the early train home, striding straight down St Swithin's Lane and over the road to Cannon Street Station. He picked up a free newspaper, looked up to check the platform for the next train, and headed off to the barriers, where he swiped his travel card across the electronic reader. No queues on the platform. *Great*, he thought, enjoying the unusual feeling of openness.

The train pulled in, and the doors slid open, allowing the few departing passengers off as James stepped aboard the small first-class compartment. The timing meant the pleasure of a seat but did warrant the unpleasant intrusion of conversation with the other passenger, a retired bank messenger who had been up to London for a liquid lunch to meet ex-colleagues.

The messenger was very animated, obviously stoked up by a number of beers at a city pub and was chattering away about how the city had moved on and changed since his day. James did wonder if this guy had a first-class ticket. As soon as he perceived a natural break in conversation, the newspaper was up and the necessary barrier in place. Within a few minutes, there was the muffled sound of snoring from the messenger, whose head had slumped forward onto his chest. James smiled to himself and wondered if he too would be similar in retirement.

Fifty-five minutes later, the train pulled into James's local station; the messenger was still asleep, and he hoped he wouldn't sleep past his stop, which he had gleaned from conversation was still another twenty minutes down the line.

James left the newspaper on the table and headed for the doors; he pressed the Open button and stalked off to the station taxi rank.

Carl was there.

"Early finish for you," Carl stated, waiting for an explanation that never came.

Carl just carried on from where they had left off this morning.

James was half-listening, checking email and contemplating the local pub for a top-up or home. Home won for the time-being, or Betsy did.

His cab crunched up the small driveway to James's not insubstantial sixteenth-century country house, he mused that had it not been for the divorce, he could have afforded a mansion twice the size. Betsy, his black working Labrador, yelped in anticipation as James's car neared the enormous wooden door.

The house help would have left at four that afternoon, so he would have missed her by about forty-five minutes. The cab driver pulled the car up beside the front door. James stepped out onto the gravel, thanked Carl, and headed for the door. He pulled the keys out of his pocket, slid the five-lever key into the lock, and opened the door to a high-jumping Betsy, desperately trying to give James a big, wet, sloppy kiss. James grabbed Betsy by the front paws and allowed the daily ritual of wet tongue to slide over his face.

He went into the kitchen, lifted a beer from the fridge, caught the news, checked the stock market, and caught up on emails again.

Hans—London, Tuesday

Some fifty-five minutes later, Hans alighted and walked from the station and out towards the countryside. He stepped off the main pathway and headed onto a small footpath heading into woodland, where he made sure he was alone and unseen. From his small business holdall, he removed training shoes and slipped his jacket, trousers, and shoes into the holdall, revealing running shorts and long-sleeve running shirt that had been hidden beneath his business attire. He took a small mirror and applied a bushy black beard to his chin.

The holdall had two straps that allowed it to be attached to his back, over both shoulders; from his hidden bushes, he checked the path and emerged as a runner and sprinted off further into the woodland for another twenty minutes.

He waited, heart pumping, for his prey, his eyes glued to his cell, which was showing that his target was getting closer. The excitement, tension, adrenalin rush was like a drug-induced high; he had waited so long to feel this alive again.

James—Home, Tuesday

James slipped out of his suit and into cords, walking boots, and green wax jacket. Betsy jumped excitedly; the lab knew they were to enjoy a long walk through the woodland.

James filled his lungs with what was now becoming once again crisper cooling air, exhaling a small mist as he strode out into the trees. He grabbed a fallen branch and launched it into the dense, almost shoulder-height blanket of bracken.

Betsy hurled herself into the green and brown mass, crunching and smashing her way through, desperately seeking out the trophy for her master.

James chuckled to himself as again he sent Betsy flailing through the undergrowth. He squelched through the fallen leaves and sat down on a large dislodged branch of a huge tree, lighting a pipe, a habit he did not share with his work colleagues but an overhang from his cigarette smoking days, and began to dwell on the day's events and the following week's plans.

He let fly with the branch again. He started to make a mental note to get a number of deals to fruition; he also needed to gear up his team for the inevitable due diligence that would follow any takeover of the organisation he worked for. He was quite looking forward to a completed deal, as this would make him a tidy sum on his share options.

There had been some recent run-ins with his American boss, Joe, but it took more than some rabid madman to upset James.

Just then, Hans struck, his lean, toned six feet two inches of muscle sliding from the shadows, and smashed James's face into the tree, breaking his neck in a single twisting motion. The crack permeated the woods; Betsy stopped, startled by the noise, but then headed back and began to search out the branch once again.

James made a small gurgling noise as he slumped into oblivion, his pipe smouldering in the undergrowth.

Hans checked the area of James's final resting place, moving his feet in a sliding motion to make it look like a slip. He tapped out the pipe and put it back in the pocket, all the time looking out for the return of the dog. He removed the tracking device from James's cell and checked his beard and eyebrows were still intact as he headed off in the opposite direction of the returning, bounding Lab, his hunting experience having been used perfectly, remaining downwind of the dog and off the track, stalking his prey.

He changed back, trimmed the wig to a shorter style, placing the trimmings into a plastic bag. He headed back into London on the next train, this time to London Bridge. Once again, he headed off along the embankment, found a busy pub, and ordered a lager. He drank about half the pint and headed to the gents, where he switched the jacket, removed all of his new black hair, and placed it in his holdall.

He left the pub and walked along to the Oxo Tower; he took the lift to the brassiere bar and ordered a dirty vodka martini as he took in the sights overlooking the Thames. The rush was still with him. He took in the attentive glances of the beautiful young women willing him to stare back and perhaps invite them over. *Not now*, Hans thought. *Some other time.*

Upon returning to the hotel, he decided to have another drink at the bar. Now back in his room, he cut the wig and beard into small pieces and systematically flushed them away in the toilet.

He slept like a baby.

David—New York, Tuesday

Melissa was not working this evening, and David had planned dinner at Hakkasan; they both really enjoyed the Asian fusion menu coupled with the warm and busy atmosphere.

Melissa had long, jet black hair, very bright blue eyes, and a perfect complexion of pale porcelain-like skin. She was exceptionally slim and about five feet eight inches tall. Her family stemmed back to Scotland, and she was regularly mistaken for either Irish or a dark-haired Scandinavian.

She recently celebrated her twenty-second birthday; David had arranged a surprise party for her at the Gansevoort Park Rooftop, where many of the guests ended up in the pool during a steamy July evening.

She and David had met at a club where she had been singing in the piano bar; David had been buying champagne for a number of colleagues, an all-male group that had been mesmerised by Melissa's stunning vocal performance, coupled with a tight, figure-hugging, satin red dress that accentuated every move of her perfect body, taut from dancing lessons and daily workouts.

David had sent over a glass of champagne, and Melissa had waved and mouthed a thank you. When she finished her set, she had come over and thanked him personally; it was obvious that both liked what they saw, but Melissa left without further interaction, knowing that David would be back.

And so the start of their relationship had begun, and David returned to the piano bar the next evening, this time on his own, and he and Melissa managed to grab forty-five minutes of getting to know each other at the bar. Numbers were exchanged, and the two began a whirlwind of dinners, clubs, the park on Sunday afternoons, and early-morning bakery/coffee shops.

Melissa, although twenty-two, was going on thirty-plus in maturity; she had been brought up in a small town in Illinois. She had learned to sing in the church choir and had progressed through performing arts school, pushed on by her grandparents; her father had died in a car accident when she was eleven. The push of her mother and the loss of her father at such an early age had given Melissa a drive for life but an underlying need for a secure and strong alpha male around her.

Her mother was diagnosed as bipolar many years ago; her mood swings had pushed Melissa away, although Melissa she took the time to check in with email and phone calls on a weekly basis. Mum had drifted in and out of relationships and had taken up painting landscapes, which with some savings left by the grandparents and the insurance paid the rent. Melissa had long since given up on talking about her mother; the last couple of boyfriends had been told that she was estranged from her mother and had no contact. This was a lot easier than explaining, and Melissa had no intention of putting David through the humiliation that she and previous boyfriends had gone through when Melissa had tried to include her mother in their lives.

Melissa had moved into David's apartment in trendy Tribeca after two weeks, and things had been blissful.

David arrived home from the office at seven and had caught Melissa in the shower; he dropped his Armani suit onto the bedroom floor and headed to join her. He shed his other clothing, slid the door open, and entered the double cubicle as she turned and threw her arms around his neck and kissed him full on. His hands cascaded down her back, and he cupped those exquisite buttocks in the palms of his hands and pulled her gently into him as his lips moved down to caress her slender neck just below her ear. He was already rock hard and began biting softly into her neck as she stretched up. Their tongues danced with each other, shared in their mouths as they teased in and out.

Melissa slid her tongue down David's bare torso and then up to his right nipple, which she pulled in between her teeth, sending a shiver down his spine. She slipped to her knees, pulling David's foreskin back slowly with her hand as she licked his shaved balls, moving her tongue slowly up and pushing him into her mouth as she massaged his testicles. David pulled her up and pushed her onto the double sink top as he slid into her very moist slit.

Melissa put her arms around his neck as he lifted up and penetrated her much deeper; they both gasped. David was so hard, he felt he could hold her upright without leaning on his arms. The love making finished up on the bed, which was now soaked from their wet, entwined bodies.

It was now eight o'clock; David had ordered a limo to take them to dinner, which he had booked for 9.15. They liked to eat late and have a few drinks before dinner if they could.

Melissa lifted her lithe body off the bed and headed back to the shower to finish off. David sat up, picked up a towel, and dried himself down as he checked his phone for emails. Melissa began towelling herself in the bathroom; David kissed her arching white back as he headed to the shower to shampoo his hair.

They hadn't spoken more than two words to each other; sheer lust and attraction had swamped them.

David finished up in the shower, dried his hair, and headed into his own section of the large walk-in wardrobe. He picked out a cream silk shirt, black linen Armani suit, and dark brown brogues. He also picked up a cashmere overcoat, as the air was beginning to chill quite noticeably when he had arrived back to the apartment ninety minutes earlier.

Melissa was ready, her long dark hair was like a shining light of crystal, framing her beautiful face. He could just make out the solitaire diamond earrings, a present he had given to her on their first month anniversary, a stunning black Chanel dress, cut just above her knees, and black patent Christian Louboutin shoes.

"You look absolutely beautiful, my darling," David said. "You look good enough to eat."

"Why, thank you, and you just have," Melissa said with a chuckle.

David's phone vibrated into life, signalling that the car had arrived downstairs.

"Will we be walking any distance, David?" Melissa asked, worrying about her shoes.

"No, just a few feet to the car and the same at the other end," he responded.

With that, Melissa picked up a black wrap, threw it over her bare shoulders, and clasped a small black purse in her right hand. She headed along the corridor to the large door. David slipped his phone, wallet, cash, and the little Tiffany box into different accommodating pockets in his trousers and suit jacket and followed with his coat over his arm. He opened the door for Melissa and locked it securely behind them as they headed to one of the two elevators. Melissa pressed the call button, and within seconds, they were on their way down to the lobby and the waiting limo.

"How was your day?" she purred.

"Yeah, okay," David responded, never giving anything away.

The driver was on the sidewalk and opened the rear passenger door for Melissa to glide in. David slid in beside her, traffic passing on the other side would have made an entry difficult. They cuddled into one another and held hands as the driver climbed into his seat.

They confirmed the venue, and the limo eased out into the flow of traffic.

The ride was a lot smoother than the stop-and-go acceleration of the yellow cabs darting for spaces in the traffic flow; the driver took a steady approach and kept the same line in the moving river of cars.

Twenty minutes later, they were outside the canopied entrance to the restaurant.

They had been getting on so well recently; Melissa had had an inkling that this evening would be special, and she was going to be proved right.

Earlier in the day, David had visited Tiffany's to collect a huge five carat diamond solitaire. It had taken several visits to pick out the diamond and the design, a purchase built up from the rare casino wins where he had immediately put away the cash as a deposit, plus he had cut down on the coke.

David opened the door for Melissa, and they headed into the low-lit hall towards the reservations desk. He gave his name and said they would have a drink at the bar before being seated.

"Not a problem, Mr Kettner," the young girl at the desk said. "Just let us know when you would like to be shown to your table."

The two walked hand in hand along the corridor separated from the main restaurant by black wooden oriental partitioning; through the small square apertures, they could see that the candlelit tables beyond were packed. David stepped up to the black stone-topped bar; Melissa managed to find a spare stool and climbed up on board, watched by a number of men in the bar.

"Hi, what would you like?" the barman asked David.

"A bottle of Dom, please, two glasses," replied David.

"Great, just let me fill an ice bucket for you."

David put his crotch on Melissa's knee as he sidled up to her, showing the other men in the bar she was his.

They drained the first glasses, and the barman topped them up.

After twenty minutes, David asked to be seated, and the two were shown to their table; the ice bucket followed behind them, carried by one of the waiters, who had also placed their flutes on a tray and carried them to their table.

Suddenly, three violinists appeared, and the restaurant table was covered with dozens of red roses. David went down on bended knee, handed Melissa the Tiffany's box, and uttered the words, "Will you be mine forever and ever?"

The restaurant was still and quiet.

Melissa began to cry and immediately replied, "Yes, of course," to rapturous applause and cheering from the other guests; she snapped open the box to reveal the enormous fancy yellow solitaire, supported on either side by more large diamonds. She wiped tears of joy from her beautiful cheeks as she leant in to hug and kiss David.

David went on to explain that the bank was being sold and that he would come into a great deal of money, and for safety, he had decided to change identities to protect them from the threats of extortion and kidnap.

Melissa was on a cloud and not quite understanding what David was telling her; it just passed over her, and she thought about an idyllic life away from the nightclubs, a life at last with the charming, beautiful man of her dreams.

David wanted to leave the country quickly and set up life in Europe, something the two had talked about many times before. He said that this dream was now a possibility but would need to be done quickly; they would leave with little luggage, given that they could buy whatever they needed, now that he was coming into money.

Hans—London, Wednesday

Hans checked out of the Connaught, as he had arranged a meeting with a supplier in Brussels. He boarded the Chunnel express at St Pancras, London. It was now whisking through the Kent countryside; it was mid-afternoon, and the sunlight streaked through the windows, causing Hans to squint at the flickering brightness.

He sat opposite a young redheaded girl with blue eyes, in a black tee shirt tapping away on her laptop. The girl's mobile phone started to sing "You've lost that loving feeling."

"Hi, Suzie," she answered the call.

No wedding or engagement rings, Hans noticed, surveying her delicate fingers. The caller was jabbering away, obviously business, as Suzie spoke about her agenda. She was on her way to a meeting in Brussels the following day, something to do with department stores and apparel.

Hans picked up his newspaper but was not reading it; he was more intent on listening to Suzie's conversation with her work associate. As he peered over the top of the paper, they made eye-to-eye contact; the afternoon sun caught both of their eyes, and they shone a brilliant blue. She smiled, mid-conversation.

"When is your print run?" she asked.

The eye contact continued as Hans returned the mutual smile; Suzie brushed her free hand through her long red hair, her pupils blackening as the intensity of Hans's stare continued.

The rumble of the train and the excitement of the eye contact aroused Hans.

Suzie finished her call and looked back at the beckoning computer screen; work or Hans? Work ... for now.

Hans decided alcohol was a good remedy, but *Not a steward in sight*, he thought as he stood and turned in the direction of the bar. He turned back to Suzie, saying, "I'm off to ease the burdens of the day with a drink; can I bring you one back?"

A quick smile beamed across his face; Suzie looked a little apprehensive but melted with his smile. "Dry white wine," she said, "if you insist, but I'm an ABC girl."

Hans looked puzzled.

"Anything but Chardonnay," she said, beaming.

The break was made; the inevitability of sex was upon both of them.

Hans returned with a beer and wine, and the two of them began to chat, initially about the weather, the train, where they came from, and then on to Suzie's work. She was a buyer for a large department store in London and was visiting several suppliers in Belgium which provided printed fabrics and chocolates.

They arranged to meet for supper in Brussels; Hans was at the Intercontinental and Suzie at the Radisson, quite close together and pretty good for a stroll down to the Grand Platz and the cobbled streets that housed many restaurants.

At his hotel, he checked into his messages and took down the details of hit number two, another banker, working for a subsidiary of a large US group. If Hans had checked further, he would have noted that the subsidiary was in fact owned by the same bank as James's, hit one, but he hadn't. This guy's name was Jack, an American.

Hans thought about the day and Suzie; he unpacked and went for a stroll. Now back at the hotel, he dozed for an hour and then showered. He called home; things were fine, the kids were missing him, but all was well.

He slipped into some jeans, a polo shirt over a white tee shirt, and brown sports jacket and threw some gym kit and trainers into a small shoulder holdall. He left for the Radisson.

Hans walked purposely into the hotel lobby and looked up at the huge atrium; glass-sided elevators moved up and down its walls. In the centre of the atrium was a restaurant and bar, alive with the chatter of many different languages. He dropped his bag with the bell desk and took a ticket receipt.

Suzie arrived a few minutes later, looking even more beautiful than before, dressed in tight jeans and a white top, showing a very firm and tanned midriff, with a jumper slung over her shoulders. The evening was still pretty warm, and the walk down to the Gran Platz was covered.

Hans took hold of her hand, smiled, and kissed her cheek. "Hi, you look great," he said.

"You too," came the response.

They walked out of the hotel still hand-in-hand, crossed the road, and entered the glass, domed-shaped shopping arcade.

"How about a drink in the Grand Platz and back for some food in the lanes?" Hans proffered.

"Sounds great," Suzie replied.

"Any preference on food," he asked. "Do you like shellfish?"

"Love it; moules frites for me," said Suzie.

"And for me," replied Hans.

The couple were like two teenagers, just allowing the atmosphere wash over them, not a care in the world for the next few hours, both realising that this was a chance meeting that would end as quickly as it had started.

Hans bought a couple of beers; they sat out in the main square, their table warmed by a gas heater, admiring the buildings, and Hans Suzie's midriff. He started to talk about South Africa and its wonderful beaches and scenery.

Suzie gazed intently into his eyes; eye contact was unmoving, and no one else was there with them. Conversation covered a multitude of things but no mention of wives, husbands, boyfriends, or kids.

The Grand Platz was busy with milling tourists, taking in the magnificent square and buildings.

The evening was now very much upon them, and the air was cooling; they both slipped hand into hand and walked from the square to the cobbled streets where many restaurants had a wonderful display of shellfish and fish on ice outside. They chose one and walked into what resembled a wonderful old room from a medieval castle, with large oil paintings on the dark wood-panelled walls and one of the largest open fireplaces, pumping warmth into the busy room, either had ever seen.

Hans ordered mussels for both of them and an ice-cold Montrachet wine, having lightly teased Suzie on her lack of Chardonnay exploration, as she loved it. Suzie spoke about her life being brought up in the Oxfordshire countryside. Daddy was a high-ranking director of the store where she worked. Hans sucked in the vibrant nature of Suzie's conversation and sheer life force.

They finished another bottle of wine; Hans paid the bill, and they strolled back to the hotel in the chill night air. Hans cuddled Suzie into him, goose pimples now on her neck and nipples like stalks very visible from under her sweater.

There was no need for more conversation as they entered the hotel elevator together; Suzie pressed the button to take them to her room. Hans began to nuzzle into her neck, small tickling bites as she shivered from the attention, not from being cold any longer. This continued along the corridor until they fell into her room. Soft kisses to her lips now and then the gentle penetration and the meeting of their tongues, both now exploring each other's mouths, with no notice of the garlic and wine that had been consumed.

They helped each other out of their clothes and jumped onto the bed, with Hans continuing to nibble at her neck and ears. Eventually, his hand glided down to the tremendously moist mound between Suzie's legs; he then slowly moved his tongue to her bullet-hard nipples and further downward until she was writhing under his touch. She didn't last much longer, as she was catapulted into the most explosive orgasm she had ever experienced, shaking and writhing.

Suzie grabbed hold of Hans's throbbing penis and glided her lips over its tip, then pushing it into her mouth, in and out and round. She rolled Hans onto his back and straddled him, slowly sliding down on him, and then riding him wildly until she once again exploded in delight. Hans lifted her quivering body onto her knees and slid into her from behind, and both enjoyed a combined orgasm as he too let go.

Joe—New York, Wednesday

Joe and Peter, the CFO, had spent years gently massaging the figures, releasing and increasing provisions, hiding losses until they could be taken in better years or hidden in acquisition accounting. Never spectacular highs or lows, just steady year-on-year profit growth. The shareholders were happy; they were a safe pair of hands, never a problem. The rewards had grown with the performance; the share gifts and options were considerable.

Joe flitted in and out of the stock market screen, monitoring his considerable share portfolio. With the benefit of insider information, he was able to add 20 to 30 per cent returns in a matter of weeks. He had a never-ending hunger for more and more; greed had overcome any consideration for an early retirement, and the power had become intoxicating. Joe felt bulletproof, above the law.

He usually acquired several companies a year, swallowing them up into the main company and then building up huge provisions in the acquisition accounting, basically taking huge amounts of money out of asset values to provide for future potential liabilities that never materialised, so that these could then be taken as profits in following years or to hide losses he had incurred on other business. This accounting could hide many areas of underperformance in the business, and they had become masters of it.

Joe was looking at his screen with Peter, when Tony entered the room.

"Bad news from the UK," Tony said. "James is dead, an accident whilst out walking the dog."

"Jesus!" Joe and Peter said in unison.

This is going to be a bad month, Joe thought. "What the fuck happened?" he snapped.

"We have some sparse detail, but essentially, he fell and broke his neck," said Tony.

"Jesus," they said again.

"Thanks, Tony; catch you later. Can you find out if James had a family?" Joe said as he turned to call Pat one of his personal assistants. "Pat, get me human resources and tell Frank to join us in my room, immediately."

John Schroder—Los Angeles, Wednesday

John Schroder was the head of Joe's office in Los Angeles, covering the West Coast of the States.

It was Wednesday evening, and John and the rest of his senior team had spent all day preparing a presentation for the banking division's CEO. Joe and his two bag carriers, Peter and Frank, would be arriving in LA late tomorrow afternoon. Any presentation had to be concise and hit the point. Joe's attention span was like that of a gnat, and if a point could be misconstrued, it would be by Joe.

Joe had once called his whole sales force pathological liars because something in a report could be taken two different ways. Obviously, the reported item was true, but because it could be taken to have a different interpretation, which Joe had immediately hooked onto, and the forthcoming explanation from the vice president of sales was not sufficient, Joe had torn into him and the rest of the team. The members of the credit board just sat stum, knowing that any interruption or attempt to ease the situation would probably mean their instant dismissal. There was no tolerance with Joe.

Joe also liked the sound of his own voice, enjoyed having his ego massaged, and relished any situation where someone he knew was in trouble or could be wound up. Joe liked to dish it, but woe betides anyone trying to give any back.

As such from the mass of management information available to the unit, John and his team had distilled this down to the following:

- welcome
- financial performance, year-to-date versus budget
- new business performance and deals pending completion
- portfolio performance and any issues
- staff update and issues
- close

All neatly on a total seven pages, with some interesting gossip on staff, not documented but to be discussed, and some opportunities to get some deal changes agreed for some juicy fees. Joe was always a lot more amenable face-to-face, and anything to do with fees seemed to get his blood up.

The team also rehearsed who was to cover what; all were clear that only one person would speak on each subject. There would be no interjections; no one would make any interpretation or use the line "what he is really trying to say …" or anything that might undermine the message or be misunderstood in any way. They were a team, and if anything needed to be picked up on, it would fall to John and no one else.

John also had a secret weapon: Jessica was his head of marketing and indeed now headed the division's total North

American marketing strategy. Jessica was twenty-seven, with long curly brown hair, brown eyes, and a slim body. Joe had taken quite a fancy to Jessica when he had met her two years ago, when she was a marketing assistant. Joe made sure she attended all of the meetings when he was there, both internally and externally. He often placed his hands on her shoulders when she sat in on meetings in the LA office boardroom, and he had her shipped off to New York for two months to learn more about the organisation. Jessica had been promoted in New York. Coincidently, the head of marketing in New York was caught fiddling his expenses whilst she was on assignment and was fired.

Jessica had been quizzed many a time by John, out of earshot to anybody else, about her relationship with Joe, but nothing was ever forthcoming, just a knowing smile. John was astounded when she received a two hundred-thousand dollar bonus after her first year in the new role, but he made sure she was there when Joe was in town.

John had worked for the bank for twelve years; he had previously headed up the local Wells Fargo office, and Joe had heard from the industry that John was doing great things in LA for Wells, whereas Joe's office always seemed to be in second place. Joe made a direct approach to John and charmed him over lunch, promising him the world, a clean sheet of paper, substantial salary, and a very large sign-on bonus. The latter had happened, but once John joined, it was "My way or the highway" with Joe. That said, the money was extraordinarily good, so John put up with everything Joe and his processes had to throw at him. After all, they only spoke twice a week, visits were quarterly, and outside of that, John and his team were out of the daily grind and intimidation that the New York employees were put through.

John was a complete petrol head and had bought an Aston Martin DB9 Volante, the drop head, when they had been first introduced into the States. He was several changes in and had been looking at the DBS version during the week. He needed a good bonus to persuade the wife that the additional one hundred thousand dollars for effectively the same car plus a few bells and whistles was worthwhile.

How the British, well, it had been Ford that had introduced the DB9, and now the Koreans, who owned the iconic brand, could build such a car ideal for long drives in the sun was beyond him. He had been to England many times and was sure summer consisted of no more than three days a year; getting anywhere by car was a complete arse ache given the traffic, small two-lane roads, narrow country lanes, and endless roadworks.

It was now six fifteen in the evening, and John stepped out into the bank's parking lot, having said his goodbyes to whoever was left in the office. They had sent a nine-page report on the perfume company to New York before Joe and the guys had left, so they could read this on the plane. John would then further summarise the position when they met tomorrow. He arranged for a six-seater car and would head over to meet the trio at the airport, but now he was heading home for dinner with his stunning wife and ten-year-old daughter.

His parking space was under the building, where the bank had parking for twenty-two cars. The Aston Martin sat there in all its splendour, surely the most beautiful car in the world. This version was midnight blue, a dark metallic blue with an understated sparkle, similar to the stars in an early evening sky, where the stars were easy to pick out due to no light pollution from a major city, something he had seen when in Bali. The canvas roof was dark blue, and the interior was cream leather seating with dark blue piping and carpets. The top of the dash was blue, as was the leather steering wheel.

He slid the crystal key into its slot, stepped on the brake pedal, and pushed the starter button. The engine throbbed into life, six litres of V12 muscle. He never left the handbrake on and prodded the R (for reverse) button on the dash, pulling majestically out of his space and slowly up the ramp to the exit, so avoiding scrapping the front spoiler on the concrete ridged floor. He stabbed the park button and waited for the barrier to raise, a slow process but the part he liked best. With another grinding few inches for the gate to go, he pumped the accelerator, the exhaust bafflers opened, and the noise in the confined space resembled a fighter jet accelerating to Mach 3, as a melody of car alarms sprang into life around the car space. It was sheer bedlam, and John loved every millisecond of it as he lurched the car onto the road beyond and headed for home.

John was a keen runner and regular marathon participant, and he ran every morning before heading into the office; he would also run in the evenings given the chance, but not tonight, as he had dinner with Joe tomorrow and wanted to dedicate this evening to family.

Lucy, his wife, and Lucinda, his daughter, would have cooked dinner together to surprise Daddy, but he already knew, having been tipped off by Lucy, to ensure he would make all of the right compliments. John began to realise that his earlier thoughts on English traffic may have been overdone as he sat in the LA exodus, and flashes of acceleration from the Aston were few and far between. The car was also dwarfed by the SUVs, all guzzling more gas than the six litres under the Aston's hood, with their grinning kids looking down into the Aston's cockpit.

He was listening to a CD mix put together by Lucinda and genuinely worrying about tomorrow's visit as Pink exploded into "Let's Get This Party Started," which brought a big grin to his face.

New business opportunities in LA had all but evaporated over the last quarter; the portfolio of clients was beginning to see some weakness, and like most bankers, John lived beyond his monthly salary, with recovery from the excess from the annual bonus, which was all at the whim of a madman named Joe.

The ninety minutes disappeared, and John dabbed the button to open the gates to home. At last, an open piece of road, as he revved the car along the three hundred and twenty feet of drive.

Lucy and Lucinda had heard the car; Lucinda rushed out, as she was very excited that Daddy would be sampling her cooking.

They had decided on spaghetti carbonara, a mix of diced bacon, sautéed onions, diced garlic, mushrooms, pasta, Parmesan cheese, and egg yolk; Lucinda had loved cracking the egg and separating the yolk. They had also made their own garlic bread. John loved Italian; most Saturdays, they descended on San Carlo's, their local and best Italian restaurant, where they were treated like royalty. Lucinda loved it as the waiters treated her like a princess. The owner, Giuseppe, would always make sure they had a great booth, and John had regularly seen Cameron Diaz, Drew Barrymore, the David Beckham family, and many other Hollywood and sporting luminaries in attendance.

Lucinda was a precocious little imp of a girl, with flowing, long blonde hair, blue eyes, and a little freckled nose.

"Daddy," she said, "I have cooked your favourite for dinner, it's taken me hours."

John knew that was not possibly the case, but he contorted his face into one of awe and amazement at this feat. Lucinda jumped up and kissed John and took his small leather case from him.

"How was school?" John asked.

"Fine," she responded.

"What did you get up to?"

"Nothing really," she said, uninterested.

"Oh, glad we pay so much for nothing," John said with a smile on his face. But this sarcasm was lost on Lucinda, whose only aim in life at this moment was to get Daddy to the dinner table as soon as possible.

Lucy was at the door and stepped forward to give John a hug and a kiss.

Lucy was thirty-four, a stereotype of LA, with long blonde hair to the crack of her perfectly formed arse, one deep blue and one deep green eye; she was five feet six inches tall and had been working in underwriting at Wells Fargo when the two of them had met. Initially, the atmosphere had been a formal and frosty one.

New business and underwriting never mixed well, but John had proved time and time again, he was a company man. He wanted safe deals, not fast commission earning transactions that lined his pockets without thought for what might happen in the future, a theme Lucy had seen in so many other salespeople; get the deal on, if it went wrong after that, it was the portfolio managers' problem. "After all, it was still breathing when it was paid out."

So the normal friction between sales and underwriting mellowed, and they really began to get on. It was the late nights in the office pulling the deals together and a few drinks afterwards that cemented their relationship into something more.

"How was your day, darling?" she asked knowingly, snuggling into him.

He cuddled her back and just shrugged his shoulders and frowned.

"We got all we needed done, but with Joe, you never know how things will go. I understand he was in London last week; they are not doing too well. They have a propensity for company cars and mobile phones and other perks. Apparently, Joe took all the company cars away, the gas allowances, the lunch perks, and was in discussion about the mobile phones, when the local managing director said something like phones are a fashion accessory for the staff in the United Kingdom.

Joe bounced off all four walls, and Frank hid under the boardroom table; John smiled to himself at this folklore story.

"Ouch, so what happened?" asked Lucy.

Lucinda had dumped John's bag in the hall and was bouncing around quite impatiently.

"I think he wanted to fire a few people," John said, "but the European laws are pretty onerous, and the local human resources manager did a great job in telling Joe it would cost him a lot more if he fired the people without proper process.

That said, the local guy won't get a bonus, no matter how good their performance is."

He disrobed his jacket as he came through the hall and headed towards the large open-plan kitchen.

"Hey, something smells great," he said.

Lucinda grinned from ear to ear.

"We'll dish up in fifteen minutes," Lucy said.

"Great, I'll just get into some jeans and be straight down," John said as he headed up to their bedroom.

"Wine?" Lucy asked.

"God, yes. I'm going to need it," came John's response, over his shoulder.

Lucy headed to the glass-fronted wine and champagne refrigerator and picked out a local pinot, opened the bottle, and poured two substantial glasses.

Lucinda had set the table and was lighting a couple of candles. *Kids' fascination with fire,* Lucy thought and had to repeat what she had said a thousand times: "I don't want you messing with lighters and matches when an adult isn't around, Lucinda."

"I know, Mom," snapped back the reply, Lucinda's face looking like she was chewing a wasp.

The polished black granite table had been set out with two large candles, now burning brightly, three gold placemats surrounded by spoons and forks, and a couple of mats in the centre of the table to support the garlic bread, Parmesan cheese, salt, and pepper. Lucy had diced some fresh coriander, as John loved this flavour and would sprinkle it across the pasta with the Parmesan. Lucinda wasn't so sure, as anything green was a no-go area, and she would also make sure that her own serving would be devoid of mushrooms if possible; onions and garlic just about passed muster.

Lucinda would ensure a layering of Parmesan that would extinguish any other taste.

John slipped off his shoes and laid them on the slanted shelf in the wardrobe; he hung up his suit. He had had this daily task beaten into him by Lucy, as his previous habit of leaving jacket downstairs, suit trousers on the floor, and shoes anywhere they dropped had driven her mad. He pulled on a pair of jeans and left his off-pink shirt tails out. He checked his emails but didn't bother to respond to anything. He ambled back down the stairs and sought to eradicate any worrisome thoughts about tomorrow from his mind.

Lucinda was in Abercrombie joggers and tee shirt; more importantly, Lucy was in a pair of figure-hugging jeans, what an arse, Victoria Beckham's latest, and a waist-hugging white lace blouse, probably from Abercrombie and Fitch. She had no bra on, and her silicon-fuelled boobs thrust her nipples forward like a couple of nuclear warheads. Her tanned bare feet and natural but buffed toenails added to the effect. *Yum*, John thought, *how lucky I am*. He would have his tongue in there tonight.

Lucinda was dishing up, ensuring the mushrooms were heading in her parents' direction.

John came in from behind Lucy, put his arms around her waist, and thrust his crotch into her backside; he nuzzled down and kissed her neck. He felt a shiver go through her body. Lucinda was oblivious, still counting out mushrooms.

"Time to sit down," Lucinda said as she and Lucy carried the pasta and garlic bread to the table. John was already sat down and had slugged back half of his wine glass by the time they laid out the food. Lucy placed the wine bottle in the cooler and moved it in John's direction.

The rest of the meal was spent congratulating Lucinda on a masterpiece of culinary skills; it indeed was good but was obviously given Lucy's oversight.

It was time for Lucinda to hit bed; school tomorrow. She carried on, oblivious to the time constraints; she just had to do this and do that, until Lucy erupted, "Bed. Now," and then there was the peck of a kiss tonight, and she was gone.

The second bottle of wine was open, and John had slumped onto one of the lounge sofas and started flicking through the channels. For once, he avoided the news and sought out some romcom that the two of them could snuggle up to and watch together. It would make a change from the sci-fi that John would normally watch. *Was* Alien vs. Predator *not a romcom?* he asked himself.

He flicked through the list and settled on a film called *50 First Dates*; this was about a girl, Drew Barrymore, who could only remember a day at a time, following an accident. Adam Sandler was the suitor, generally a bit of a buffoon in John's eyes, but having seen Drew in the flesh, he thought it would be a worthwhile use of time.

Lucinda was now tucked up in bed, the dishes were in the washer, the table cleared.

Lucy and those tight jeans sauntered across the room, glass of wine in hand. She placed the glass on one of the side tables and jumped John.

"What's on the TV?" she asked.

"Dust," John said, waiting for the slap.

"Ha, ha, so what we watching?" Lucy said, playfully patting his face in a faux slap.

"*50 First Dates*, something about an Arab and his love of date trees," John joked.

"Oh, greaaaaaat, or is that grate, as on my teeth?" she said.

The film kicked off, and the two cuddled into one another on one of the four large cream sofas. The movie was soothing and sentimental. Sandler was okay, Drew superb.

"So, what are your plans for tomorrow?" Lucy asked.

"Finish up and make sure the presentation shows us in best light," John said. "Pick the guys up at the airport, dinner with the team, arse licking as best as I can. Then Thursday, we have a difficult meeting with a defaulting client, the perfume guy retail chain."

"Well, your arse licking is second to none. What's the problem with the perfume client?" Lucy asked.

"Typical in this market: too much leveraged borrowing and revenue falling off a cliff, as people cut back on non-essential expenditure, but I also suspect people are shopping more in stores, where they can get all they want at one time, as opposed to specialists, where they don't have the time for the touchy-feely experience. Also, Joe has really allowed them a lot of rope, but at the end of the day, I will get the blame if it all goes south." John sighed and took another gulp of wine, which was now quite warm.

"I'm sure you'll get it sorted. Let's head for bed," Lucy said.

"Yum, good idea," came John's response.

TV was off, lights doused, and the home secured. The two headed up the stairs, John nuzzling into Lucy's behind as he climbed.

Hans—Brussels, Thursday

Hans awoke at six in the morning; the sunlight was streaming through the window, as they had not drawn the blinds. They had had little sleep. Hans looked down at this beautiful and yet fragile girl; what fun they had had exploring and learning about each other. He put his jeans, shirt, and shoes on, picked up the room key, and headed down to get his holdall.

Back at the room, he threw on his gym kit and strolled off in search of the hotel gymnasium, with water bottle in hand. Hans headed towards the treadmill, did a few stretching exercises (although he was still fairly well warmed up), and stepped onto the rubber pathway. He pressed the speed button a number of times and took himself up to a fast walking pace; five minutes later, he increased the speed again and began pounding along the black, cushioned belt. He would run ten miles this morning; there was no pause, very little sweat, and he finished up looking like he just had a quiet stroll in the local park.

Hans took the stairs back down to Suz's hotel bedroom and slid the card to open the door. She was still in dreamland.

He showered quickly, dressed, and kissed her on the cheek. Suzie rolled over and gazed into his eyes; she knew it was goodbye and threw her arms around his neck. He was strong; his body didn't even move under her weight as they hugged and kissed.

As he left, she realised he had brought a bag with him. "Cheeky bastard," she smiled to herself.

• • • • • • • • • ● • • • • • • • • • • •

Hans was to meet with two of his Belgium suppliers, one for a coffee and continental breakfast, another for a leisurely lunch. He had agreed to meet his first appointment, Archie, at the hotel restaurant, where they had filled their plates with ham, cheese, and croissants.

Archie had brought along some chemical samples that they were looking to have manufactured in South Africa, plus a mix of other testers that Hans had requested.

The conversation was all in English; Archie's grasp of the language was excellent.

Archie had been born in Antwerp and now lived close to his company's chemical plant. Hans had met him twice before, and they shared and updated stories on their kids. Archie had three boys, ranging from four to twelve years old.

The meeting was at a conservative European pace, and the two discussed parameters for a mutually beneficial deal, although nothing would be decided here and now.

Archie and Hans finished up and parted company.

It was now just gone ten in the morning, and Hans was feeling quite jaded, what with the travelling, exertions from the previous evening, and the settling of food in his stomach.

His mobile blipped, and he answered the call. It was confirmation that his hire car was being delivered to the

hotel as arranged. Hans had decided that he would visit
Bruges and some of the Belgium countryside after his lunch.
The car was dropped off at the front of the hotel. Hans
signed the paperwork, took the keys, and parked the car in
the hotel car park.

The lunch meeting had been arranged for noon at one of
the restaurants on the side of the Grand Platz. Hans decided
to take some time out in his room, and after stripping down
to his underwear, he laid out on the bed and phoned home.
Sabrina answered as if she had been expecting the call at
that second.

"Hi, darling," they both said in unison. Sabrina had a fit
of the giggles, and Hans had to wait for her to calm down
before getting any sense of conversation.

"Hey, hey, calm down and let me know what's new," he
said. "How are the kids?"

"Everyone is fine here," she said. "How are you, and
what have you been up to?"

Hans recounted his travelling, looking around Brussels,
the weather, and the fact he had another boring lunch
meeting coming up. He explained that he would take a
run out to Bruges, a beautiful town about an hour west of
Brussels.

"I wish you were here with me," Hans cooed.

"Me too, but we couldn't have left the kids. It's not a
good time for me to travel just now," she said.

Sabrina updated him on the boys' latest school reports,
which were all relatively good. Nothing much else was
going on.

They kissed their goodbyes, and Hans decided to doze
for forty-five minutes before his lunch appointment. The

alarm on his phone woke him at eleven twenty, and he thought it best to take another quick shower before heading off to the lunch meeting.

Jacques was already at the table and stood up to warmly embrace Hans as he walked over.

"Great to see you again, Hans, how are you keeping?" Jacques asked.

"You too," Hans responded. "Things are good, and with you?"

Once again, they got down to business; Jacques had also brought some chemical samples, which Hans had asked for.

They both decided on a sea bass fillet for a main course and shared a bottle of sparkling mineral water.

The rest of lunch was uneventful, and they finished at just before one thirty.

Hans placed the chemical bottles into his holdall, alongside the others and some smaller containers that he brought with him from South Africa.

Hans was all of a sudden abuzz; a new life had been breathed into him. It was time, and time was tight.

The samples, on their own, were quite innocuous, but when mixed together, they would create a nasty gas, which would cause significant drowsiness to anyone inhaling the mix in a confined area.

Jack—Brussels, Thursday

Jack Ashurst had worked for the bank for nine years and had been transferred to help with European operations two years ago. He was thirty-six and had been going places. Things had started off well enough, but Europe was overbanked, and the recession was biting. He was under some pressure to get things moving in the right direction, and this stress was beginning to tell.

Jack was fluent in French; he was Canadian by birth but had gained US citizenship some years back, together with German, and this in itself built a strong respect amongst the European clients and introducers; that said, many wanted to try their hand at English in any event, the recognised language for business by all bar the French.

However, respect and a good working relationship was not enough to win business. The bank's quirky and inconsistent credit process had left many a deal in tatters at the altar. The main problem was the divisional CEO, Joe, who would agree on things one day and then change his mind the next; he would also increase pricing on deals, not by slight amends but by massive hikes. This added to the general distrust of American banks in Europe, which was primarily due to four major factors, often recited to Jack by many of the Europeans he was trying to do business with:

1. American banks leave in their droves when things get bad; every recession, they pack their bags and head for home. The umbrella is never there for the rainy days.

2. American banks always know best; there is only ever one way to do things, just like in the States. This is not the United States of Europe.

3. American employees don't speak the language and really don't understand the culture.

4. American financial institutions are always seeking to make a fast buck at the expense of the client. This latter part had gained some prevalence, with many of the US hedge funds entering Europe, buying up European bank lending debt to local companies at a discount, defaulting the loans, and effectively taking over the businesses for very little, known as loan to own, something unheard of in Europe and particularly in Germany, where the local banks now refused to do business with many of the American lenders.

So Jack was tarnished by a very deep coat of distrust of the organisation he worked for.

He had just completed his monthly report for Europe; combined with the UK figures to be sent to the US, these did not make healthy reading.

Jack had moved his wife, Carey, and five-year-old-son, Max, to Europe with him and had become more and more distant from them as he struggled with the complexities of doing business in Europe and the expectations placed upon him by the bank. He had always been an extremely confident individual but felt it very difficult to juggle everything at the same time. Already at the forefront of his mind, this wasn't the United States of Europe, and US-style banking was frowned upon, as were the expectations of large fees.

He didn't quite know how to explain this to his wife and had fallen into the same old routine of saying everything was fine, but both of them knew that it wasn't. Jack couldn't bring himself to tell her he was struggling to cope; he was used to just taking it on and everything turning out great.

Jack was also beginning to question what life was about; at first, it had been quite natural: work and provide. Work was key to the latter, and everything else would fit into place. Then there had been the overseas assignments for long stretches, and he had begun to miss his family. Then the move to Europe, tearing Carey away from her family and friends, and although he had promised to be there for her, he was just too busy trying to make the business work. This was impacting on his relationship with Max, who he wanted to spend more time with.

Jack kept telling himself that things would improve, but they never seemed to go the right way.

They lived in the suburbs of Brussels, and Jack walked to work most mornings. He had left both Carey and Max sleeping when he left at six o'clock this morning. Jack was five feet ten inches tall, slim, athletic build, with ginger hair and blue eyes. He was wearing a black Hugo Boss suit, light blue shirt and tie, buckled, black shoes, and a charcoal grey, cashmere overcoat and black scarf. He carried a computer case filled with his laptop and a melange of working papers and reports.

Bob Renterson

The walk was just under twenty minutes, and he bought a coffee on his way. The sky was slightly overcast, but no rain was predicted. That said, weather forecasts were usually as effective as economic forecasts.

The Brussels office was spread across two floors in a terraced office block, just four stories high. The building was of red brick and had probably stood there for over a hundred years, although the interior had been gutted. The bank had fourteen staff at the office, including Jack; there was an American senior vice president, Sandra, who had been flown in to head up the underwriting team, although they had no authority, and as such, it was a team to provide analysis on deals and put them in a format that was acceptable for consumption in New York. The rest of the office was a mix of Belgium, French, and German nationals.

He got a few emails out of the way in the morning, proofread the reports, and ordered a sandwich for lunch.

Hans—Brussels, Thursday

Hans had checked out Jack's apartment and surrounding area the night before; he knew which car Jack drove and exactly where it would be parked. He knew when Jack would be leaving for his afternoon appointment; the information was flawless. Hans headed off at pace towards Jack's address; he didn't want to risk driving and not finding a place to park, and he was there in under fifteen minutes. He pulled a hat from the bag and slipped this onto his head and slid on his sunglasses.

There was no one about; schools were not yet closed, people were at work, mothers were on their way to pick kids up, but he didn't want to be seen, and the hat and glasses were enough to shield his face, just in case something went wrong. There was always that possibility; although nothing had gone wrong before, fate could always intervene.

He approached the car park gate, swiped the card reader with the card that had been delivered to his hotel, and jumped to bump the CCTV camera so that it faced the wall. There was no one viewing any screen; it just looped on to a hard drive kept in the telecoms, Wi-Fi, and alarm system cupboard in the basement of the building.

He saw the silver BMW parked in bay six; it hadn't moved from last night and probably hadn't moved for a week or so. Hans quickly slipped into the car. He had been given the BMW's alarm transmission signaller; all he had to do was press the button, and the doors clicked open. How they were able to get these details did surprise him, but anything that relies on electronics can be copied or manipulated, if you have the right skills.

He opened the holdall and took out two small containers, which were joined together at the hip; these looked like the double oxygen bottles on a scuba-diver's back and had a tube stopper that covered both tops. Hans took the tube off and poured some liquid from one of the samples from Jacques into one container. He then took sample two, which had been supplied by Archie. He replaced the tube, placed the containers in the drink holder of the car, and checked his watch for the time. The tube would gradually mix the two liquids, and at the same time, the containers would dissolve over time, and the mix would create the gas. All that would be left would be a small amount of unidentifiable residue, even if they found anything; the rest would have evaporated quite quickly. These he placed in the ventilation system. For completeness, he slipped his hand under the rear of the car and pierced the fuel tank very slightly.

Hans then relocked the car, left the garage, and headed back to his hotel, replacing hat and sunglasses into the holdall when he was comfortable he had not been followed or noticed.

He walked into the hotel car park, opened his rental, repositioned the seat for comfort, checked the mirrors, and engaged the engine. He pressed down the clutch, shifted the car into reverse, released the handbrake, pulled the car out of its place, and headed out of the hotel and drove back towards Jack's apartment. As he pulled up outside and settled down to wait, he saw Jack walk past at quite a pace and into the apartment building.

Jack—Brussels, Thursday

At least this afternoon, Jack had the opportunity of a new business meeting. This was out of town, and he would need to get a move on and get to the car, as it was a longish drive. He packed up and headed back to his apartment; Carey was out and Max at school when he returned back home to collect the car. After the meeting, he had a conference call booked with the New York office, which was running six hours behind Belgium on time. They, the US, just didn't seem to realise that he had done a complete day's work and more when they came on the calls that had become more and more frequent.

The last call had been particularly unpleasant, with all fourteen of the Brussels office team on the call when Joe, their CEO, had questioned whether they were, to quote, "running a fucking charity" over there, and he would be over to cut some cloth. When Joe was in those moods, you knew to say nothing unless expressly asked to do so.

Jack realised that he was now running late, and he rushed down and out to the car parked in the basement of the apartment building, threw his briefcase into the back, and jumped into the car. He got a faint smell of petrol, but that was not unusual in the car park.

The car's engine lurched into life as Jack turned the key, he plugged his mobile in and tapped the accelerator, urging the car forward to the exit. The sliding door screeched up into its housing, and he pulled the car out onto the side street and sped off in the direction of the main ring road. He was soon out on the highway and accelerated past several vehicles. The road was quite clear.

He didn't notice the small red Volkswagen a mile or so back that was tracking his every move. About twenty-five minutes into the journey, he began to feel quite drowsy. Too cold for the window down, so he turned down the heat and turned up the fan on the ventilation system. He was dreaming about summer, a picnic in the park; he was teaching Max baseball.

The car slammed into the central barrier, spun over several times, and as the petrol hit the exhaust pipe, it burst into flames. There were no cars immediately behind, and the little red Volkswagen pulled off the slip road about half a mile back.

Several vehicles were now driving up to the scene and slowed to see the burning wreckage; one stopped and obviously called the police.

The police found nothing untoward, no other cars, no skid marks, an accident caused by a wandering mind, perhaps, or just too fast so as not to miss the planned meeting. The Belgium police cleared the debris quickly; what was left of Jack's body was in a body bag in the ambulance. The firefighters had secured the burnt-out shell of the BMW, and it was now being hauled onto the back of a transporter. The entire road had been cleared quickly, and traffic was flowing again in forty-five minutes. Belgium was full of Eurocrats, and they hated to be kept waiting.

Joe—New York, Thursday

Linda had booked Joe, Frank, and Peter onto an afternoon flight out of New York for the proposed meeting in LA the next morning. The three would meet up with the LA team upon arrival.

There had been a number of meetings during the morning, and the three had discussed the latest performance of this LA perfume retailer, which was not good. Revenues had fallen steadily over the months, and Joe wanted his money back.

Linda called through to remind Joe that he should be leaving in fifteen minutes; she would repeat this every five minutes, knowing what Joe was like.

"Thanks, Linda," Joe replied, smiling as he spoke.

On the third call, Joe and his cohorts grabbed their overnight bags and marched out of the offices like three gunslingers heading onto the street, with Joe in the lead and Frank and Peter a few feet behind him; the image dissipated with the wheeled trolleys trailing behind them.

Around the office, there was a noticeable sigh of relief as the tension eased, like waiting to be hit by a tornado that just misses your house. "Yes!" Joe had left the building.

A bank limo was waiting in the basement car park; the driver took each of their bags and placed them carefully in the trunk. Joe climbed into the back seat, Peter in the front passenger seat, and Frank next to Joe in the back.

Joe grabbed a water and slugged this back like he had been lost in the desert for days.

The car pushed up to the metal barrier, which sensed the waiting vehicle and shuddered into motion, rising to the ceiling. The driver eased the car out onto the street and into the flowing traffic, yellow cabs squealing out of its way, seeking out a foot of extra space. The occupants paid no attention to what was going on outside and really paid little attention to one another, as they shuffled papers and looked at their phones.

Much of the first thirty minutes of the journey out towards the airport was spent in complete silence, just the tap-tap on the BlackBerrys permeating the air.

The car was now out on the main highway, graffiti covering much of the concrete on the outside. A light drizzle started, and the windscreen wipers began their automatic whir, adding to tap-tapping as background noise.

Check-in was painless; a flash of Joe's frequent traveller card for this airline, and all jumped to attention. He enjoyed the fuss.

The three walked through concourse and headed to the lounge. They had a forty-five-minute wait, and Frank and Peter were looking forward to grabbing a few sneaky Jack Daniels and Cokes. Joe frowned on drinking, other than expensive red wines over dinner. Frank and Peter usually slipped the Jack in and topped up with a little Coke. Joe wasn't that stupid, but he said nothing and suspected that they also sneaked down to the hotel bar, although he had never caught them, both before and after his dinner sittings. That said, the three were past the fragile relationship where Frank and Peter feared for their jobs; they knew too much, not that they would ever dare say such a thing, but they played the game, and Joe acknowledged this.

The lounge was busy, but they found four seats together and invaded those, coats on the spare chair and bags to the side. Frank asked Joe if he wanted anything from the courtesy bar. Joe mumbled a "No" as Peter and Frank hustled off to the Jack Daniels.

They returned with drinks and peanuts in hand and spread out on the seating.

Joe was checking the stock markets on his phone, having checked in with emails and sent his wife a text saying he was at the airport and boarding for LAX shortly; he would call when he landed and hoped to speak to Joe Jnr before bedtime on the East Coast.

Frank and Peter woofed their drinks back, like thirsty dogs after a long walk, and headed back to the bar for a top-up. Joe looked them up and down like some smelly substance had landed on the bottom of his shoe.

The flight was called fifteen minutes later, and the three advanced, in formation, down to the gate, with Joe in front.

The three were in the first row of first class, Joe against the window, with Peter on his side and Frank on the opposite aisle seat, next to two hundred and twenty pounds of Californian woman chomping peanuts that she had immediately demanded from the air hostess.

The taxi to take-off took forty-five minutes, quite fast, Joe thought, and they were in the air; the plane was buffeted as it entered the low cloud cover, but things calmed down as they hit clean air above the grey.

Joe picked up the briefing notes for the perfume deal meeting and began scribbling some thoughts.

After he finished, he turned to Peter to discuss the latest financial performance of their division. It was always strange that all three knew what was truly hidden in the numbers, but like gamblers they ignored or denied the losses and looked just at the wins and the potential wins. If the shit hit the fan, the business would have to make hundreds of millions of provisions, but they were in control.

Peter – New York Thursday

Peter had been the chief financial officer of a smaller finance company that Joe and Frank had acquired some ten years ago. He was now sixty-three and weary of the games, but he had five kids and fifteen grandkids to think about, plus a wife he loved and whom loved him, but neither could envisage a situation where he was home full-time.

He was a genius with numbers; they would buy a business for, say, $50 million; generally, they would be buying at a discount to asset value, given the sellers were keen to exit. Even so, they would often buy businesses above asset value. He was, under US financial law, allowed to treat this cost of goodwill as a capital purchase and write the cost off over twenty years, making sure the purchase agreement segregated the purchase price into the allowable compartments. So true assets were down-valued, but the goodwill was inflated. Yet the assets or the loans they were acquiring would usually repay in three to five years. Thus, they were able to see the purchase price come back much quicker than they were accounting for; this allowed them to hide the poor performing loans in their portfolio. The business was always seeing an increasing profitability, but if it all stopped at a point in time, the realisation would be that there was no asset profits left to meet the ongoing write-down of the original purchase price.

Peter had written an example for Joe some years back:

> $50 million purchase price
> Assets (loans) $50 million
> Structure of deal:
> Loans written down to $35 million in value.
> $15 million attributed to goodwill, written down over twenty years.

Fifty million dollars of loans redeemed over three years meant that the $15 million, less the three years of write-down, would now be $12.75 million, was still shown as an asset but only on the basis that the acquired business continued to make new loans based on the goodwill and enterprise value in its business.

Thus, they had made exceptional profits within the first three years. Most acquisitions withered under Joe, given that clients acquired in new portfolios were not used to such heavy-handed relationship banking that Joe insisted upon, and it was only the continued trail of acquiring other businesses that hid the reality.

Therefore, the business would have booked $50 million in cash flows and returns and made $12.7 million dollars profit on this much earlier, but this still had to be made back from future profits over the next seventeen years.

Peter smoked sixty cigarettes a day; he was involved in practically all of Joe's meetings and credit committees. He had a bush of grey hair, black eyebrows, blue eyes, was clean shaven and was Joe's equivalent height. He had a New

Jersey drool and given the drag on cigarettes, any sentences were long drawn out, but he was always considered and on the nail.

When Joe acquired his business, there had been several other bidders, and one of the young guns on a competing team, seeking to impress his boss, sat next to him and asked the executive team at Peter's finance company how they went about getting their new business.

Before the sales vice president could reply, Peter had said, "I think that will cost you fifty thousand dollars. If you need to know how to generate new business, we are always pleased to help."

The young gun reddened up, and the boss was furious; they put in a bid but missed out. Just as well for Peter, who probably would have been on the exit list.

Peter, ironically, enjoyed the comfort of money, but his mantra was never buy a depreciating asset over $35,000. He and his wife had bought one car in the last eight years, which they still had. He had, however, acquired much of the local neighbourhood to house his family; all of his kids lived within ten minutes' walk.

Joe and Peter congratulated themselves on the numbers and both drifted off into a light sleep.

Hans—London, Thursday

Hans caught the train back to London and returned back to his hotel, prior to leaving for the US the following day. Sabrina was fine and keeping everything warm for him; he should hurry home.

Hans was now completely topped up and ready to return home; perhaps he wasn't enjoying this as much anymore. He thought about his father, Klaus. Hans was the image of his father in looks, and perhaps this dark side of Hans came from his father's personality gene.

Klaus had been a philandering alcoholic; he was always away on business, and this was when Hans's mother, Katherine, seemed most at peace. Hans enjoyed these stress-free periods. When his father was at home, it was like a war zone. He would become very aggressive and smash things in the house; the more personal the items to his wife, the better. Hans used to hide in his room, shaking, not knowing what to do or where to turn. Luckily for all around, his father disappeared off a cliff one night whilst out driving in a drunken stupor. There wasn't much left of the car, but the police were surprised that there was no evidence of any attempt to brake; Hans knew why.

At eighteen, Hans joined the military and embraced the opportunity to join the Special Forces. "Seek and destroy at will" was their own squad motto; this was arduous training, and in the days of Apartheid, they had carte blanche to do anything they liked. At first, it was hard, but after some innocent white kids were killed by blacks, he just cracked and became an android killing machine. He was in charge of an elite squad, trawling through the townships at night, assassinating any potential political thorns and radicals.

As the political environment began to change, Hans had become restless at the lack of opportunity for what he now considered some form of blood sport and game.

This had become a drug, a need so deeply imbedded in his psyche that fulfilling this rush consumed his every moment. He felt suffocated by its draw but in some way liberated and empowered by its release.

Outwardly, he was as normal as anyone, but some of his team knew that things weren't quite right there when they were out on their covert missions.

As time moved on, the army put him out to grass; he had a lot of counselling to bring him back, but something had stuck, and this something had to be fed.

Even though the relationship with his father had been strained, he had been groomed to take over the family business, and this is what he did. He was very good at it: ruthless when he needed to be and charming at other times. He maintained contact with some of his ex-servicemen colleagues; some had drifted into murkier roles, mercenaries and hit men. Here on one drunken night, he had discovered, although he had always thought it was the case, this darker side. He sought contact with the people who moved in these circles and over time became a major player in international hits.

He had several agents who would contact him from time to time; initially, it was sovereign spy agencies wanting certain people out of the way, either through a direct hit, making a statement, or an accident. He had become a master of what he considered an art. Gradually, he began to get work from large corporations and crime organisations, no side ever knowing who was who. He was able to move about the world on business without suspicion.

Family life and age were beginning to mellow this kill-or-be-killed cancer that was eating at Hans, and he was beginning to feel more in control of himself (not that he had ever felt out of control).

Perhaps now was the time for more help; what would Sabrina feel if she knew, or his boys? He began to slow down his work rate, taking jobs on a need basis to plug this part of his life that he could never share with anyone else. This was a dirty but deadly secret, perhaps not as bad as a murderer, rapist, or child killer; strange how Hans categorised this in a business-need sense. He would laugh at himself sometimes. Surely, murder is murder; these people had wives and kids, and were in many cases just fighting for a good cause or had upset the wrong people at the wrong time. But it filled his void, his need, and he had been able to compartmentalise his life. This was a game, a thirst that required quenching, a buzz, a thrill.

His cell phone vibrated; this he wasn't expecting. This was a twenty-five-pound phone he had bought with a pay-as-you-go SIM card. It was Suzie; he had given her his number. After all, the phone would be gone after this little business trip had finished. She was in London and wondered if he had returned.

"Hi, Hans, just to let you know that I am missing you, or should I say parts of you," she said.

He hesitated for a moment but then suggested she could reacquaint herself with certain parts of his anatomy, which were on the rise, at the Connaught.

He ordered a bottle of Dom Perignon Rose, still and sparkling water, and canapés for two. Suz arrived; she had tied her hair up and wore a black leather jacket over a charcoal grey cashmere sweater and tight black jeans, complemented by knee-high leather boots. He thought she looked stunning.

John Schroder—
LAX, Thursday

John arrived at LAX with plenty of time to spare; his PA had kept him abreast of the flight timings, checking on the internet. The car dropped him off at the arrivals area, swung out, and went off to park on the perimeter until John called confirming their arrival. The driver would then be outside in a few minutes and thus avoid the traffic cops moving him on, time and time again.

On the way to the airport, John had received a call from Sam, his head of underwriting in the LA office. Sam's twelve-year-old daughter had fallen off her bike, and it looked like a broken arm. He was angling to cry off from the dinner. John was sympathetic but knew Sam's wife, Karyn, was fully capable of looking after the situation.

"Sorry to hear, Sam. Poor Michelle; hope all else is well. Where are you now?" John asked.

"We are here at the emergency room," Sam said. "Michelle has been examined, given some pain killers, and will be going to X-ray shortly. It seems to be broken."

"Is Karyn with you?" John probed.

"Yes, she actually brought Michelle in," Sam responded.

"Look, Sam, I appreciate you feel you need to be there, but this is Joe's first visit in over three months, and you know he always wants the senior team at the dinner. To be honest, he ain't going to be easy to handle, and I need you at my side. Remember Marty?"

Marty had been one of Joe's trusted lieutenants in New York and worked alongside Joe for eleven years. Joe was godfather to Marty's two kids.

Eighteen months ago, Joe had bought an operation in London. He had charmed the seller and existing management team with a spiel all the existing team had heard tens of times before: "We are a family of companies; we take the best processes from the businesses we buy and replace our own processes across the board. Obviously, if our existing processes are deemed better, we implement them into the new family member. Nothing is sacred, but like anything that involves change, it's never easy. We have done it so many times; we have a well-worn and tested way for people and companies to join us. It's just like when you buy a new pair of shoes; they pinch a little bit at first but soon are worn in, and they become your best and most comfortable pair of shoes."

As soon as the money had changed hands, Joe implemented his processes, and anything or anybody not needed in the acquired entity was discarded like a used tissue. Frank had passed on a story that the head of credit in London had given Joe a copy of their controls and underwriting procedures on the day the business was acquired.

Joe looked him in the eye and said thank you as the three-inch file was dispatched to the waste basket, adding,

"We won't be needing that anymore. I'll get someone to send you ours."

Good money kept the staff motivated, but as Joe said many times, "I don't pay you to come to work to be fucking happy."

Joe had even ordered switching off the computer system of one acquisition after transitioning the clients to his own, but instead of running in parallel to ensure all was working well, he said no. Saved him $1 million a month in costs, but the new clients had major losses of receipts in the new system for a period of six weeks, which meant their overall borrowing increased by $72 million, more money for Joe in interest.

Anyway, back to Marty: Joe had a regime of meetings for breakfast every morning at seven before he and the team descended on the target. There were usually about ten of them doing due diligence on the acquisitions, supported by accountants and lawyers. Religiously, they would return to the hotel at six o'clock; dinner was seven thirty. Frank and Peter would find the nearest pub and slope off for a couple of the warm beers London had to offer. Joe would always monitor anyone who needed an early restroom break during dinner and assume they had been drinking; this could mean the death of your career. Peter and Frank had got this down to a fine art and always hit the restroom at seven twenty-five.

They had been in London for ten days. Marty had worked in London several times previously; he had lived in Knightsbridge for seven years whilst being employed by Credit Suisse First Boston. Joe had pencilled Marty in to head up London and ultimately Europe. A great move for Marty, who was keen to get back to London, and the relocation also entailed a huge pay increase. On the tenth night, he had told Joe that he was catching up with some ex colleagues in the London market. What he hadn't made clear was that he wouldn't make the dinner. Also, the next morning, he missed the breakfast; too many beers from the night before, but he made the car taking them to the target's offices for their further meetings.

Joe never spoke to him again. They flew back to New York, deal done, and Marty sat in his own office for three months, never invited to any meetings about Europe, never a word was uttered. Marty left and was now with a third-rank bank, in the wilderness, so to speak.

"Got you, John; thanks for the pep talk. I can't afford to lose this year's bonus, which is probably the first thing Joe would seek to implement. I'll be there for dinner."

The phone clicked dead, and Sam hurried off to make his excuses. Karyn would frown but wouldn't make a scene; that would come later, in bed. Luckily, Michelle was in a wheelchair and about to be taken into X-ray, and Sam said that only Karyn was allowed to join her. He kissed both of them as he swung round and headed to find his car.

Joe—LAX, Thursday

Joe had dozed for an hour or so on the flight and now was wide awake as the plane began its descent into LAX. He had taken in the Grand Canyon some time before, which never ceased to amaze him (and for anything to amaze Joe was amazing in itself). Now they were over Los Angeles, which was bathed in afternoon sun and a low-lying haze, not quite the smog of old.

He was looking forward to the mental battle that would be JJ, the CEO of his client. They had met many times before, and Joe had built a typical relationship whereby he was lavishly entertained and rewarded by the client for granting increased lending facilities. After all, Joe made the money for the bank; it was his and his alone for the taking. JJ had been exceptional; hookers galore, usually models from the perfume photo shoots were in play, insider trading tips on several computer gaming companies, where JJ knew the CEOs very well, and of course a steady monthly supply of the best perfumes in the world for Joe's wife, plus aftershaves for Joe.

The landing was, like the whole flight, uneventful, and they were first off and met at the exit by John Schroder, the head of their LA office.

"Hi, Joe; great to see you," John beamed, arm extended for a handshake, making sure that Joe knew he was the centre of attention, something not lost on Frank and Peter.

Joe shook John's hand. "Hey, good to see you in the flesh, John; this perfume deal looks like shit."

John's face reddened; Peter and Frank said their hellos but looked at the floor. It was never wise to make any comment. Joe's opinion was never questioned, and certainly there would be no suggestion the perfume deal was in a shit state because Joe had lent it too much money, without recommendation from the LA office, following nights out with JJ, with whom Joe, like many clients, had a very close relationship. If only they knew just how close.

"The car is out front," John said, knowing not to prolong the discussion.

John had organised the six-seater limo, which was now perched outside the terminal exit; with no bags to collect, the four had finished their hellos and headed off to the exit doors. The driver greeted his new guests and grabbed the bags, stowing them in the trunk.

John realised Joe was in one of those insular moods; best not to interject into those deep thoughts, so he concentrated on Frank and Peter, who were both in good spirits. If he didn't know better, he would have said they had been drinking.

It was late afternoon, early evening in Los Angeles, and the sun was still warm. The New Yorkers didn't acknowledge the change in the climate but just discussed business.

Peter and Frank were always charming company, but Joe was the boss, in fact, the catalyst to making things happen or not. John needed the me time with Joe, but he had learnt over the years when the best time was to embrace this, to brown-nose, massage Joe's ego, and now was not the time. Joe was in his own world, and intrusion here would cause bad feeling, although Joe would probably have forgotten about everything within hours. Any sting from Joe was felt for some weeks, if not longer, by his staff.

Frank and Peter had caught up on what was happening with the LA staff, and when they started on who was shagging whom, Joe perked up and slid into the conversation with a smile on his face. There were fifty-eight people in the LA office; over the years, it had become one of the most profitable parts of Joe's empire, both for the bank and also for Joe personally. He had bled the local businesses very well for gifts, but more importantly, there was a strong propensity for the West Coast businesses to slide in performance, most probably due to the fickle nature of the population.

This meant that Joe had engineered the collapse of many a company, on the basis of defaulting on loan covenants resulting in big fees; he then provided funding for friends and family to take these businesses over at substantial discounts. The bank didn't have to take any write-down, although the quality of the loans remained suspect, as the companies carried on trading. Joe took a slice of any returns, and his associates generally ended up with significant capital gains when they sold the companies on, or in many cases just sold the assets of the company and disappeared with the cash, leaving creditors out of pocket and in some cases the bank as well. This latter position was always orchestrated by Joe, who knew what the bank could afford to take in provisions against bad loans.

"Yeh, big disaster in the office yesterday," John said.

Peter and Frank were on the edge of their seats.

"Fuck me, but Steve has been shagging three of the girls in the office. Different age groups, different departments, but all on the same client team; they had been out at the client's annual staff party, got pissed, and went on to a club. They all found out that Steve had been seeing them at the same time. Luckily, he wasn't there, but yesterday morning, they came in and confronted him, and then all hell let lose when Connie realised that she was the only one he hadn't shagged, and she was so fucking jealous she ripped into all of them, given she felt she had been given the come-on and had not received the same treatment as the others."

Joe was relishing every second.

"I need to get Steve a transfer," John said, directing this at Joe, now realising he was engaged.

"Not in my fucking office, the dirty little shit," Joe retorted, loving it.

Peter asked, "Isn't he married?"

The whole car laughed.

"Yes, and with three kids," said John, realising he now had the senior team of the bank in his coven.

"Shit," was said in unison.

"We'll have to promote him to justify the move," Joe said.

"Anyway, tell me about the women in question," Joe carried on, his eyes wide with interest.

John went into their intimate details:

"Grace: twenty-seven, blonde, true one as reported back, five feet nine inches tall, emerald eyes, thirty-four D cup, enhanced, fit, slim, tanned, oh yes, an analyst.

"Marilyn: thirty-five, redhead, blue eyes, no freckles but porcelain skin, large arse but firm and rest of body all trim, small tits, works in new business.

"Skye: twenty-one, and yes, she likes looking at the sky, blonde, not matching collar and cuffs, mousey, probably a thirty-four B, blue eyes, clear skin, tightest-looking arse in jeans, in sales support.

"Connie: thirty, two hundred pounds, brown hair and eyes, pretty face, she's been working eighteen hours a day on Steve's latest deal, whilst the others partied. He had his tongue down her throat one night after an office do recently; she took this as they were now an item. Underwriter on the deal."

"I assume the deal has been declined by the underwriter," Joe said, easing into the atmosphere of hysteria.

The car carried on its journey towards Beverley Hills and the Beverly Wilshire Hotel. Joe was already looking forward to the paid-for entertainment but would have to entertain the troops to a dinner first.

John had booked a table at the hotel and invited his senior team, to include Steve but luckily none of the girls involved; there would be twelve of them for dinner.

The car drew into the hotel entrance. The driver stepped out immediately and ensured Joe's door was opened first; he had been prebriefed by John. Joe stepped out and stretched his legs; the air was warm, but the entrance was covered, so this would add a few degrees.

The bags were repatriated with their respective owners. John was ready for the evening festivities to start.

Joe took his overnight bag and headed in towards the check-in desk. He gave them his details and was checked in before anyone else joined him at the desk. As Peter and Frank floundered across the reception, Joe waved them off and said he would see them later in the lobby.

"Joe," John said, really ignoring Peter and Frank, "I'll meet you in reception; as you know, dinner is booked for eight thirty."

"Yeh, we'll be down at eight," Joe responded for everyone. "Don't go to the bar, will you?"

"Happy to take in some of that fine wine you choose, as you always do. Later, Joe," John oozed.

Joe disappeared towards the elevators and was gone. The plan had worked well; Frank, Peter, and John had loitered around the entrance and waited for Joe to check in. They too secured their rooms, but the aim was to head to the bar and catch up with John whilst enjoying a few more Jack Daniels and perhaps several beer chasers.

John filled them in more about the deal meeting tomorrow, but outside of that, it was more of a social catch-up and the opportunity to drink more.

Joe decided to grab a quick shower. Afterwards, he sat at the desk in the lounge of his suite and called home to speak to his wife.

The discussion with Monica was detailed but devoid of emotion. Joe Jnr was fine, and the house had not burnt down since he had left.

The three veterans of Joe's empire stood at the bar and chinked glasses as a toast to each other, or the company; they hadn't really clarified what they were toasting.

Peter and Frank finished off their drinks and headed up to their smaller rooms to get ready for this evening, leaving John at the bar.

John took the opportunity to call home and spoke to Lucy and Lucinda.

Both were well and missing husband and father.

The trio descended on the lobby as arranged; John, following a well-timed restroom break, was there with all of the LA team waiting for them. The team all lined up to greet Joe and the New Yorkers; they all knew each other already. Both Joe and Jessica lingered over their greeting, Joe kissing her on both cheeks, very close to her lips.

Joe wanted Steve sat next him, so he could grill him a little more about the office liaisons. Jessica sat opposite; Joe was in his element.

The evening went well. Joe always bought a really expensive red wine; he chose Opus this evening, quite fitting for the Californian venue. Generally, he preferred Old World French wines and seemed to have a great knowledge of these, always named by region as opposed to grape variety. For instance, as his team had learned, Chablis (white burgundy) is Chardonnay, Sancerre (white Bordeaux) is Sauvignon, Bordeaux red (claret) is usually a blend dominated by cabernet, and burgundy red is pinot noir.

However, he would only buy enough to cover two glasses each, and if ladies were present, they were afforded just one glass. Tonight, there were twelve of them, two women, so Joe had established he needed twenty-two glasses and ordered four bottles, based on getting six glasses per bottle, and the waiter eking out what he could, there should be a few glasses free. Joe made it clear that four bottles was the limit, and if they wanted a tip, they should pour conservatively. Still and sparkling water was in abundance, and the team knew the protocol.

Joe had finished interrogating Steve and moved his attention to Jessica. John was out of the loop but was having a good conversation with Peter and Frank.

Dinner was finished by ten. Joe said his goodbyes, arranged to meet up for breakfast the next morning, and was gone.

Steve had been suitably grilled throughout the evening and thanked John sarcastically for sharing his problems. Steve, John, Peter, Frank, and Sam headed to the bar, the rest of the team leaving to get home. Sam had confirmed Michelle had indeed broken her arm, but she was now safely in bed at home. John saw Jessica to her cab, just in his own mind to make sure she wasn't staying the night, but there again, Joe wouldn't risk the compromise. Sam would have to do a lot of making up to his wife to get back to a decent level of points, but his mood had been mellowed by the wine; he had made three glasses without detection, and Joe was now gone.

Sam quipped at John, "Thanks for putting me right in it at home. As we all know, we husbands are always in the shit, it's just the depth that varies, and right now, I'm up to my nose and still sinking."

John laughed and said, "Get the drinks in."

Peter headed out to find the restroom; as he traversed the corridor, he nearly fell into the two models making their way to the elevators. "Wow and yum, think I know where you two are going," he said under his breath.

Hans—London, Friday

Once again, they had a great night. Hans had left Suz sleeping soundly and headed for Paddington and onwards to Heathrow Airport.

Hans sipped a spiced tomato juice in the executive lounge at Heathrow, whilst waiting for his flight to the States.

The flight was called; Hans put down his drink and grabbed his briefcase. The airline had bumped him to first class, and he laid back into his seat and took a glass of Bucks fizz. "Prost," he said to himself under his breath. Hans began to think about the multiple assignments that lay ahead of him. He always insisted that details of each individual target were given to him after the successful completion of the previous hit; this ensured the overall mission would not be compromised should he fail for any reason. He knew there would be four assignments, all adult men; he would never do women or children.

It was rare to have more than one at a time, but times change, he chuckled to himself.

Take-off was eventless.

The stewardess asked him what he would like for lunch. "The king prawn salad, followed by the fillet steak, rare, please."

"Any wine, sir?"

"Um, another champagne, and I'd like to try the Rauzan Segla with the fillet, please."

His mind wandered away from the air stewardess's backside and began to drift back to his earlier days in South Africa's equivalent to the Navy SEALs or special forces. His skills and senses had been moulded into a fearsome killing machine, and if it were not for this hobby, this drug, he probably would have gone insane some years ago. *Perhaps I already was,* he thought, chuckling to himself again. The stewardess turned and smiled back at him; that was more than a courtesy smile, he thought.

Following lunch, Hans checked his business itinerary; this was the bona fide business for his company and would act as the perfect cover for his visits, meeting with suppliers in New York, Los Angeles, and San Diego.

The flight was due to land mid-afternoon local time on Friday, and he had the weekend free. Hans stretched out on his "bed" and slept deeply for a few hours.

The flight arrived at JFK in cloudy conditions.

Hans had eventually cleared passport and customs control but had been questioned heavily and for some time. These Americans have an immigrant population the size of a small country, and they give him a hard time, he thought. As if Hans would want to stay in this country for any longer than necessary.

Joe—Los Angeles, Friday

It was five in the morning; the entertainment had left about three hours ago, as the bedside phone shrilled and awoke Joe.

"Hi, sorry to wake you, Joe," said a very apologetic Linda.

"What the fuck time is it?" Joe asked.

"It's eight in the morning here," Linda said, struggling to calculate the three-hour difference. "I've an urgent call; it's Sandra from the Brussels office in Europe"; adding the Europe part seemed important to make sure Joe knew where Brussels was. Linda didn't really have a clue.

"Oh okay, put her through," Joe said and was transferred to Sandra, the senior vice president who worked in Brussels.

"Hello, Sandra, what's up?" he asked.

"Hi, Joe, sorry to trouble you, I didn't realise you were in LA. Some really bad news. I'm afraid that Jack has been killed in a car accident," she said. Joe knew she was crying.

"Jesus, what happened?" Joe asked.

"We don't know much detail, but he was on the way to a client visit and had an accident on the highway." Her voice was quivering.

"Sandra, close the office for the rest of the day and let the people go home. Let me have Jack's wife's details. I need to speak with our human resources people and will get back to you on your cell phone later. I am so sorry; what bad news," Joe said.

"Okay, I'll do that and wait to hear back from you," Sandra said, and the phone went dead.

"What a week this is," Joe mused and jabbed at Peter's room number on his phone. He told him the news, followed by Frank, who was deeply asleep or drunk, given the incoherent conversation.

Joe called Linda back and asked her to inform the head of human resources and also told her to send a basket of fruit, wine, and cheese to Brussels.

JJ and Joe—LA, Friday

Joe entered the breakfast room, as arranged, at eight that morning. He looked invigorated but sad. His immaculately pressed suit was light grey with pink pinstripes; he had a white collared and cuffed light grey shirt, pink Hermes tie, and black tasselled shoes.

Peter, Frank, John, and Sam were already seated, and all looked the worse for wear. Peter and Frank still had the same suits on from yesterday, Peter in charcoal; his trousers had double creases from a sloppy introduction into his room's press. Frank was in black but with a few crumpled creases.

Joe sat down and ordered some sliced fruit.

"Right, guys, what's the plan for the meeting this morning?" Joe began.

John had not been told about the European deaths, and he took over.

"Well, as you can see," he said, "we have three clear covenant breaches looming. Our asset cover remains very strong; we have taken security over the inventory of perfume and have had a recent going-out-of-business valuation completed by an external specialist firm.

"This shows that we have about 125 per cent cover to our loan," John added, "but our position is worsening as the company is finding it difficult to extend credit terms with its suppliers and is selling the more popular perfumes quicker, which means the inventory of perfume will gradually diminish in value, given the fast-moving brands will be sold and the slow movers will become a greater proportion, thus diluting the value. We also need to make sure Britney doesn't start shaving her head again."

He went on, "We don't have any additional security, nothing from JJ, such as guarantees or personal assets, but we know he must have some substantial assets, given how much he has been taking out of the company in the last few years. At this time, he has declined to give us any other comfort."

"What is the company forecasting?" Peter asked.

"Well, we have the added benefit of coming into Xmas," Sam said. "As such, this will generate significant cash. We could probably support some direct purchases of perfumes from key suppliers to make sure the stores are stocked properly. I would like to see if we can get a one million five hundred thousand dollar guarantee from JJ and take a fee of five hundred thousand dollars to cover the covenant breaches and change in facility terms. Beyond Xmas, figures look overoptimistic, given current trading. We might want to consider an exit in January; we'll collect the cash into a lockbox controlled by the bank; this will give us considerable control."

"Okay," Joe said. "We are all agreed that this business has to go through the seasonal uplift for the best result. If JJ plays hardball, and he will, given he knows that we need to get Xmas out of the way, we should insist on putting in a restructuring guy to work alongside JJ and his team if we don't get the guarantee."

They had a plan, but it would be fluid; things had changed dramatically after Joe and JJ had been in one-to-one meetings before, but Joe wouldn't allow this to happen this time around. He had his bodyguards, and it was time to play the game.

John had suggested that Joe catch up with a number of other introducers and clients whilst he was in town, but Joe had declined; he wanted this meeting out of the way, and they would get a branch performance update over lunch.

The hotel had said they would sort cars out for the twenty-minute journey to their meeting. Joe stepped out to the back of the hotel with the team to be met by two black stretch Rolls-Royces, probably a million dollars of metal, John thought, waiting to take them to their destination. He had booked a restaurant for lunch near the client, so they could leave after the meeting finished and walk to lunch.

John had arranged for them to be picked up at the restaurant; bags were collected from the hotel, thus allowing Joe and the guys to head directly back to the airport.

Joe slid in through the open rear door; he could literally stretch out horizontally, and his feet wouldn't touch the back of the front seats. The depth of the black carpets enveloped his shoes as he cradled back into the leather seat. John had managed to get into the back with him and would use this as quality butter-up time. The other three took the rear car.

Obviously, there was no engine noise, just a feeling of cushioned motion as the cars left the carport of the hotel and effortlessly accelerated towards the perfume client's head office.

John got a number of things agreed with Joe; Steve's transfer and promotion was sorted. He had a number of amendments to deals that Joe could agree to, all so much better than a fourteen-person committee; these too were accommodated.

The two cars entered a huge white arch, which was the entrance to the cobbled courtyard to JJ's head office building. Apparently, the building had been home to one of the major film studios in the twenties.

The drivers stepped out like a dance team in unison and allowed their cargo to disembark.

"When do you need picking up?" one of the drivers asked.

"We'll probably okay for the return," John said, thanking them.

The sun was hot, Joe and the other New Yorkers basked in the glory. The white deco building was in a horseshoe formation surrounding the red cobbles.

There was a fountain of three angels at the apex of the courtyard, and gardens of bright green bushes with spectacular red blooms acted as a moat to the offices. No one had any idea what the flowers were, hibiscus maybe, but no one really cared.

Joe looked around to ensure he had his army right where he needed them and headed towards the twelve-foot-high, double mahogany doors, covered above by an overhang, which would take them into the building's reception.

The reception area was at least two thousand square feet of opulence. To the opposite far wall was a mass of varying artwork; Joe suggested to Sam that they get the wall valued, but Sam said a lot of the artwork was actually owned by JJ's wife and lent out to the company.

"Still worth knowing," Joe said.

The walls, not covered by paintings, were clad with solid oak panelling. The floor black and cream marble tiles, cascading into the middle floor design of the company logo, an intertwined eagle and dove holding perfume bottles. To the left was a spread of brown leather Chesterfield sofas, surrounding a number of antique coffee tables. Beyond the Chesterfields was a huge fish tank; it must have been twelve feet long and six feet high. To the right of the fish tank were another set of huge double doors; Joe knew these led into a private bar room, complete with international-size pool table, covered in burgundy baize. The bar had been installed by JJ for private entertaining of suppliers, so they could discuss deals without the fear of being overheard; it was also where JJ's chief executives mentioned the insider trading situations that Joe had benefitted from so well. The bar staff had usually been carefully chosen, most probably from one of the local modelling agencies, both boys and girls.

The perfume industry seemed particularly gay and bisexual, so these distractions of scantily clad bodies serving drinks and canapés always helped the negotiations.

Once again, the dimly lit bar was oak panelled and had a plush dark cream carpet and brown leather lounge chairs and sofas.

The air was awash with sweet-smelling fragrances. Back in the main reception, the team spun to their right and headed to a bank of three large antique desks, adorned with green and brass table lamps. Beyond the lamps and behind the desk were four of the most beautiful women the guys had set eyes on; for Joe, this was probably an exaggeration and would probably have to be the most beautiful he had seen today. All four wore the same black suit, with a whiff of a white blouse that ran adjacent, but probably covered an extra inch of modesty, to the lapels and the grand canyons of silicon cleavage perfectly centred between the lapels.

John stepped to the fore, but before he could utter a word, the black-haired girl to the right on the central table had stepped up and out to greet the entourage. She must have been six feet tall and wore black heels which clicked on the marble as she made a perfect gangway walk forward. They all stopped and took in this marvel of God's creation.

The woman pushed her hand forward, directly and purposely to Joe.

"Hi, I'm Shelly," she purred, "and you must be Mr Scattini."

Joe thrust out his hand, loving every millisecond of the attention. Shelly's hair was cut short and swept back with gel, framing her lovely features. He could see that she had deep green eyes, with a touch of hazel, a lovely little snub nose, eyebrows that had been styled to an inch their life, and full eyelashes. Her light foundation had specks of glistening gold that caught the light from the floor-to-ceiling windows. The other major protrusion from this lithe body was her glossed red lips.

The handshake lingered; a bead of sweat ran down Sam's face as he anticipated his own greeting.

Joe, eventually, was disentangled.

"Yes, and this is Frank, Peter, John, and Sam." A fundamentally different Joe, they all thought. Wow, he had remembered everybody's name, and all of a sudden, they existed.

Shelly did the rounds, explaining that she was JJ's head office manager and was really pleased to meet everyone.

"We have let JJ know that you are here, and I'll take you up to the main boardroom straight away," she said, keeping direct eye contact with Joe.

All the guys nodded, in between drooling, and would have followed Shelly blindly over the nearest cliff if requested to do so. She turned on those heels, causing a grate on the marble, and clicked towards the large corridor to the left of the desks. There the marble gave way to the same dark, cream carpet that Joe knew was present in the bar, and the only things that could be heard now were the movement of the black skirt across Shelly's backside and the heavy breathing following behind. To the right were two elevators with wood-panelled doors. Shelly pressed the request button, and one of the elevator's double doors opened to show once again more wood and brass. To the back of the elevator was a bronzed smoked mirror, and Joe noticed that all of the men were checking out their own appearances before returning their attention to Shelly.

The building itself was three storeys high, and the boardroom was on the third floor. Shelly guided them down the long corridor. In the middle of the building was a domed atrium, allowing shards of light through the stained glass and straight down to the reception three floors below. Joe, John, and Sam had seen the atrium many times, but Frank and Peter had missed it completely from below, too preoccupied. The corridor curved on either side of the atrium, and on both sides were doors leading into similar-sized boardrooms. Shelly directed them to the left; this room bowed out across the courtyard they entered. Full floor-to-ceiling windows were covered with slated wooden blinds that dimmed the room. An oval walnut table took centre stage, surrounded by twelve carved chairs.

In the centre of the table was a polished brass globe of the world. Shelly slid the lighting controls, and subtle spotlights in the ceiling illuminated the room with distinct circles of light.

Through the open door came one of the in-house catering staff, a fit young man with blond hair, in black trousers and shirt.

"Good morning," he said. "We have a selection of coffee, tea, iced tea, juices, sodas, waters, plus a selection of fruit, croissants, and Danishes on the cabinet behind you. We also have a selection of bagels." As he said this, another black outfitted man pushed a small trolley into the room with said bagels.

The first man asked what each of the guests would like to drink; the other laid out plates, cutlery, and napkins.

Once Joe's team had been served, the men left. Shelly gave Joe a sweet smile and said, "JJ will join you imminently, with Angela, our chief financial officer, and Tara, our head of retail sales. Lovely to meet you all, and should you need anything, please press zero on one of the phones." With that, Shelly was also gone.

Joe always thought people bugged their own boardrooms with listening devices; he had done the same with many a meeting room and listened in before meetings and also when clients had asked for some out time. Had worked wonders for his negotiations.

He didn't really care if anyone was listening in and said, "Fuck me, we are paying for all of this." No one externally was listening, and the rest of the room didn't say a word.

JJ swept into the room, flinging both doors open, followed behind by Angela and Tara, two very proficient operators and both stunning looking, but they had to be, in this shallow beauty industry.

JJ had on an open-neck white linen shirt, tan coloured designer suit, and brown loafers. Both women had their hair tied back in a pony tail. Tara, a blonde, was sporting a navy jacket and cream skirt, Angela, with light auburn hair, wore a dark charcoal trouser suit. They both carried folders and leather notepads. JJ just carried himself and headed directly to Joe for a handshake and then an embrace. Joe caught the scent of Joop, one of Joe's many favourites, as JJ's cheek brushed his own.

"Great to see you, Joe," JJ gushed. "Been a few months. How are things?"

"Yes, you too," Joe said. "Times are difficult, but we are holding our own and supporting our clients and the market by doing some good deals."

Joe and the local team had met everybody before; Peter and Frank had met JJ in New York but not his team.

The five bankers, each in turn, shook Tara's and Angela's hands; Peter and Frank exchanged business cards with them.

JJ and the girls sorted out coffees only, JJ having seen that Joe and his team had already been served.

The atmosphere was good; the bank team sat down, and the perfume team on the opposite side of the table, with JJ taking a marginal position at one end of the oval.

"So I know you have the latest figures, guys," JJ started. "And things continue to be very difficult. We are in the middle of a number of promotions, which are seeing good footfall in the stores; revenue has increased recently, but at the expense of profit margin.

"Angela will just summarise the latest figures, and Tara can give you an update on where we are at the front end," JJ said.

"Fine," Joe said.

The figures were discussed, the upsides, the downsides, room for improvement, supplier support, discounts, the run-up to Christmas, creditor pressures, and the current cash flow.

Ninety minutes later, they were in the endgame; the restructuring officer had not been mentioned, given no final decision on the guarantee had been made by JJ. A personal guarantee was needed for further support, but JJ wanted time to consider. Covenants were restated, but the bank maintained reservation of rights (i.e., it may well have agreed to forebear, but it could still take action immediately if need be). Fees of five hundred thousand dollars were glazed over but would be taken the next day from the client's account, effectively increasing the loan.

The meeting was finished; a number of items had to be followed up. Sam summarised where they had got to and what had been agreed. He would also follow up with an email to all parties.

JJ wanted to show them a new store design and some product ranges. They all descended to the second floor, where JJ displayed a mock-up of the new proposed layouts. A number of film stars and singers were coming to market with new brands. All marketing spill and crap, as far as Joe was concerned; he wanted his guarantee and his money back in the New Year.

JJ caught Joe to one side and said, "Joe, we have enjoyed some special times, very special times together. I would have thought this will make sure we have your continued support?"

Joe was pissed at this and took it as a veiled threat of exposure, but he remained nondescript, saying, "We always seek to look after our clients in difficult times, but the past is the past, and we need to look to see what can be done in the future." He dropped those dark cold pools directly into JJ's eyes. *Don't fuck with me.*

JJ didn't pick up on the animosity.

"You guys free for lunch?" JJ asked.

"No, we have to catch up on other clients," Joe said, shutting down the conversation.

The meeting was over; they said their goodbyes, more especially to Shelly, who was at her post in the reception area.

They explained that they didn't need any cars and walked out into the bright midday sun. They headed out of the courtyard and turned left onto the sidewalk towards the reserved restaurant. Silicon Valley was out in full force, as all took in the sights passing them by. No one volunteered to start a conversation.

Joe was agitated and kept a pace ahead of the four soldiers trailing behind him. He knew where he was going; he had been to the same restaurant with JJ half a dozen times before.

They arrived at the restaurant, wilting in the heat. Joe said he preferred a table inside with the air conditioning, and they were taken into a conservatory styled room with white wooden shutters, fans spinning in the ceiling, and the much-needed cooled air.

Waters all round. They ordered a selection of light salads and protein, rather than bulky carbs.

Once this was done, Joe disappeared to make a call and was gone for fifteen minutes, leaving the team to digest the meeting and otherwise catch up on sport and other items they had missed yesterday.

Joe returned to the table as the food arrived, and the rest of lunch was taken up by John's presentation on the branch performance. Joe took in the numbers.

"John, the market is tough," he said. "We need to make sure we don't lose our arse on some of these deals. We need to stop throwing shit at the wall and hoping it sticks. You and your team have and are doing a good job."

And that was it, an anti-climax all round. No explosion, no expletives, just acknowledgement of the market, the branch, and the people involved.

John was happy; that'll do. No bruising criticism, no tantrums, and thank God, he didn't have to go back and sack anybody. Usually Joe's visits preceded a necessary number of sacrifices "If you can't make the revenue, there is only one thing I can cut: the staff" was the mantra.

The waiter announced that their cars had arrived, and the New Yorkers stood as a team and prepared to depart. John was expected to pay the bill. John and Sam shook their hands, and John told Sam to get the bill. He would then sign off on it and followed the trio out to make sure the car had their bags, which it did.

Sam joined John on the sidewalk with a big grin.

"Well, that wasn't too bad, was it?" Sam said.

"Actually, very pleasant," John replied.

Joe was notorious for sacking people on a whim. In the States, employment laws allow this draconian cull; that said, the European model made it practically impossible to sack people without cause; thus, even if you were making heavy losses in Europe, you could end up just closing down, as the restructuring costs are astronomical. There are good arguments for both; in the US, it means you are flexible on your feet, but Joe abused this. He wasn't looking to save the business; he just wanted people to be in fear of their livelihoods. Europe protects this, but it also puts in barriers that make cutting staff very difficult if you really do need to save costs quickly.

On the way back to the LA office, John recounted a story in the Joe folklore to Sam.

"Joe had been in Paris for a conference some years ago. Concorde was flying at the time. Joe had become more and more agitated about being in a different time zone and not being able to yell at someone. He started calling the New York office at two o'clock French time, 8 a.m. on the Eastern seaboard. No answer until 8.57 a.m., and that was one of the secretaries. Joe was livid that whilst he was away, everyone was shirking hours and coming in late. He liked his people in before 8.30 a.m.; their start times ranged from 8.45 to 9.15, but Joe didn't care.

"Apparently halfway through his week, he booked onto Concorde, flew back, and waited at the staff entrance from eight o'clock and began sacking people at 8.46 a.m. Word got out, and staff were coming up the back stairs and in through the client entrance and heading for their desks, head down. Joe wised up to this when he came round the main office at 9.10 and caught a few stragglers. He then headed back to the airport and caught Concorde back to the European conference. He is a bloody madman," John concluded.

But now, he was gone, and John and Sam slumped back into their seats, exhausted. They may have a quick beer before heading home.

Martinez—Colombia, Friday

Martinez swaggered alongside the huge pool that overlooked his estate. His gazelle-like legs, tanned nearly black, dropped from his sky-blue shorts and led down to dark blue moccasins. He wore an unbuttoned white silk shirt and large black sunglasses.

Armed guards were everywhere; his fortress was better protected than Fort Knox: movement detectors, infrared cameras, land mines that could be armed from the control room, radar, and surface-to-air missiles. The Americans were not breaching this defence to kill Martinez, as they had killed his brother five years ago. The estate also had its own airfield and helicopter pad; the latter gave a short hop to Martinez's grand one hundred and twenty-five-foot motor yacht, called *Assilem* (many assumed it meant *Asylum*).

Martinez was six feet four inches, lithe, with oiled, swept-back black hair and dark pools for eyes. His face was handsome with a bone structure reminiscent of a rugged mountain range, a perfect set of bleached teeth, and a smile that would melt any woman's heart, but his eyes never smiled, giving an air of menace and putting the fear of a demon into anyone receiving a glare in the wrong circumstances.

The big M was entertaining, and the lunch had cascaded into the mid-afternoon. His kids were at school; their mother had died at the same time as his brother, not that Martinez had been upset (it saved him the trouble), and the nannies were under strict orders to keep them away from the pool area and the back of the mansion when they arrived back.

Covertly, a number of local politicians, judges, and police chiefs had been ferried in via helicopter to join Martinez for a lavish lunch. The Alaskan snow crab legs, lobsters, and fillet steaks had made a mark, washed down with Cristal, Petrus at ten thousand dollars a bottle, and the King Louis XIII cognac now flowing with coke mixers, at two thousand dollars each in their Baccarat crystal decanters. They had planned to meet on M's yacht, but the ocean had become choppy, so the decision was made for the party of twelve to be entertained within his compound.

The estate was positioned on the top of a small hill, overlooking the grounds and a small village to the rear, which it loomed over like a medieval castle.

On the four distinct corners, round turrets of some six stories rose into the sky. The walls were painted a light pink; to the rear of the property, there were five arches that rose to support a large terrace overlooking the pool.

The pool was Olympic size, with Jacuzzis at either end, raised some eight feet, with waterfalls cascading from them into the pool. Surrounding the pool were large sandstone slabs and beyond these lush green borders.

There were three dozen young girls around the pool, all topless and in different coloured G-strings, strutting around in heels. The combined weight of the eleven guests was probably double that of the girls, but that wouldn't stop the impeding sex fest, all covered by the discreetly placed cameras around the pool and the pool house, where there were five rooms made up with small beds.

One of M's aides stepped through the crowd with a phone in hand.

"There is a call for you, sir; the States, something urgent. My apologies."

Martinez took the phone without comment, saying, "Hi, what is your problem?"

After listening for a minute, he said, "Well, consider that problem dealt with. Get the details I need onto the network I just gave you. Adios."

Martinez made the necessary arrangements and returned to the party.

David—New York, Friday

Today was the day the $20 million arrived, as anticipated. David initiated the complex web of money transfers, to eventually pick up the funds in Switzerland; the Caribbean or South America would be obvious, but Europe should be relatively safe to start a new life, was his mindset.

David had booked flights for Mexico; from there, they would fly to Brazil, change passports, and head to Argentina. From there, they would return to Europe, landing in Madrid. He had left his Danish car for delivery to his hotel in the Spanish capital; he would then drive leisurely through Spain, France, Italy, Switzerland, and then Germany to Copenhagen. He and Melissa would be able to take in some the splendours of the Old World on the way to their new lives.

David felt sure that the first part of his plan could be achieved before anyone suspected foul play. In his mind, it was impossible for anyone to track the money to Switzerland, anyway. His aim would be to move some of the money onto Denmark, where his Swedish ancestry should lose him in the crowd. Melissa was a gorgeous blue-eyed brunette, but initially she would have to change to blonde; they would learn Danish together.

Sergey—Moscow

Moscow was deep in snow, and the temperature had fallen to twelve below. People shuffled through the icy streets in their yeti-type booted feet, fur coats, and hats.

A black sports utility vehicle, with blacked-out windows, slid to a halt in a dimly lit side street in the red-light district. The front passenger window slid down, and a blond man popped his head out to survey the area. He opened the door and stood alert in the street, peering all around, like a hunter looking out for game on the savannah, albeit a very cold one, as snow settled on the shoulders of his black suit. His breath span out like swirling cigarette smoke.

The engine continued to purr away in the large SUV, with the double exhausts burbling out grey fumes into the coldness, as the blond nodded to the unseen driver. The back doors of the car opened, and another black suit stood in the road as a grey-haired man in his late fifties stepped onto the pavement, immediately joined by the blond and another bodyguard. They made their way to a door being opened to embrace them (the driver had called to alert the residents that they had arrived).

Two of the suits and the fur coat were whisked into the blue-lit doorway and were gone. The blond suit jumped back

186

into the SUV, and it too was gone, crunching through the settling snow.

The trio of men were led through a burgundy-coloured curtain and immediately took in the warm air filling their lungs; they were then led into a large room where a dimly lit chandelier hung from the black ceiling, lighting a glass table surrounded by plush burgundy-covered chairs and sofas.

In the middle of the table sat a shiny ice bucket filled with two magnums of Cristal and two more of vodka, surrounded by glasses and various mixers of orange, cranberry, lemonade, tonic, and Red Bull.

The men watched as the tattooed man who had led them in disappeared back through the curtain without a word as two beautiful lingerie-dressed women swept into the room like some magic trick.

One of the women took the coat from the older man, and the suits stepped back into the shadows with their backs to the walls.

The grey-hair stood by one of the chairs and eyed the girls and the bristling curtain at the same time. Once again, the curtain revealed a tall man with gel-backed black hair and piercing blue eyes, smiling with the whitest teeth that added extra light to the room. He was followed by three more men with short-sleeved shirts, more tattoos, and shoulder holsters.

The toothy man grinned even wider as he embraced the older man.

"Admiral, how have you been? It's so good to see you once again," bellowed Sergey, the teeth.

"You too," the admiral said with a scowl, wishing things were back like the old days rather than having to deal with the rats that had risen up from the sewers in recent times. This body language was not lost on Sergey, but his physical demeanour did not betray his thoughts, unlike the admiral, who seemed to wear his distaste on his sleeve. However, business was business, and money was money.

The young girls proffered drinks, and vodkas were poured for the two men as the girls had champagne from beautiful crystal flutes.

Sergey was finalising the delivery of a retired nuclear submarine with the fleet admiral. This was for delivery for his friends in Colombia, for more elaborate drug running around the world. Sergey didn't really give a damn what they wanted it for; his turn on the deal was millions of dollars, as was the admiral's.

The vodka flowed a few more times as the men engaged in small talk and stared into each other's eyes like cats look at mice.

"So where is the sub going to end up?" the admiral asked.

"Nowhere that will concern Russia and its people, Admiral. Trust me; you will never hear about this submarine again." Sergey did not want the admiral to know anything about his clients.

The admiral, however, buoyed now by the vodka, was still being unrealistic in his price expectations. *He should be more careful,* thought one of Sergey's aides. Sergey had an unforgiving bad temper and had blown away an ex-KGB colonel during an argument over fifteen hundred dollars.

Sergey's own father had been a senior-ranking KGB officer, unknown to the admiral, and he now worked for his son in one of Russia's largest crime enterprises: drugs (both legit and illegal), alcohol, guns, nukes, ships, sex, and the list went on.

The admiral and Sergey sat in a private room reserved for VIPs and raunchier experiences at one of Sergey's nightclubs; the five bodyguards stood in the background, and at least fifteen others patrolled the club with machine guns, carefully out of sight of the patrons enjoying the lap dancing in the main auditorium.

The two negotiators ate caviar washed down with the iced vodka, and now eight of the club's dancers straddled both men, and the admiral's hands wandered all over two of the young girls' thighs and breasts as he listened to Sergey negotiating delivery of the item.

The vodka and girls were putting the admiral at ease, and suddenly, the extra million dollars didn't seem so important, especially as he had seen Sergey's flash of anger an hour earlier, when they seemed to have hit an impasse.

The admiral realised that both sides had a good deal, and he leant over and whispered into Sergey's right ear that $10 million, as his commission, on top of the agreed purchase price, plus the two girls for the night would finalise the deal; his people would then be in touch with the logistics.

Sergey smiled broadly, flashing those teeth; he nodded, and they shook on the deal.

Sergey said the club and its resources were at the admiral's disposal as he and his men headed for the curtain, leaving the two girls behind them. The admiral embraced the two girls and drew them to his lap, whilst snapping fingers to the suits, who covered the two hidden camera lenses as they headed beyond the curtain to maintain sentry duty just outside.

JJ—Los Angeles, Friday

It had been a long day at the office, and JJ had just about had his stomach full. JJ recounted the day and developments of the last year in his head; he wanted to get things straight, so that he could explain them to Jenifer later. Revenues had been steadily falling over the last six months, and cash was tight. He had met with the CEO of the bank's finance division many times over the four years they had been a client, and historically, all had gone very well.

The meeting in the morning with the bank was not a good one, and as an aside, he had mentioned the good times to Joe, more so in frustration at the lack of further support rather than in malice. The bank entourage had left the meeting with little by way of conclusion but were pushing very hard for repayment of their current facilities and his personal guarantee.

The sun was still high in the sky as JJ left the office and jumped into his Porsche Targa. He was five feet ten inches tall and kept in relatively good shape, swimming daily in his pool both before and after the office. He had swept-back, sun-bleached hair and a Californian tan which sat well with his blue eyes and well-proportioned Roman nose. He was always clean-shaven, looked young for his forty-six years, and most days wore linen suits, in summer colours and linen white or cream shirts and brown loafers.

He threw his jacket into the front trunk compartment, knowing that with the glass roof swept back, he was in danger of losing it to wind turbulence.

He slid into the seat, turned the key, and revved the air-cooled engine. He slid the roof open, slipped on his aviators, and engaged the reverse in a well-rehearsed ritual as he slew the car across the parking lot, with the screech of tyres just before the traction control slipped into action. He headed for the interstate. He fancied a few cooling beers on his way back home.

The Porsche, gun metal grey with black leather, gobbled up the highway at a steady sixty-five miles per hour; the main traffic would be several hours away and behind, until JJ left the built-up area of LA and progressed into more sedate surroundings. He eased the car up to eighty miles per hour.

The afternoon sun beating down on his tanned brow made JJ feel good, and he smiled to himself as the car growled further forward. JJ turned up the CD tracks, playing Fleetwood Mac and breathed in the rushing warm, moist air.

Beer or home, he kept thinking to himself. Beer became more provocative as the journey progressed, and after fifty-five minutes, he eased the car onto the slip road and headed for an English-style pub about fifteen minutes from home, with red phone box on the outside and dust-covered floors on the inside.

He knew the pub well and met friends there for drinks on a regular basis. Today, he would be ahead of the pack, but he wanted, needed some time to think things through, alone.

He eased the car into the pub parking lot, slid the roof close, and disengaged the key, once again in one slick movement. Sunglasses were kept on; he decided to have a beer on the terrace and left his jacket in the car. As he walked across the lot, he saw a black SUV pull in next to his car. He could not see the occupant, as the windows were blacked out and his sunglasses added to the incognito of the passenger (or passengers). The SUV's engine idled for a few seconds and then came to a halt. No one emerged immediately, but he guessed they were probably talking or emailing on their phone.

JJ walked around the outside of the pub towards the garden and stepped up onto the wooden, planked terrace, which already had a clutch of drinkers, a few ladies finishing up on lunch, a couple of guys who had obviously been in situ for some hours, and a further two sets of couples, either on holiday or in some form of tryst away from their mundane married lives.

The waiter recognised JJ and proffered a table for two in the far corner, half in the sun and half shaded by an umbrella canopy. JJ smiled his thanks and asked for a Heineken before he had even hit the seat.

He positioned himself to put his face and shoulders in the sun, with the rest of him covered by shade.

The waiter appeared with iced water, the much-needed beer, and a small dish of peanuts, with the aim of not only lining the stomach for more beer but the salt exacting further urges for liquid refreshment. He placed these on the metal table and proceeded to pour half of the bottled beer into an iced glass. As soon as this ritual was finished, JJ grabbed the bottle and topped up the glass, making sure the gassy head was kept to a perfect minimum, and gulped several mouthfuls in quick, blissful succession.

He surveyed the pub's external walls, covered in emerald green climbing plants, smothered with bright, purple blooms, of which he had no knowledge, surrounding the open French doors which led into a covered orangery, leading into the main bar and restaurant beyond. He moved his gaze to survey the other patrons but wasn't really paying too much attention, as his mind drifted back to business and how best to tackle the issues he now faced.

He had kept much of the decline in the business away from his wife; he hadn't wanted to worry her and really felt the blip would be over and done with very quickly, but it had just continued to balloon out of control. They had used a lot of the increased bank funding to better their lifestyle, having taken funds from the business in increased salaries and benefits.

Much of the money had been frittered away on living, and little was shown in asset value, although Jenifer had an impressive art collection. They had both felt business would always be good and increasing.

The second beer arrived and was beginning to have a pleasant numbing effect, coupled with the sun, which even with the tan was bringing a redness to JJ's forehead and nose.

JJ texted Jenifer and said that he was at the pub and perhaps they should catch a bite to eat or just a few drinks there later. Jenifer was just thirty, and the two had been an item for six years, having met each other through business;

she was in merchandising sales for one of the large cosmetic companies. The attraction had been immediate, initially for some of the typical reasons of younger, beautiful, and confident woman meets even more confident, wealthy man. Jenifer was the same height as JJ, with long slender tanned legs, blonde hair down to her pert buttocks, medium but enhanced breasts, green eyes, and flawless complexion. They were parents to twin four-year-old boys, John and James, both blond, blue-eyed tearaways that would be with their nanny now. Jenifer would be playing tennis, hence the text, but should be good to catch up for dinner or just a few glasses of wine.

The terrace area was down to the two guys who had been there for some time, whose conversation was getting louder and louder; it was now four forty-five, and there was probably another hour or so before a new steady stream of clientele would arrive, bringing in some of JJ's and Jenifer's friends and the end of his contemplation time.

He grabbed a handful of peanuts and dropped them into his mouth, dusting the salt from his hand on his suit trousers. He beckoned the waiter for another Heineken and began to think about how best to tackle the business woes. "What else did they want?" continued circulating around his head. After all, he had already negotiated better terms with suppliers, reduced overheads, and launched sales campaigns, but still these savings and changes were far from catching up with the lost revenues.

Jenifer—Los Angeles, Friday

Jenifer had just finished a doubles tennis match at the prestigious tennis club just twenty-odd minutes from her home, where she and her partner, Dawn, had smashed their opponents by three sets to one in the time that they had allowed themselves, which followed an earlier coaching session. Six to four, six to four, five to seven, six to one. Jenifer and Dawn smiled and congratulated each other as they moved to the net to shake hands with Lynda and Bella. All four were blondes (only one a natural), with lithe, fit bodies and sparkling white, straight teeth.

The four pulled their white jogger bottoms on over their solid, little buttocks, slid their racquets into bags, and headed to the sun terrace for a drink. They pulled up their chairs and, as was custom, all four iPhones in various different cases, gold, silver, mirrored, and pink, were pulled out to check for messages. A waitress brought iced water to the table but struggled to gain any eye contact, or indeed any type of acknowledgement from the table.

Jenifer raised an eye whilst dabbing away and knew that the girls would all share a bottle of iced Chardonnay; she pointed out a Californian favourite from the wine list to the fidgeting waitress.

There was a text from JJ, a lot earlier than she would expect; she responded, but a shiver sped down her spine. The girls were now back into their own company; they sipped their water and exchanged updates on things happening in their lives, from holidays, husbands or boyfriends, kids, and pets. No mention of the humiliating defeat from either side. The wine and chiller arrived in good order, and the waitress poured four small glasses; measures were kept to a minimum, as the wine would lose its coolness as the surrounding temperature warmed the liquid quickly.

Jenifer had driven down with Dawn, her neighbour, in her Cadillac Escalade, and given the unease she was feeling, she whispered to Dawn that she would need to be away fairly quickly.

JJ—Los Angeles, Friday

JJ's phone buzzed, and he picked up the return text from Jenifer; she was heading home to see the boys, have a shower, and catch a cab to the bar for six thirty-ish (she was rarely on time). Jenifer hoped all was okay, given the early finish at the office, but looked forward to catching up. JJ ignored his emails, placed the phone back onto the table, and took another slug of the beer.

JJ flicked back through the years to when his father had owned a couple of pharmacies, which had been the bedrock of the large retail conglomerate that he oversaw to this day. His father had died ten years ago, a massive heart attack, aged sixty. Nothing heredity, so the doctors had confirmed, but probably stress and lack of exercise. JJ's mother was sixty-eight and enjoying life flitting between JJ's and his two sisters; between them all, they had seven grandkids for her to dote on.

He finished up his third beer, motioned the waiter over, and explained he would like to book a table for dinner at seven o'clock for two. The waiter had seen him several times before but was relatively new on the staff; in any case, he realised JJ was a regular customer and said he knew it wouldn't be a problem to squeeze him and his companion in later on. JJ explained that he needed to get his jacket from his car and would be back momentarily.

The waiter said, "No problem."

He slipped his cell into his trouser pocket whilst heading to the car park. He saw the SUV first, which was still next to his car and covering it from view as he strode across the relatively empty lot. JJ grappled for his keys in his pocket and instinctively pressed the open button, hearing the single blip of the car as the doors were unlocked. He walked in between his car and the SUV, leaning into the passenger compartment to flick the front trunk compartment open to get to his jacket.

As he stood back up, he heard the SUV window slide down, and he turned to look as the bullet exited the silencer of the automatic pistol and struck him centre temple, causing a small pink spray of blood as JJ's head jerked backwards, his knees buckled, and he slid down the side of his own car. The SUV window began closing as the engine kicked into life and then reversed slowly, turned, and headed for the exit. It turned back onto the highway and was gone.

It was twenty minutes later before JJ's body was spotted by a couple departing from their car. The emergency services were on-site twelve minutes later.

Jenifer—LA, Friday

Bella was talking about a holiday she was planning to Europe next year; she and her husband were looking to take in Rome, Venice, Paris, and London over a three-week break. Her spouse was one of JJ's friends based in the entertainment business and had some business in London.

Jenifer was a little subdued, out of the ordinary for her.

"You okay?" Dawn had whispered to her, whilst pretending to listen to Bella.

Jenifer just nodded.

Lynda was paying attention. "Yes, Zack and I went to Rome and took in the Coliseum, the Spanish Steps, St Peter's, Sistine Chapel, and the Trevi Fountain, where we made a wish. No, his didn't get any bigger."

Dawn laughed at the joke at Zack's expense, Lynda's long-term partner; Jenifer was not quite sure what she had missed, and it certainly had passed completely over Bella's head.

"Sorry, need to dash," Jenifer said to Lynda and Bella, who were just pouring another mouthful of wine into the empty glasses.

Jenifer and Dawn air-kissed their goodbyes to their beaten opponents and headed to the front of the clubhouse, where the Escalade had already been brought to the fore by the valet and was waiting for them.

Bags were thrown into the back, and the two women stepped up into the large black beast of a vehicle. Jenifer clicked the car into drive and headed back to the gated development of houses that was home to both of them. She mentioned that JJ had suggested a visit to the Sergeant's Arms and wondered if Dawn and Dan, her husband, might like to join them for dinner a little later. Dawn would check in with Dan and let Jenifer know, but she thought it sounded an excellent idea.

Jenifer pressed the remote, and the huge gates to the development swung open, like Moses parting the waters; she dropped Dawn at her door, at the base of a long sweeping drive. Dawn grabbed her sports bag and reconfirmed that she would let Jenifer know when she had heard from Dan, who was still in the office and had yet to respond to an email she had already sent.

They waved each other off, and Jenifer pulled away and headed the six hundred yards down the street to her large brick driveway. The car slid to a halt just outside of the double wooden doors, and Jenifer, bag in hand, slipped her keys into the door and stepped into the white marbled hall. She heard *The Simpsons* playing from the boys' den, coupled with the squeak of her tennis shoes on the floor as she popped her head round the door.

"Hi guys, have you had a good day?" she said to the back of their heads.

Silence.

"Hi, Mom; great to see you," she shouted as two heads jumped with shock at the loud, unexpected interruption.

"Hi, Mom, *The Simpsons* are on," they said in unison.

"Really?" Jenifer said as she bent down and hugged the boys, who grimaced and wriggled to ensure that they didn't miss a millisecond of Bart, who himself was watching Itchy and Scratchy, the latter getting decapitated, on television.

Jenifer squeaked into the expansive white kitchen and said hi to Gwen, their nanny, who was stooped over the stove making the boys' dinner.

"Just going to take a shower," Jenifer said. "Can you call a cab for forty minutes to take me down to the Sergeant, please?"

"Yes, Jenifer, will do," Gwen said. "Would you like anything to eat before you go? There's plenty."

"No thanks," she replied. "I had a salad at the club, and we'll be eating out later."

She spun round and bounded up the large sweeping staircase, enveloped by black metal railings. She dropped her bag on the bed and headed for the shower, where she turned on the circular, ceiling-mounted head and then undressed, throwing her clothing into a wicker laundry basket.

The en-suite bathroom was covered completely with large sandstone tiles, with under-floor heating, one mirrored wall, and gold Italian fittings.

Jenifer slid the shower door open and felt the caress of the warm water ease the knots in her neck and shoulders. She lathered the fruit-based body rub and spread it across her muscled tummy; the shower shot cold, and Jenifer felt a spasm that enveloped her body. Something was seriously wrong, but what? She shook her head; the shower warmed again, and she finished washing and conditioning her hair, still in a state of feeling somehow vulnerable. She stepped out and took one of the large brown Egyptian cotton towels. Jenifer called JJ's cell but got no answer. She dismissed the uneasiness and sat down to dry her long blonde hair.

She decided on mainly white, pulling on a lacy white G-string, white jeans, and blouse and picked up a cream cashmere cardigan, finished off with white pumps and no socks.

The boys were at the kitchen table, tucking into roast chicken and miscellaneous vegetables (the latter not seeing much inroad).

She saw the cab on the CCTV monitor, which sat on the kitchen counter, pulling up behind the Escalade. Jenifer kissed the boys goodnight, explained that Daddy would see them in the morning, and said goodbye to Gwen.

Jenifer's cell chimed; JJ, she thought, but no, it was Dawn confirming that they would join the two of them for seven forty-five later. Jenifer stepped out and into the cab. She confirmed the pub as the destination to the driver and tried JJ to ask him to add another couple to the table order, but still no answer.

The driver pulled out onto the main road and headed towards the gates, which swung open, and he sped off in the direction of the pub.

The evening was warm, and the sun flickered through the cab windows and off Jenifer's sunglasses as she squinted into the screen of her phone, lifting her shades from time to time so as to read her messages properly.

As the cab neared the pub restaurant, the driver muttered something to himself; the parking lot was sealed with yellow police tape, and two police officers waved him past. Jenifer looked up and saw a sea of flashing, emergency vehicle lights stacked together in the lot. Across the tarmac was a line of crime scene investigators in white body suits, covered head to toe and wearing masks and glasses.

"Oh, my God," she gasped. "Stop here, let me out." Jenifer slipped the driver twenty dollars and didn't wait for change. She immediately felt the uneasiness flowing back into her mind.

"Sorry, ma'am," said a tower of blue police officer at the entrance to the pub. "There has been an incident here, and we are interviewing customers. The venue is likely to remain closed for this evening."

"My husband is already here," she said with wild eyes.

"Oh, okay. Please wait here. What is his name?" the tower asked.

"JJ, or John James Henderson," Jenifer said.

The police officer stooped his long neck into the foyer and spoke to another one of the milling police officers, who disappeared into the darkness beyond.

Within minutes, a detective appeared in the doorway, behind him stood a policewoman. The way he looked at Jenifer made her body buckle at the knees. He took her hand, which she gave instinctively, and said, "Please come this way."

The front of the bar was empty, and she could see a small crowd of customers in the main restaurant, many sat at tables making statements to the many officers.

Jenifer was ushered into one of the plush booths; the detective and policewoman slid in on either side of her. Jenifer was shaking.

"I understand you are here to meet John Henderson," the detective said, really a statement of fact than a question. He proffered a driving licence at Jenifer. "Is this your husband?"

"Yes, yes, what has happened?" Jenifer asked, not blinking; the policewoman slid closer to her.

"I am so very sorry, but your husband is dead. He has been shot," the detective said as Jenifer's body shook with total uncontrollable motion and tears welled in her eyes. She could not talk or comprehend what had been said to her; this wasn't possible. He had texted her; he was always there. Why, why, why?

The policewoman tried to comfort Jenifer, but she brushed her arm away.

"This cannot be possible," she cried. "I don't believe you."

"I am so very sorry," both officers said in unison.

Jenifer's world crashed around her.

"Do you have any family or friends nearby who can help? As difficult as it may be, it would be of great assistance if you could answer some questions now," the detective said.

Jenifer nodded numbly, her mouth moving, but no words came out.

Joe—LAX, Friday

Joe sat in the executive lounge at LAX, watching Frank and Peter subtly hiding the liquor bottles with their bodies as they poured this into the glasses before topping up with Cokes.

The meeting with JJ had not been a good one, and Joe was getting more agitated, which was not good news for anyone that had to be around him. They had left the lunch with the LA office team and headed back in silence to the airport.

Many of the flights east had been delayed due to bad weather somewhere in Middle America. This was also adding to Joe's bubbling anger.

"God damn it, nothing seems to work in this God-forsaken country when you need it to," he said to no one in particular.

Peter and Frank mellowed as the day dragged on and the bourbon did its job.

Joe called home and informed them that once again, the airlines were not making his life any easier.

Several hours later, the flight was called for boarding, and the passengers were urged to get a move on, as the gate would close quickly.

As the trio picked up their bags and headed out of the lounge, the TV was broadcasting a live news bulletin from the Sergeant's Arms, just outside of LA, where a prominent local businessman had been shot dead. There was no apparent motive; his wallet had been found intact in his jacket. An unconfirmed report had come in, saying it had all the hallmarks of a gangland execution, but why this would be the case with a businessman in a very affluent area was open to speculation.

Hans—New York, Friday

New York was alive, vibrant, and enhancing everything bad and good known to humankind, all in one great city.

Hans strolled into the Hilton's lobby, where he had arranged to meet the chief purchasing officer from one of his company's major customers. Jed was in his late fifties, with a gut that hung out over his belt in all directions; he sweated gallons, which was very evident when he stuck out his podgy hand to welcome Hans with a handshake. Jed was always happy to get out at any time, and once he heard that Hans was over, he suggested a Friday evening in New York, as opposed to his company's suburban offices.

"Hey, how you doing?" Jed said as he squelched his hand into Hans's palm.

"Great, you?" Hans said, rescuing his hand as quickly as possible and wiping his palm off in his trouser pocket.

"Yeh, great, thanks. Let's get a beer."

They headed for the sports bar, a little like a very fit Don Quixote followed by his Sancho Panza.

"The American fascination with sport washed down with weak beer, hot dogs, and pretzels; what a contradiction," Hans muttered to himself.

There they all were, the stop-offs between work and home, the out-of-towners on business, tourists, the all-knowledgeable, multitalented sportsmen.

"Thought we could just catch some of the game," Jed said, "and I've booked us into Ben Benson's for a steak at eight. What yer drinking?"

"Just a cold beer will be great." Better get into the evening, Hans thought, whilst marvelling at what a feat of civil engineering that belt was, holding in a potential tsunami of fat that could take out the bar if it snapped.

The bar was dark, lit by the eight large plasma screens showing a mix of sports. Hans was a little bewildered as to which game they were supposed to be catching, given there were three sports and several different games showing.

Jed ordered a lager pitcher with two glasses and disappeared to one of the white linen-clad tables on the side wall, which supported a hot plate, laden with hot dogs, bread rolls, and ketchup and French's mustard.

He returned with a plate of four dogs, sides of caramelised onions, ketchup and mustard in little bowls, and a mass of paper napkins.

"Help yourself," he said.

They discussed business generalities between touchdowns; now Hans knew they were watching an American football game, with Jed sliding the hot dogs into his cavernous orifice.

The bar was packed; the air had turned warm and moist, defeating the air conditioning that had not been adjusted. A crowd of office workers and businessmen were staying at the hotel. There was a little whooping when a female flight crew visited for a few drinks before going to their rooms.

Eight o'clock came around soon enough, and off they trotted to Ben Benson's.

Jed ordered a huge lobster for the two of them to share as a starter; he literally sucked every last morsel out of his half-shell, smothering everything in melted butter and squeezed lemon juice. The mix of butter and lemon dribbled from the left side of his mouth, as he snorted for breath down onto his shirt, the midsection and armpits of which were covered in sweat. He followed up with a steak that dwarfed the plate and allowed no room for the fries and zucchini, which arrived in separate bowls. Hans settled for a Caesar salad after the lobster, which still came with two large grilled chicken breasts.

Jed continued to wash dinner down with beer after beer, clutching his bottle with greasy paddles of fingers as he glugged down half at a time.

Amazingly, Jed decided to forgo a sweet.

He was in town for the night; he didn't get out much and wanted to relish every minute.

They finished up in one of the local microbrewery pubs. Jed wasn't into walking far, and Hans was feigning jet lag. They had another couple of beers, and Hans had said his goodbyes and decided to stroll back to his hotel, the Peninsula on Fifth. He was greeted at the door and headed off to the elevator.

· · · · · · · · · ● ● · · · · · · · · · ·

The next day, Hans decided to take in some of the sights; he caught the ferry from Battery Park over to Liberty Island. The Statue of Liberty was closed for renovation but still an impressive sight. The weather was cold but clear;

the ferry was packed on its way back to Manhattan but the crossing smooth. Hans walked out of the park and up towards Ground Zero; he had pre-booked through the hotel concierge. The foundations of the two towers were preserved in two huge square holes; water flowed on all four sides to create spectacular waterfalls, manifesting their own rainbows.

Hans touched the names of the fallen, carved in the polished granite, and spent several minutes of silence contemplating the enormity of this event and the impact on the families of the victims and the rescue services. He caught a cab back to his hotel.

The jet lag caught up with him, and he dozed on and off throughout the night.

Joe—Weekend

Pat, one of Joe's assistants, had been to the accounts department on Friday to raid the petty cash tin for Joe's weekend expenses: twenty-five hundred dollars a week for thirteen years, never missed; she arranged for the money to be delivered to Joe's home.

It was his niece's birthday party this weekend, and all of his family, friends, and some work colleagues were invited to his palatial home at the Hamptons.

Monica had worked with a number of party organisers, and what an elaborate collage of entertainment and themes this Sunday promised to be.

Monica and Martha had arranged the party for Gabriella's fifth birthday, under strict instructions by Joe to make it better than anything before, and spare no expense. Gabby was the daughter of Emilio and Giovanna. Emilio was a few years older than Joe but had remarried after his first wife had died of cancer some twelve years earlier. Giovanna was a pretty thirty-two old and had been a waitress at one of Emilio's restaurants. Emilio had dyed jet black hair and dark brown eyes; he was a couple of inches taller than Joe but looked forty-five. He was wearing brown chinos, a cream ruffle-neck sweater, and brown check sports jacket. Emilio's two boys from his first marriage were both married themselves now.

Joe had been married before but had had no kids; he was godfather to all of his siblings' children, of which there were now fourteen, and he relished the role. He would regularly take the boys shooting and golfing, the girls' horse riding, and was always on tap to listen to them. He was the archetypical Mafia-styled godfather; everyone pandered to his neurosis, his need to be the top dog in anything and everything he did.

Everyone just said yes when they were supposed to; they listened to his every word, like he was a deity directing his followers.

His whole family was in attendance. Joseph Snr walked tentatively across the lawn, stabbing his cane in front of him, to one of the large marquees. He stooped over, facing the ground, staring up from time to time through large pebble glasses, searching out family in the melee of Joe's friends, work colleagues, and smattering of neighbours; who attended to gawp at what Joe had rather than any deep friendship.

Joe's family were all of similar height, bar his father, and were dwarfed by many of the other attendees at the party. Joe surveyed the area like a watchdog, and anytime he ended up in conversation, he would always make sure he was on a higher part of the garden or on steps above the others he was conversing with.

There were three large marquees laid out on the lawn; the sun was shining, but the temperature remained in the low sixties. Overall, it was a pretty good day.

There were two lifeguards patrolling the heated pool area, the sides of which were open, as dozens of kids jumped in and out of the steaming water.

One marquee had been laid out for a late afternoon lunch; one was for guests to chat, drink, and share canapés; and another orchestrated like an old-style fairground, with stalls offering up myriad games for kids and adults to play. Candy stores and hot dog stands were also in abundance.

Joe was surrounded by a familiar entourage of Frank, Tony, and Peter from the office. Giuseppe and Alonzo had caught up with Joseph Snr and had found him a chair to sit on. Maria was busying herself with the kids, helped by her husband, Mario.

All in all, there were about two hundred and twenty guests, and Joe lorded over all, like Napoleon surveying his troops.

Joe caught up with Maria, Giuseppe, Tony, Alonzo, and Emilio and their families. Over the years at the bank, Joe had financed several restaurant chains; when they had missed a beat in their payments, Joe had foreclosed the loans and arranged for the businesses to be sold on to his family at favourable terms. The family were now owners of sixteen New York-based eateries and five large bakeries, which supplied many of the hotels and restaurants in their area. If Joe did any lending to hotels or other restaurant groups, he made sure that they bought baked products from his families' businesses.

You scratch my back and I'll scratch yours; the Italians kept a very close-knit fraternity.

About an hour into the festivities, Joe, Giuseppe, and Joe's management team of Peter and Frank had disappeared into his study, where they huddled together and talked through the events of the last few weeks.

Monica overheard Joe, just before he left, mentioning something about a perfume retailer that he wanted Giuseppe to run.

Monica was keeping an eye on the mass of kids that were running feral across the lawns and trying to catch some of Joe's prized koi carp from the ornamental lake farther down the manicured lawns. Some of the more responsible parents were now trying the get to kids back to the marquee, and Monica had asked one of the bouncers to position himself at the lake, to ensure they didn't lose any of their little guests or indeed a fish.

Joe Jnr was in the fairground with several boys from the neighbourhood. They were all at the shooting range, having just smashed each other about on the dodgems, that had been laid out with the latest high-tech air rifles. Several of the fathers were already trying to outdo each other on the range.

David—New York, Weekend

David and Melissa spent Saturday packing, and it was now early on Sunday. David had made it clear that they would only take two hold bags each. This, ironically, wouldn't be a major problem for Melissa, who only wanted to make sure her shoes were in attendance, but David would lose scores of expensive suits and many clothes that were still labelled and unworn, so Melissa would have to cut back.

So this was it; their combined lives shunted into one hundred and sixty pounds of luggage, plus whatever they could wear and carry. That said, between the two of them, there was a tremendous air of excitement, marked with trepidation.

David had cancelled his lease, but it would run for a few more months, already paid; the apartment was rented as furnished, but David would leave behind some personal electrical items such as coffee machine, juicer, and other miscellaneous furnishings.

They were now ready to start their new lives abroad. Melissa burst into tears with both happiness and sadness: a new life with David but leaving her life and mother behind (even though they were not close).

David, of course, knew nothing about the mother, but deep down, he felt it would be impossible to risk coming back to the States. He drew her close to him, and he could feel the warmth of her tears against his shoulder, seeping through his linen shirt.

"Hey, what's up?" he soothed.

"Nothing," she said trough the tears, "just strange feelings; so happy, yet so worried, nervous, but I do so love you and really want this."

"Hey, we are in this together, and I so love you too," David said as he cuddled her closer into his chest.

His phone buzzed with the arrival of the car to take them to the airport and the beginning of their new life. They stacked their carry bags onto the wheeled luggage and checked around the apartment to make sure they hadn't missed anything. They clutched the handles of two bags each and zigzagged towards the exit, scuffing the wall as they went. They staggered into the corridor with the bags swaying their handlers from side to side, as if they had caravans in tow.

Melissa mouthed a goodbye to the apartment. David was already spending the money.

As the elevator opened onto the lobby, David saw one of their neighbours coming in, obviously from the night before.

"Hi, Cheryl," he said, grinning.

Cheryl blushed bright red "Oh, hi, David."

The driver piled their bags into the trunk; the two sat back into the black leather and held hands as they headed out of Tribeca, on the first leg of their multi-stop escape.

They passed effortlessly through the city and out on to the busy highway to JFK. They were silent, looking at the graffiti on the highway bridge pillars as they moved steadily forward.

The driver dropped them at the terminal, where their bags were deposited just opposite the first-class collection desk (a few extra dollars, but why not?). They checked in kerb side and headed into the terminal building.

David had arranged a quick stop off in Mexico for the two of them, using their real passports, and then on to Brazil, where they would spend the day, the next day, they would use their new passports and identities to fly from Rio to Buenos Aires and then to Madrid. David should receive confirmation that the money had reached his Swiss bank account on Monday.

The airport in Mexico City was a complete buzz; once in the transfer lounge, they decided to have something to eat before their next flight.

They arrived in Rio, the battered cab got them to their hotel, where they would spend the night before the flight tomorrow evening out to Argentina.

No need to unpack; Melissa had wisely packed one day's clothing in the top of one bag for the two of them.

They both moved to the terrace and took in the sun and the vista of blonde beach and blue sea.

David had already mentioned the change in identities; Melissa would now be Lisa Johansson, wife of Larus Johansson, aka David. Lisa was an American wife of a Swede, and they both had Swedish passports courtesy of the Swedish embassy official in the States who had taken the necessary bribes. David was fluent in Swedish, having learnt this from his mother. Lisa/Melissa didn't have to be. Now she knew why he had taken some head shots of her in her blonde wig, which she would need to wear from tomorrow onwards.

David would sport a shaggy mop of blonde hair, which was three or four inches longer than his normal style, and he was now sprouting a couple of days of stubble.

He had taken all of his watches with him but, given Rio's reputation for muggings, had not worn any of them since he left the States.

He squeezed her hand as they strolled along the beach in Rio, the sun beating down on their backs as they looked at the sectioned beach, with its body builders and beach volleyball.

"Some toned bodies out there," Melissa said.

"Just like yours now, and mine in about three months. Anyway, make the most of it because we head for Europe tomorrow evening," he said.

"Is there anything you need to tell me about all of this covert operation and different passports?"

"Nothing, you need to worry about, darling. Everything is fine."

Melissa nuzzled into David's arm. Life was good, and she was already planning for a family.

Tomorrow, they would head to Argentina and then fly to Madrid.

Hans—New York, Sunday/Monday

The gym beckoned the next morning, and Hans took in Central Park after working out.

Back in his room, Hans checked in; he had been given details of the third target and his itinerary for the next two weeks; the agent obviously had contact with a source who kept detailed tabs on these employees so they would know who was where and when. Target three was Todd Baker, from Chicago, and he had booked a long four-day weekend in St Lucia's Jade Mountain, a resort overlooking the lush greenery of the Pitons and the small bay. Hans thought St Lucia would be a lot easier than orchestrating an accident in a US city.

He immediately arranged for a few days stopover at the resort; he was lucky on availability, as he was to leave on the Saturday morning, and the weekend was busy. He was booked into JC1, a sanctuary room; he managed to get in a night prior to Todd's arrival on Thursday. *Perfect*, he thought. Now all he needed was a suitable partner to take with him, as Jade is famous for honeymoons, second honeymoons, mistress liaisons, and romantic trips away, so a lone male would raise unnecessary suspicion.

Given the timing, an escort would have to do. Hans trawled through escort agencies in the NY Yellow Pages and linked his laptop onto one of their websites to review photographs and CVs, the latter detailing what these young women would do for money.

He needed someone to travel and spend a few nights away with him, and there she was: Cheryl, five feet seven inches, blonde, green eyes, classically educated, and all services. The booking was arranged, but understandably, Cheryl wanted to meet a few days before the trip to make sure she wasn't going off with the local axe murderer (how she would ascertain this over dinner, God only knows).

Hans had said he was staying at the Peninsula and arranged to meet for cocktails on Monday evening, on the terrace bar overlooking the city; it was now Sunday evening.

He had another lunch meeting tomorrow and decided to sleep in until ten in the morning and head for a workout in the gym before lunch.

He stretched out on the huge bed, turned the television on, for noise distraction rather than watching anything in particular, and began to take in the last few weeks.

His heart was pumping; he had felt really alive, at a high. However, now he felt remorse, perhaps a little fear of being caught. He couldn't put his finger on it. This drug habit had subsided over the years, and given the last two kills, he had felt suitably topped up, but a job had to be finished to ensure another was forthcoming, although he now declined many opportunities.

Back in South Africa, he had spoken to the Army psychiatrists; they had had quite a team interested in him, but in the end, this hunger always returned, an addiction that needed to be fed.

David (Larus) and Melissa (Lisa)—Sunday/Monday

David and Melissa ate in their Rio de Janeiro hotel the night before, made love in the massive bed, and finished off the evening chattering away about their future on the terrace of their room.

Melissa was keen to find out more about Denmark and its capital city. David explained it was an easy-going society, distinct weather seasons, on the coast with a population of over two million, with more restaurants and bars they could hope to visit in a lifetime.

David was relaxed and explained that he had set up bank accounts in both Switzerland and Denmark and that he would add Melissa as soon as they settled in Copenhagen. He had flown to Switzerland on many occasions for business and set up a numbered bank account, introduced by his father. When he visited his mother in Sweden, he had spent a few days in Denmark, and with his new passport and a letter of reference, he presented himself as Larus Johansson to Danske Bank. He had produced a reference letter at his own bank and then opened up a bank account. Danske had checked out his reference and he, of course, had been able to confirm that Mr Johansson was a long-established and respectable client, who had worked in the States but was now heading back to Scandinavia.

They had awoken early and ready for the next leg of their journey. Melissa was now blonde. They had thrown their mobile phones into waste bins on the beach the night before.

David had booked their own car to the airport (the hotel still had their real names), and they would fly into Buenos Aires under their new identities and then later onto Madrid.

David had booked a hotel in Madrid for a few days, and then they would drive to Copenhagen.

The journey to the airport was a laborious drag; both were still tired, and conversation was light, which they were comfortable with.

The couple checked in as the Johanssons without a problem and headed for the first-class lounge. The largesse would eventually help their searchers, as they would start with the first-class passenger lists of all airlines to narrow their search.

The hop from Rio de Janeiro to Buenos Aires was over in the blink of an eye.

They boarded the Iberia flight to Madrid, which would take them to their new lives in Europe. They were at the front of the 747 and would be in Madrid the next day.

The flight over the Atlantic was a turbulent one, and neither managed to get much sleep. David had overdone it on the champagne and was in dire need of rehydration and aspirin to take the pounding away from behind his bloodshot eyes.

Melissa had adjourned to the restroom, to clean her teeth and moisturise. *Wow*, she thought as she was so tired, her shoulders sagged. There was another seventy-five minutes to go.

It was early morning in Madrid as the seat belt lights flicked on with a bong. Melissa had managed to doze for the last forty-five minutes and woke with a start, but surprisingly refreshed. David had raised his seat, placed his blanket in the locker, and was pulling on his shoes. He smiled down at Melissa, so beautiful, still cocooned in her seat.

"Good morning, ladies and gentlemen; as you can see, the captain has turned on the seat belt sign. Please return to your seats, ensure your seats are placed in the upright position, and close all tray tables. Our entertainment system will now be turned off. Please shut down all electronic equipment and ensure all luggage is placed in the overhead locker or under the seat in front of you. Restrooms are no longer available for use, and we will now be checking the cabin to ensure your seat belts are securely fastened."

The message was repeated in Spanish.

"Good morning, this is your captain. As no doubt you are aware the ride over was a bumpy one, but we did benefit from a significant tail wind, which has meant we will be thirty minutes ahead of schedule; also, Madrid air traffic control has been kind to us, and we have a direct slot in, so I anticipate we will be landing within the next ten minutes. Thank you for flying with Iberia, and I wish you all a safe onward journey to your next destination.

"Cabin crew, doors to manual and seats for landing, please." The captain clicked off to concentrate on getting the aircraft on to the runway.

One of the stewardesses leaned over to David and asked if he would mind pulling up the window blind to his left.

He obliged, asking himself, *Why, so I can see if we miss the runway or another plane is going to hit us, then rush and warn the cabin crew, who are behind locked doors?* But rules were rules, and he was just irritable given the lack of sleep.

As he lifted the blind, he squinted as the brightness hit his eyes.

The landing was low key; the reverse thrust shot through the plane's engines, and brakes were applied as the captain aimed for the exit slipway several hundred feet in the distance.

"Welcome to Madrid, where the local time is 8.33 a.m.; if you are transferring to another flight, please head for the transfer lounge in the main building. Thank you once again for flying with Iberia, and we hope to see you again soon."

The aircraft was brought to a rest at its gate; the engines died, and the seat belt lights flicked off. The cabin was busy with people putting on jackets and coats, mobile phones buzzing into life, and luggage being brought down from the lockers.

David took down Melissa's hand luggage and set it at her feet; he placed his arm across her delicate shoulders and snuggled into her.

The gantry was at the door, and the first-class passengers were allowed to exit. The Swedish passports didn't get a second glance from the Spanish border guards. David and Melissa headed to the luggage hall and had their four bags within twenty minutes. David had attracted a porter, who lifted their lives onto a trolley, and they proceeded through the customs unheeded and out towards the taxi rank.

Outside, the sun's rays were beginning to warm the morning air. Melissa had a light tan cardigan on over a cream tee shirt and was wearing denim jeans. David had black jeans, a black tee shirt and a bronze/brown jacket.

David had booked the five-star Ritz Hotel in the centre of Madrid for a couple of days and felt that they had now covered their tracks very effectively.

His car had been stored with a specialist storage firm; they would deliver it at the hotel when they were ready to leave.

The journey to the hotel took forty-five minutes; David had been to Madrid many times before, both as a kid and on business conferences. Melissa had not even been to Europe, so she was in wide-eyed awe and disbelief at the magnificent wide boulevards overlooked by beautiful sandstone and white buildings that had stood long before George Washington had become the first American president.

As they headed further into this beautiful city, renowned in Europe as the city that never sleeps because the locals head out to dine from ten o'clock in the evening and party all night, she turned to David and said, "Wow, what is that? It looks like a massive sports stadium."

David smiled at this little lost girl in a new world.

"That is the world's richest soccer club's stadium," he said, "the Santiago Bernabeu; it's one hundred and fifty feet high, seats over eighty-five thousand, and is home to Real Madrid. I have been there a few times to watch one of the world's greatest grudge matches, when they play Barcelona."

"Impressive, but so strange to see it strutting out next to the buildings like it does," she said.

The car pulled up outside the enormous, majestic Ritz Hotel, a huge curved, white building, with black topped turrets, that has stood for over a hundred years.

Their luggage was unloaded immediately; David paid the driver and tipped the doorman with a five euro note. The doorman gave David a receipt for the bags and said, "Please show this at check-in," as he opened the door for Melissa and David to enter the hotel. The couple walked into the huge reception area, with marbled floors and large pillars to the ceiling.

David had booked a suite, and they were escorted up to their room. The large door opened into a lounge area, scattered with antique furnishings and enormous paintings. The carpet was cream and the walls decorated in luscious gold leaf wallpaper, framed by wooden rails. The ceiling must have been twelve feet above them, with a huge crystal chandelier dropping some four feet from its fixings in the ceiling plaster.

David and Melissa enjoyed the night at a tablao, basically a restaurant with a stage, where traditional flamenco was performed. Melissa loved it; everything was so traditional. She had kindly unpacked some of David's clothes for their evening out, still trying to keep things in some order. She had even taken out his gold Breitling watch and set the time; its automatic movement had stopped due to not being worn for some days. They finished early, by Madrid standards, as they were both jet-lagged.

Hans—New York, Monday

Hans dozed and awoke at nine in the morning; he would call home later. He went to the gym on the top floor, worked the weights for an hour, showered off at the pool, and swam twenty-five lengths. He could see that the weather was good and clear outside as he peered along the avenue from the pool room windows.

Lunch was a bore but necessary. Further deals were cemented and opportunities discussed.

Joe—New York, Monday

It was coming up to lunchtime in New York, and Joe had been invited out by one of the clients, together with Tony, their account manager. The restaurant had been pre-booked, Joe assumed by the client.

Tony walked up to one of Joe's personal assistants and said, "Hi, Pat; how are you today?"

Tony was forty-two, five ten, one hundred and eighty pounds, with a charming personality and smiling face. He had worked for Joe for seventeen years and worshipped the ground he walked on. Tony was married to Carole, also an ex-banker, and they had two kids, seven and ten, the younger a girl called Sandy and the older boy, and you may have guessed it, Joe. Joe, the boss, was godfather to both.

"Pretty good, thanks, Tony," Pat replied.

Pat was fit as a butcher's dog, twenty-six, with long flowing black hair and beautiful deep brown eyes. She was petite, probably five feet four inches, and in perfect proportion. Her complexion was flawless, and she was always immaculately presented, dressed in anything Saks had to offer. All the office guys knew she was off-limits.

"How's the mood in there today?" Tony asked, gesturing at Joe's office.

Pat smiled and said, "Hey, pretty good today, for a change." It was with a wry smile, as she had blown Joe off in his private restroom thirty minutes beforehand and thus knew he would be in a pretty good mood.

"Will you let him know the clients have arrived? There are the two of them: Jeff, the CEO, and Paul, the CFO. I suggest we have forty-five minutes in one of the meeting rooms for an update and then off to lunch," Tony said.

"Sure," Pat said, licking her lips. She dialled through to Joe. "Hi, Joe; the clients have arrived. we'll show them through to meeting room 1." There was a muffled grunt of response from the other end of the line, and Pat nodded to Tony.

The clients had been led into the meeting room and were helping themselves to a soda as Tony walked in, hand extended.

"Hi, Jeff, Paul; how's it going?"

"Hey, good to see you, Tony," Jeff said as both took turns shaking hands. "Well, you would have seen from the figures for the last quarter, it has been pretty good; how's your family? Any holidays recently?"

"Family is good; we managed a week in Aspen skiing earlier in the year, but nothing else planned. You look well, Jeff. Been away?"

Jeff smiled, and the tan highlighted his bleached white perfectly crowned teeth.

"Took the pack to Florida for a few days and caught some rays at Disney," Jeff said. "Took me a week to recover."

"And you, Paul?" asked Tony.

"Hey, someone has to do the work," he said, grinning with not-so-white teeth. "Nothing yet, but hope to get away to the Caribbean later in the year."

Jeff was in his mid-fifties, six feet tall, as mentioned an impressive set of pearly whites in his mouth, blue eyes covered by some heavyweight lids, in turn covered by some bushy grey eyebrows, thinning grey hair, and a small paunch pushing at his white shirt.

Paul was in his late forties, face looking a little drawn, no tan, slight grey pallor which was accentuated by the obviously dyed black hair. Brown eyes and trim, after an hour or so at the gym every day. Height was about five ten. Dark grey suit and also white shirt and silver patterned silk tie.

Joe waltzed into the room, and all immediately stood to attention. "Hi, guys, good to see you both. Good results. Let's catch up quickly and get out of here for some lunch," Joe ordered.

Paul quickly dished out four small presentation packs from his black leather carry bag and handed them round. Their company manufactured water and chemical purifying systems, steady growth with new orders and applications.

Paul presented the figures, with Jeff embellishing and selling the performance. As expected, the company was growing quickly, and the business's working capital needs were coming under pressure. They needed more money to continue this growth. The company enjoyed a $55 million loan package and wanted an extra $10 million for growth; most would be covered off by the additional collateral, in receivables and inventory generated, but an element was to be covered by the growing profits and the resultant cash flow.

Joe and Tony had known the company and the management team for nine years; they had steadfastly, if not boringly, always met their performance targets and delivered on their strategies.

The additional money would be paid back over eighteen months.

"Agreed. Two hundred and fifty thousand dollars in fees, payable now, and three hundred and fifty basis points, 3.5 per cent over Libor, interest plus five thousand dollars per month for additional monitoring. Now lunch," Joe said, "and you guys are paying."

There was no further negotiation, take it or leave it. They took it, shook on it, and Paul checked his pocket for his wallet as they got up to go.

Tony would do a file note, and Joe would sign it off. Money would be available that afternoon.

Tony had booked his favourite Italian restaurant, just off Fifth Avenue but some way from the office, and although Joe wasn't for wasting time in cars, this was fine as the client was paying. Joe picked up Peter, the division's chief financial officer, on the way out. "Hey, free lunch and two hundred and fifty thousand dollars," he said, deliberately within earshot of the clients.

Peter knew never to be unavailable for a client lunch; this was an order, not an invitation. Joe loved having an entourage, and the more, the merrier.

Tony had anticipated additional numbers and had forewarned the restaurant to expect four to six people. There were two cars waiting to take them to their destination.

After they arrived, still a little walk away due to traffic congestion, Joe stepped from the car and immediately headed off in the direction of the restaurant, daring the scrambling entourage to catch him up. He marched through the crowds in his tailor-made cashmere-wool mix suit, white collared and cuffed pink shirt, Hermes tie, and twelve hundred dollar tasselled black shoes.

There had been the inevitable dialogue of small talk, dotted with individual expectations of how the economy would fare, but Joe knew it all already; after all, he was Joe.

They reached the restaurant, Luigi's, and were ushered in by the head waiter, who gushed, "Tony, so good to see you, thank you for joining us again, Tony."

As the two kissed cheek on cheek, Joe thought, *Tony this and Tony fucking that; ignore me like some lackey of Tony's, you shit!*

To the perceptive, a nuclear explosion had just gone off inside Joe, but to his guests, he remained a sea of calm, occasionally adjusting his diamond cufflinks to ensure the stitched initials on his three-hundred dollar shirt could be seen. The other participants stole the odd glance at the eighty-thousand-dollar gold and diamond Rolex as it caught the light.

Joe listened and then exploded with a tremendous, educated insight into the economy's movements, everybody hanging on his every word.

Nothing from Peter; he would listen intently and nod when a nod of support was needed, never missing any signal to agree or disagree when required. Lunch was finished quickly, in inimitable NY style, some iced teas, no appetisers, no sweets, and back to work. The clients headed off in their own direction.

Joe strutted off in front of Tony to the waiting car; a huge blond man stepped out of a jeweller's shop without looking and collided with Joe, nearly throwing him off his feet. Tony tried hard not to laugh out loud.

Pat could tell lunch had not been a great success and tried to sooth the atmosphere.

"Hi, Joe, would you like anything … to drink?" she asked, hinting seductively.

"No, thanks, Pat; compose a staff email, now," Joe said, ignoring her undertones.

"To all staff," he dictated, "Luigi's Restaurant, just off Fifth Avenue, is not to be used by any of the bank staff for entertaining. Note no receipt from this restaurant will be reimbursed henceforth."

When the email hit his screen, Tony finally realised what had happened, but he had missed it during all the adulation at the restaurant. Best to keep his head down, he thought. Don't mention it, and all will be forgotten over the next few days. "You get used to it," he mused.

Hans—Monday

Hans left his lunch meeting and called into a jeweller on Fifth Avenue, where he bought Sabrina a beautiful thirty-five-thousand-dollar diamond bracelet, something he would need to be careful about hiding when going back through South African customs, but he was rarely stopped; they had bigger fish to fry.

As he stepped out onto the street, he bumped into a strutting little man.

"My apologies," he said.

The man stared at him with disdain and carried on.

Martinez—Colombia, Monday

Martinez had been checking through the accounts in the morning, validating with his accountants that his drugs revenue outstripped the GDP of many Third World countries.

After the CIA had assassinated his brother, Martinez had taken over the family empire. He was ruthless, especially when dealing with the Americans. Now forty-two, he was deemed the most powerful of the drug barons, with an army on call that would make any tinpot dictator stand at least two feet taller.

He picked up a call on his cell: "The package was destroyed in Los Angeles," the caller said. "There were no other problems."

"Thank you," Martinez said, hitting the red button on his cell. The hit in LA had been taken care of.

One of Martinez's money men approached him at the pool.

"Marti, we have a problem," he said.

"What?" Martinez replied, eyeing the accountant suspiciously.

"A substantial money shipment has not arrived at its destination following the complicated money laundering programme; it's not been stopped by police or government. We believe it's an inside job."

"How much?" Martinez asked.

"Twenty million dollars," he replied.

Martinez's face looked like a tropical storm, but his voice remained calm.

"Who?"

"Seems we lost it in New York; David, the vice president we deal with there, hasn't turned in for work today."

"Get on to it," Martinez barked. "Was it part of the Russian shipment?"

"Yes, it was the final deposit for the Russian shipment; that's why we picked it up so quickly. We went to David's apartment and tracked him to Mexico. We guess he has changed passports, and we are working on that with our customs and police insiders."

"Good, keep me updated. I'll speak to the Russians, but we will have to line up more money."

Martinez had a number of large shipments of cocaine bound for a number of destinations and was keen to get this new mode of transport sorted as soon as possible.

He checked his watch and knew that he could get Sergey; it was late evening/early morning in Moscow. He flipped open his phone and called Sergey's number; a young woman answered, and he could hear music banging away in the background. The woman asked him to hold.

"Martinez, my friend, how are you?" came Sergey's craggy voice. Martinez realised that Sergey was very relaxed. *Vodka soaked,* he thought.

"I'm good, my dear friend," he said. "How are things?" He didn't want to step straight into a discussion about money.

Sergey was a little less forgiving "All good, my friend, and all running to plan; your own shipment has not arrived yet?"

"No, we have a system glitch," Martinez said, "but the delay will be no more than twenty-four hours. I wanted to tell you personally."

"Okay, my friend. I hope not a major problem? I appreciate your personal call. I look forward to cementing our transaction." One of the girls was now rubbing up and down on Sergey, and he was keen to end the call. "Any other issues, let me know; have a better day tomorrow, my friend. Bye," and the phone clicked dead.

Martinez didn't enjoy dealing with the Russians; they had no class but were a necessary evil, and they had most of Europe sown up in respect of distribution. He put his phone and sunglasses down on the table and slipped out of his shoes and shirt, which he threw over the back of one of the poolside loungers. He sought out his son, who was not paying any attention, as he was splashing his younger sisters, and dive-bombed his unsuspecting offspring, soaking the accountant at the same time.

Joe—New York, Monday

Pat interrupted Joe's meeting with Peter, saying, "The bank's internal audit guys are here."

"Thanks, Pat," Joe said as he grinned at Peter. "Take the audit people to the large meeting room, then tell Frank to join us in my room."

Peter shuffled about on the spot a little, but there was a calm air about Joe, and he could literally hear his brain ticking into overdrive. They had had the audit team and the Fed in many times before; they were used to it and knew what had to be done and said. Joe ensured that he, Peter, and Frank were the only ones the outsiders were allowed to see alone. They were kept in the main meeting room throughout the process, not allowed to walk the floor, and any information they required was carefully logged before they received it and generally very well doctored. Joe seemed all-powerful in his ability to keep things under wraps. Any other member of staff the auditors wanted to interview was well briefed prior to any meeting, and one of the three was always in attendance.

The business was being sold; the audit team were just here to check things through before the potential buyers could go through the books in more detail. Joe had arranged that any purchaser would get only three days to interrogate the records on-site and to meet the team.

They had already received a raft of information on which to base their decision, all carefully put together, of course, and once they had bought the business, Joe and his team were confident of keeping everything ticking over as before.

Frank entered the room. "You called?" he asked.

"The internal auditors are here," said Peter.

"Why? We are just about to be sold," Frank snapped. "Don't they know we are God damn busy?"

"Just routine," Joe said, winking at both of them.

They all stood there for a second and thought about all of that bonus money they would receive from selling the business. Joe was in for $20 million, not that the other two knew, as he had been allocated $24 million, and $4 million was therefore left for the other senior managers. They also had shares that they would be able to sell at a vast premium.

"Right," Joe said. "Let's go see what we can do for these guys."

As they left Joe's room, Pat called Peter over and said, "You have an urgent message from a guy called Marti, Peter."

"This is turning out to be an eventful week," Peter said, shrugging and hurrying off to his own office. *What the hell is Martinez doing calling me?* he thought.

Peter picked up his unregistered cell phone and called Marti's contact number.

"Marti, good to hear from you," he said. "Hope you are keeping well."

"No, I'm not. I was okay, Peter, but we lost our package in the system, and David Kettner has left for Mexico. We have been trying to track him for little while."

"Shit," was all about Peter could muster. "I'll check it out and get back to you."

"Please do, and quickly, Peter. We need the money back quickly."

Peter placed the phone down and looked blankly at the computer screen; he began to shake, his heart rate increased rapidly, and a thin film of sweat covered his forehead as he took in the possible consequences of what he had been told.

Peter pulled on his jacket, grabbed his overcoat, and snatched up the cell phone. He strode past his assistant, muttering that he was popping out for an hour or so and would she let Joe know?

His mind was jumping to so many different scenarios; he wasn't quite sure how to pull all of this jumble together, but he knew he had to get things in motion quickly.

Joe and Frank dealt with the audit team; Joe was irritated that Peter seemed to have disappeared.

The day finished up with a list of client files the auditors wanted to review.

Peter—New York, Monday 2

Peter had checked all of David's files, desks, cabinets, and computer at the bank's branch office; he knew that his apartment had been searched. There had been some accounting journals made, but these seem to have rectified positions where money had been taken from some of the wealthier customers. David had tried to cover this up. Peter guessed that this was something that could be used in court by clients, whereas the money laundering would never be disclosed by the bank due to reputational risks. Even with the pilfering of client money, the bank would have been unlikely to risk a court case or disclosure to its clients; it would have settled out of court and just let David go. Nothing now would show on the clients' statements, but Peter expunged the journal entries from the system.

So it seemed to be just the $20 million. Peter thought, *Why just? To 99.9 per cent of the world, it was an enormous sum. I've been working with money far too long.* It had been distributed in such a way that no one could track it down, nor would anyone auditing the branch ever know it had been there in the first place. This branch would no longer be used; this part of the money laundering operation, rife throughout the bank but carefully managed, would be moved to one of their other managers in the loop.

Peter knew that Martinez would be calling for an update soon, and he grew short of breath as the time ticked closer. On the button, his cell rang, and he stabbed at the answer button.

"Peter, my friend, so what is the news?" said Martinez.

"Not good, Martinez," Peter replied. "No sign of the money; it seems to have disappeared into the system. Good news is that David doesn't appear to have left anything else to implicate any wrongdoing."

"Well, when do I get a refund?" Martinez asked matter-of-factly, but Peter realised the implications.

"I've chatted through with Joe," Peter said. "A refund is not possible, but we can wash money through, commission free, to make up the difference."

The line was silent, but then "Okay" came the response, then a click, and just the dial tone remained.

Peter called Joe. "M has accepted a commission-free deal."

"Good," said Joe, and the line went silent.

Hans—New York, Monday 2

The early evening had become cold and damp as Hans returned to his hotel.

He shaved and then showered, lathering his muscular and tanned torso to remove the grime of the day in the city. The warm spray hit his shoulders, and he felt the aura of relaxation spread throughout his body, as the massaging warmth spread from the middle of his shoulders up into his neck and down his back.

He dried his hair and applied some moisturising cream, antiperspirant, and aftershave he bought on the plane on the way over.

He decided on a light khaki silk suit with white linen shirt, brown loafers, and tan socks, very un-American, and not a suit to get wet in, but the sky had cleared, and rain looked unlikely.

Hans had been up to the bar earlier in the day and dropped the waiter fifty dollars to ensure he had the best table for the six thirty meet with Cheryl. It was now six fifteen; Hans checked his phone and email for messages and readied himself, glancing in the mirror. *Strange,* he thought. Here he was, happily married, paying for the privilege, but he still felt the need to make sure he looked good for the girl. He smiled and let out a small laugh; he was beginning to feel those first-date butterflies and making sure that he looked great for a woman who would probably shag a fat, bald seventy-year-old without even blinking an eyelid.

Hans left the room and put the privacy ticket on the door handle; he always hated the thought of someone in the room pulling the bedcovers down and nosing around.

He made his way to the bar and was immediately met by the same waiter like a long-lost friend, who guided him to his table.

"A bottle of the ninety-nine Dom, two glasses, and some still mineral water, please, Ben." Hans always sought out their name; it made sure that the service was even more exemplary, and both would endeavour to maintain this illusion of mutual respect, maybe bordering on assumed friendship, and of course more tips for Ben.

"Certainly, Mr Van Rensburg," came the smiling reply. Ben realised that he had a big hitter who liked him and thought about the large tip that would follow.

Cheryl—New York, Monday

Cheryl's agency had called early with her next assignment: "Great guy, from abroad, Australian perhaps, had seen your photo and CV and immediately asked for you, wants to whisk you away to St Lucia for a few days, or should I say nights."

Cheryl had gasped, "Wow." This type of thing happened every now and then, usually with regulars, but generally, it was the grind of the one- or two-hour late-night slot with some sweaty, drunk, married, out-of-towner, looking for the thing he couldn't get at home, and no, that wasn't lobster Thermidor.

Then she began to think; was he going to be some ailing, overweight pensioner or some strange S&M fiend who would cut her up and feed her to the local St Lucian fish? He had booked with an Amex Black card; this had helped stop her mind working overtime (well, just a little). At least he could be checked out, and there were still a few days to ensure that the card had not been stolen. The agency had said he sounded young, but who could really tell over the phone?

Cheryl confirmed the booking for tonight, said yes to the trip if all went okay at their meeting, and had immediately jumped on to the internet and looked up Jade Mountain (another "Wow"). Rooms had no fourth wall, all open to their own private terrace and individual infinity pools, a spa, and fantastic menus.

One of the sites mentioned hundreds of steps and stairs, so maybe he was not too old, unless they would be locked in the room for the entire period, but then he might have a heart attack anyway.

She had had a wax a few days before, and all was now settling down, no red marks down there anymore, completely bald and smooth. Cheryl was twenty-six, the daughter of a couple of doctors, but she dropped out of med school when she had met the perfect guy, who turned out to be a heavy drug user who just sucked out all her money and caused the inevitable fallout with her mum and dad.

That was five years ago now, and all was back in harmony with her family. The escort job, which had seemed to be the only way out of the debt burden, had now become a comfortable way of life. The agency protected her very well; she had a lot of free time and was picking up her studies again. She had money in the bank, more shoes than Imelda, and no emotional ties outside of family and some good friends.

Cheryl had decided on a long bath, with exotic salts and bubbles. She applied a light foundation to her flawless, very light olive skin (some Italian blood in the family history), a light red lipstick, and small amount of eyeliner. She had fantastic long eyelashes, so no work needed there; both nails and toenails had a light pink varnish, almost natural but smooth and shiny. She had been very athletic at school and college, swam every day, as well as doing some light weights at the gym. This had kept her body in great shape, nothing too muscular or sinewy, flat, toned tummy, pert backside, and her small breasts, with little pink nipples, hadn't changed since she was eighteen.

She decided, given the changeable weather, on a classic black cashmere dress, no underwear, and some black Jimmy Choos, with two-inch heels, just in case he was a little vertically challenged. These would be fine for the next day, for the walk of shame, where people would be looking at girls who'd obviously been out for the night before and were now making their way back home.

Cheryl checked her bag: condoms, lubricant, knickers, toothbrush, paste, hair brush, perfume, and morning makeup.

Small diamond, stud-earrings and bracelet, presents from Daddy, and a Breitling sports watch, with black strap. She had bought this after an eight-thousand-dollar tip for services rendered and had paid for a champagne lunch with her girlfriends.

It was now six in the evening. One final glance in the full-length mirror; she pulled on a black cashmere overcoat, pulled a silver wrap around her shoulders, checked her coat pocket for the small extendable umbrella, and left her apartment in Tribeca, stepping into the pre-booked cab to the Penn.

Hans—New York, Monday evening

Hans had chosen the table well, next to a window overlooking the avenue, catching a light cooling breeze from the open doors onto the terrace, with a good view of the entrance and also distant enough from other tables. The terrace would have been great, but Hans was not confident on the weather and had no idea whether Cheryl would be dressed warmly enough, even though they provided blankets and heaters.

There she was, five minutes late. He knew it was Cheryl immediately; he was used to analysing and committing photographs to memory. He was wondering whether he would ever get to know her real name; little did he know it *was* her real name. Ben, picking up on Hans's smile, immediately guided her into the lair.

Hans stood and took one step towards her; she was looking for a middle-aged, pot-bellied guy with balding head and then saw this apparition of a man leaning in her direction and inviting her over. *Never,* she thought, but no, he was looking and smiling directly at her.

He held out his hand. "Cheryl, darling, great to see you. Wow, you look stunning as ever."

At the same time, he drew her body into his as he kissed her on both cheeks and took in the Diorella scent she was wearing. He knew it and just whispered, "Mmmmm, Diorella, one of my favourite perfumes," with a smile that made her knees tremble.

As she was drawn in, she felt his muscular, solid arm and her hand had slipped onto his solid, concrete-hard back. Her nipples had immediately hardened, and Hans also noticed the immediate dilation of her pupils. He felt an immediate arousal below and smiled to himself that he had chosen well.

Hans and Ben guided Cheryl to a seat facing the other tables; all women like a view of the room, Hans had been taught. His gentlemanly gesture was not unnoticed by Cheryl, although given the usual knowing stares she received from men and the burning ones from wives and girlfriends, she normally preferred to keep her back to other tables. However, this evening was somewhat different; the women looked jealous of her, and there were just as many staring at Hans as at her. Yes, she was still getting the furtive glances of the testosterone-charged men, but she was all of a sudden with an equal; the two of them made a beautiful couple.

He made her feel so immediately at ease.

"I took the liberty of ordering some champagne," he said. "Of course, I'd be happy to order something else, if you prefer."

"Champagne will be lovely, thank you," she said, smiling.

Ben was there in a flash, pouring the champagne and offering water. The two chatted generally, getting the lie of the land, gently teasing one another with innuendos.

"Well, I understand I have you for the night, so we have dinner booked at Buddakan, in the Meat Packer's District, for eight thirty," Hans explained.

They finished a couple of glasses and headed down to the lobby, where Hans had arranged for a car to take them on to the restaurant. He held her hand all the way, which Cheryl found sweet and strangely reassuring. She felt very comfortable with this man.

Over a tasting menu of melt-in-the-mouth ribs, prawns, and Kobe beef, recommended by their waiter, they shared more about each other's lives, education, family, upbringing, desires, and needs. Town, family, school, and college names were carefully replaced with alternatives, most of which Cheryl had memorised and used a thousand times before. All mostly true but not enough information for either of them to be found by a stalker. Although Cheryl, she insisted, was her real name.

Hans looked into her eyes, all of a sudden serious; he squeezed her hand over the soft white linen.

"Tell me, truthfully, do you have a twin sister?" he said.

Wondering why so serious, she looked questionably back. "No, as you know, my older brother is a doctor, actually a world-renowned brain surgeon. Why do you ask?"

"I met this girl on the plane on my way over; she was practically your double, but obviously not you. A book researcher." A glint in his eye.

"Oh, so you were chatting about work?" Cheryl asked, wanting to know more.

"Yes, very interesting work, fascinating really. I saw her in the aisle coming my way and obviously thought it would be great if she sat herself next to me, and lo and behold, she leant down and explained she was in the seat next to me."

"Ha, lucky you. And no doubt typical," Cheryl said.

"Well, very lucky; I noticed that she was scribbling things down vigorously in a book, and as she stopped to think, I asked her why so animated with the writing.

"She explained that she was writing a book and had a deadline to meet. I smiled and said that must be interesting work. She was a few vodka and tonics into the flight now and began to open up about her travels and research for her book, which was about sex education. She said that many people thought the Italians were the fiery, rampant, great lovers, but she had found them selfish and lacking in any real charm, and performance was lacking."

"Really?" Cheryl was incredulous and wide-eyed.

"She had met some strange people, but she was really into her work. She went on that the native American Indian was actually the greatest lover, performing time and time again with great sensuous feeling and understanding of a woman's cravings.

"Then it was the French that were supposed to be the most charming, with their language of love, wooing women the world over, but once again, this proved to be a falsehood, as far as her research revealed. She had found that the Greeks knew the true poetry of language and had whisked her and her researchers off their feet.

"I stopped her there as I realised here was this beautiful woman explaining all about sex, and I didn't even know her name. It was Jessica. She asked mine. 'Tonto Papadopoulos' was my immediate reply."

Cheryl roared with laughter, as she suddenly realised she had been suckered into a very credible but elaborate joke.

A car took them back to the hotel, and they went to Hans's suite. He poured them both a glass of champagne, having lifted the bottle out of its ice bucket, and kissed Cheryl fully on the lips as he unzipped her dress in one easy, adept action, which dropped to the floor.

She stepped out of the dress and her shoes but excused herself for a quick shower; it had been a long evening, but she beckoned Hans to join her in the walk-in shower.

She couldn't believe the body that flowed in behind her, slightly tanned and muscles where she had never seen muscles before. A rippling six-pack and the start of an enormous muscle eruption searching her out from below his waist.

She massaged soap into his back and bare chest; he kneaded her neck, rubbed her shoulders, and gently nuzzled his tongue in under her right ear. She was getting wetter and not from the shower. She began to rub him harder in the shower and knelt down, placing her lips around his fantastic cock. He rubbed her shoulders and writhed as she carried on in her practised art. He turned the shower off and picked her up in his arms, carrying her to the bed. He lifted her up onto her knees and slid his tongue down the middle of her back, until she felt his thrusting tongue in the crack of her arse.

She had wondered many a time why men were keen to lick a stranger's arse and if their wives received the same; she was sure Hans's wife or girlfriend had it all.

Hans nestled his face in between those magnificent muscles and worked his tongue deeper into her anal passage as she pushed back against him; he then moved further down, exploring her very wet vagina and onto an enlarged clit. The rhythm was perfect; Cheryl just couldn't hold it and felt the explosion coming. She tried to keep it under wraps, but Hans knew. She turned back to him, more sucking, and pulled a condom from her bag (no need for lube).

He pulled her around once again; her knees were now on the lower bed box and her face in the mattress. He was in, filling her; her head swam. He tentatively began to feed a finger into her anus; this was fantastic, and she came, writhing, groaning, and pushing herself back onto him.

Hans was masterful, confident, in control. He pulled her onto her side and slid in, his balls on her inner thigh. Riding higher and deeper, she screamed she was to come again; no falsehood needed in this meeting, no pretending in order to make the client feel good about himself or to meet an hour deadline.

He exploded at the same time as she, and both crumpled down onto the bed.

Thirty minutes later, he was back for more, and again at four o'clock in the morning, and again at eight. Cheryl was looking forward to St Lucia.

Cheryl woke at ten; the sun was shining through the un-curtained windows, Hans was in the shower. *Wow, what a great night,* she thought.

David and Melissa—
Madrid, Tuesday

David and Melissa slept until eleven thirty in the morning. She was keen to get to Augusta Figueroa, the shoe street, to indulge her addiction, and the two remained inseparable. Although David didn't enjoy shopping for shoes, he was keen to be at Melissa's side. This was an emotional and difficult time for both of them. He bought Melissa six pairs of new shoes; she was over the moon.

David talked to the hotel's well-networked concierge and secured tickets for Real Madrid, who were playing Malaga. Real took Malaga apart and knocked in four goals, three from the maestro, Ronaldo. The Special One, Real's manager Jose Mourinho, the diminutive genius, stood on the touchline, seemingly sending signals by telepathy to his team. Melissa just took in the atmosphere, not understanding much about the game on the pitch, although David attempted to talk her through the rules and history of the club, the manager, and some of the world-class players.

Some of it sunk in; the offside rule did not, but she was interested in the history of the delectable-looking manager, together with the strutting cockerel and heartthrob, Ronaldo.

They also spent a lot of their time in some of the old bars and restaurants in the side streets, getting to know each other a lot better. Melissa marvelled at the laid-back lifestyle of the Spanish; she loved the tapas dishes of fish, meats, cheeses, and vegetables. She people-watched customers in the cafes, from her own vantage point.

The Madrid visit disappeared in a whirlwind of experiences and emotions, as if it had been minutes.

David's Danish Range Rover was delivered, as arranged, to the hotel. Their luggage was loaded into the large bay at the back of the car. The Range Rover was silver with black leather seats and sat high above the much smaller and battered cars that nipped about the city, seemingly without a care in the world.

The couple couldn't believe that Spain was in deep recession.

It was going to be a long journey, but David had planned a few stops on the way: Monte Carlo, Milan, Geneva, Munich, Hamburg, then on to Copenhagen.

Joe—New York, Tuesday

Joe was attending a local charity dinner at the Waldorf; he was actually the chairman of the charity, having been presiding over it for the last eight years. The charity provided hospital treatment for underprivileged children where Joe grew up.

Every year, Joe wrote to his clients and staff, seeking donations and attendees to the dinner; this exercise usually raised up to $2 million. All senior managers in the bank were advised to donate two hundred and fifty dollars each or risk the prospect of no annual bonus; Joe was the final sign-off for all payments.

Monica, twenty years his junior, was from a wealthy American family; she had been working for a firm of architects that designed an extension and new pool house he was building in the Hamptons. Monica was at his side as he greeted the great and the good as they shuffled through to the ballroom.

Joe had negotiated a great deal with the hotel, whereby they took a flat fee for the room hire. *It was a charity, after all,* he thought regularly. Wines and booze had been shipped in from one of the bank's (Joe's) customers, as had the catering supplies, tables, chairs, decorations, flowers, and stage, effectively all clients of Joe or related in some way.

He made a decent personal profit on the arbitrage, based on what was charged and then inflated and passed on in deduction to the charity proceeds.

He looked and felt good in his tailored dinner suit, gold bow tie, and black waist jacket and patent shoes as he greeted the row of guests with a smile. Monica was dressed in black and deep gold Yves St Laurent and probably $1 million of jewels, diamonds, and a Boucheron solid gold and diamond scarf necklace.

Tonight, Joe had his young personal assistant in attendance; business needs, of course. Linda sat silently at the table next to Joe as he entertained his guests with some charming and funny anecdotes about his working life. All of the guests listened intently, knowing not to interrupt for fear of a putdown, or at least no more invites to special dinners and functions.

Tonight, Joe had a number of up-and-coming film stars and fashion models on many of the bank's tables, the latter invited by one of his biggest fashion house clients, who borrowed hundreds of millions of dollars from time to time. Joe was given the opportunity to sample some of these models on visits to the fashion house's head office in LA.

There were a number of high-profile presenters from showbiz, and the Black Eyed Peas were to give a ninety-minute performance after all of the auctions and charity-giving had taken place.

Joe was in his element; the good and the bad of New York society were in attendance: billionaires, multimillionaires, millionaires, many of Joe's clients, and his senior staff.

The room design had been overseen by Linda and the hotel team; the overall theme was black and gold this year.

Tablecloths were black, gold napkins, gold and black balloons, and exotic-looking table centrepieces that were lit from the narrow base of a crystal vase with a subtle gold light extending up into a forest of black orchids and lilies, surrounded by ferns and branches sprayed in gold. Black and gold glass pebbles were scattered across the tables; there had been several accidents where champagne flutes had been toppled when put down on this uneven terrain, but that cheered up the wine waiters, who were selling far more champagne than anticipated, and spillage added to the consumption.

Joe had ordered Cristal for his table, a rare divergence away from French wine, and this was being gulped down by his guests, the CEO of the hospital and his wife, Frank, Peter and his wife, the mayor and his wife, a senator and her husband, and the CEO and his girlfriend of Joe's largest client, the fashion house that borrowed the $250 million.

Many other tables were topped by Joe's senior management who were entertaining their largest clients (by income, not by borrowing).

The chief executive of the hospital took to the stage; he thanked everyone for attending and expressed how important this event was for them. He centred on a couple of stories of kids in his care, to pull at the heartstrings but not stun the room into silence and loss of appetite.

The evening was going well; food choices had been pre-ordered to ensure vegetarian, vegans, shellfish allergies had been accounted for.

The main choices were:

A small taster soup of cold sweet pea, served in a gold espresso cup on black saucer.

To follow:

> Lobster Thermidor, baked in a small double-handled soup bowl and covered with cheese and breadcrumbs.
> A champagne sorbet.
> Filet mignon, seasonal vegetables, and dauphinoise potatoes.
> A taster of five of the hotel's special to-die-for sweets.

Generally, the men on all tables ate heartily and avoided the sweet. Many of the svelte (starved) models, high-society hookers, cocaine snorters, and waist-conscious partygoers left enough to feed the Third World for a week.

Joe had ordered some good French wines to complement the dishes, but the Cristal was still flowing hard.

Monica was in deep conversation with the senator and Joe with the mayor.

There had been a silent auction of donated artwork, sporting memorabilia, and holidays, which had seen tremendous uptake and had raised record numbers. Next up was an auction of similar but deemed more special items:

- a private jet for twenty-four hours.
- an eight-bedroom residence in Bermuda for a week.
- seats in the chairman's suite at a Giants game
- VIP tour and seats at the Yankees
- private yacht at the Monaco Grand Prix
- chateaux in Provence for two weeks

Joe stood at the podium, the mike already suitably lowered, and asked all to give generously; this wasn't about the value and cost of the auction prize, but charity. He underpinned that the prizes were beyond value, as nothing could be bought on the market.

There was also a raffle that would be drawn later in the evening.

The auction went on, and the businessmen in the room took the lead in the bidding.

Champagnes, wines, beers, and spirits flowed, and the bidding in many cases was driven by competition amongst the businessmen's egos, fuelled by the confidence of the booze. Wives tugged at arms, some telling their husbands to behave and some fuelling the fire to win at any cost.

The Black Eyes Peas took to the stage, and the party really began to rock, opening with "I Got a Feeling." This wasn't quite Joe's scene, but the Peas were tremendously popular and had agreed to a "cover our costs" contract.

Joe had been over to whisper into Linda's ear several times during the evening, something not lost on Monica.

The evening raised $2.2 million.

David and Melissa—Wednesday

Martinez's men found out that David had a girlfriend, Melissa, from their contacts in the mobile phone industry; both phones were off the network, having last been picked up in Rio de Janeiro.

They tracked them through to the Rio hotel, but then the trail went cold, and they checked all of the flights out over the next few days.

They checked all their sources with reference to the production of false papers and passports and drawn a blank.

Car hire company records were checked; nothing. Both David's and Melissa's credit cards were also being monitored.

Martinez's people were calling in a lot of favours and spending a lot of money, but this was more about reputation than the cost.

They checked first- and business-class passengers and tracked down a number of possible leads to other South American and European destinations, but getting passport photographs was proving difficult, and CCTV footage they obtained had proved inconclusive. The information flow was enormous, and now they were receiving data on standard-class flights and cruises.

They tracked down Melissa's only relative, her mother, and bugged her phones and were monitoring her email, having done the same for David's father.

Then, a lead from Madrid.

"Why Madrid?" Jose, the Martinez lead man looking for David, asked himself out loud.

"Dunno, boss," said Manuel and Miguel, two of his underlings, thinking it was a direct question to them.

They then cross-referenced their enquiries and started concentrating on the flight manifests in a lot more detail; passport details were now flowing in, and there were a number of potential couples and people travelling separately. This narrowed the list to seventy. They concentrated on US and Canadian passports, then someone suggested Sweden, given David's mother. Johansson looked a strong possibility, similar age, but quite a change in appearance on the photographs.

Martinez spoke to Sergey, and David's mother was now under surveillance, as well.

Hans—New York, Wednesday

Hans had arranged to meet Cheryl at the airport; she had declined his offer of a car and was making her own travel arrangements.

She had spent most of the previous evening sorting through clothes, swimming costumes, and lingerie. She had this general air of expectation and was looking forward to another liaison with this beautiful man from South Africa.

Hans sat in the back of the hotel limo as it crawled along the highway to the airport. He too had a feeling of anticipation, but this was completely different from the emotions Cheryl was feeling. The excitement certainly wasn't as intense as when he had first picked up the message about the upcoming assignment; he knew the hit after this one would be a final top-up. He was missing his family, his wife, his boys, and this fantasy was now getting to a tedious stage. His mind drifted away from all of this, and strangely, he thought of Cheryl. He would enjoy her riding him later on in the evening.

Then, he immediately switched back to the task in hand: how to do his job without raising suspicion. Cheryl wouldn't be a problem; she could be drugged and asleep as required. But Mr Todd Baker would be there with his girlfriend; it may not be so easy to get him alone; maybe a diving accident, as this was one of Todd's hobbies.

The car arrived at the airport, and the driver opened the door and pulled Hans's weekend bag from the trunk.

"Thanks," said Hans. The bill was already taken care of at the hotel.

"Have a great trip," the driver said as he stepped back into the limo.

Hans had arranged to meet Cheryl at the desk; they would check in together and head off to the lounge for a drink. Hans was in jeans, linen white shirt, tan jacket, and brown shoes.

Cheryl texted him and said she would be about ten minutes longer. Hans stood by the desk and people-watched. He was thinking that there were an awful lot of overweight people, waddling from side-to-side, like tipping Derek pumping stations, rather than walking one stride in front of the other. In Manhattan, people generally looked a lot fitter than in some of the other cities and states. Florida was a prime example of lard-arse after lard-arse.

Hans heard the click-click of Cheryl's black Christian Louboutins as she walked towards him at the desk.

She wore a broad smile, and her hair was tied back in a single ponytail, police sunglasses, silk neck scarf, and a black leather jacket, over a cream cashmere sweater and tight black leather trousers. She clutched a small Louis Vuitton handbag and pulled a small matching wheelie bag behind her.

Hans smiled, and the fact that most of the eyes in the hall were on her rear hadn't gone unnoticed by either of them.

Hans swooped in, kissed her, and took her hand baggage.

"Sorry, I'm late," she said.

"No problem, we have plenty of time. Let's get checked in and have a drink in the lounge," Hans said.

"Sounds good," she responded.

Hans thanked the check-in girl, who had quite happily been flirting with him throughout the process, and took the tickets. He took Cheryl's roll-on luggage in one hand, placed his own bag on top, and took Cheryl's hand in his other.

The two pottered off towards security.

They spent the flight to St Lucia chatting about all and nothing; the two looked like newly-weds off on honeymoon, as opposed to one of the world's deadliest hitmen and a hooker. However, to a more trained eye, the lack of luggage suggested a couple of nights of debauchery away from prying eyes.

St Lucia was hot, 82 degrees as they landed, after a stop-off in Puerto Rico.

They were picked up by pre-arranged transfer and driven off to the hotel. The roads were pretty good, as they took in the lush green scenery, until they hit the village at the base of the mountainside overlooking the blue sea. This looked like a war zone; poverty was evident, with many of the locals staring at the car as it manoeuvred itself through the narrow streets.

As the car left the village, it took a turn onto a rubble dirt track and disappeared into the undergrowth as it began a steady, struggling climb up the side of the mountain towards the hotel.

Wow, this is bumpy, Cheryl thought as she clung to the door handle on one side and Hans on the other. They finally arrived at the top, swung right onto two concrete strips, and headed up between villas to the top. Cheryl could see the idyllic beach to her left, and in the distance, the top of the Pitons scoping up into the blue sky like two pert, emerald breasts.

At the top of the hill, the driveway swirled round a central tree to allow cars back down the single track.

The driver pulled the car to a halt; three members of staff were waiting to greet their guests. A woman, Hans assumed the manager, dressed in a cream skirted suit, extended a hand and welcomed both to the Jade Mountain Hotel.

The bellboy took care of the cases, and a young girl in a red sari stood with two warm hand towels; Hans and Cheryl wiped off their hands, and the girl offered up two iced fruit cocktails.

The manager chatted through details about the hotel, and once they finished their drinks, they were invited to follow her and the bellboy up the small paved walkway to the main rooms.

The hotel had been built into the mountainside, and walls were of large polished rocks. They crossed a small bridge and went into their room. Dark mahogany wood covered the floor. To the right was a large king-sized four-poster bed, with netting on the sides. On the bed were rose petals and two towels ornately shaped into entwined swan necks. Just beyond the bed was a large infinity pool overlooking the ocean, and up a few stairs to the left, the open-plan bathroom and beyond a Jacuzzi and balcony. The room was walled on three sides, but there was no fourth wall. The room was completely open overlooking the beach, the mountainside, and the majestic Pitons in the distance.

Waiting to welcome them into their room was their own personal butler.

"Hello, I am Ranjit," the butler said. "Let me show you the room and explain our amenities."

"Thank you," Hans said, nodding.

Cheryl listened intently, whilst taking in the stunning views.

"Anything you need," he began, "please take this cell phone. You can call me anytime. If you need a ride to the restaurant or picking up from the beach, dinner in the room, or drinks, please let me know."

Hans tipped Ranjit twenty dollars, said thank you, and asked that they be booked into the penthouse restaurant for the evening.

It was now late afternoon, and Cheryl suggested the two of them share the Jacuzzi. Hans didn't require a second invitation.

Once again, the sex was mind-blowing, and the fact that the room had no fourth wall made it seem they were actually out in the open, a big turn-on for both of them.

Hans rolled over and reached out for his cell as it wriggled across the bedside table. He read the coded message: "Todd Baker contract is terminated. Do NOT go ahead; return to New York and await instructions for Los Angeles." Hans sighed, and Cheryl nuzzled into him and asked if all was okay.

Hans smiled down at her. "All's fine, just a business deal that I don't have to get involved in." He did actually feel a sense of relief and decided to enjoy the next couple of days.

They spent most of Friday on the beach, where they also snorkelled and wind-surfed. Lunch was Caesar salads and several glasses of wine each.

Late afternoon, they adjourned to their room and enjoyed a dip in the infinity pool, which ended with another great session.

Both showered and got ready for dinner. Many of the weekend guests had arrived, and the restaurant was busy; there was a lot of noise from one particular table, where three American couples had got together. The life and soul was a guy called Todd.

Hans smiled a wry smile to himself.

Sergey—Moscow, Thursday

"Hello Sergey, I am very pleased with the acquisition that we have concluded," Martinez said on his cell. "Thank you."

"A pleasure," replied Sergey, "and thank you for the final payment. We are now training the men you have sent over, but the captain and several of them you employed are already very proficient."

"Good to hear," Martinez said. "Sergey, I need your help on a delicate matter."

"Not a problem," he replied. "How can I help?"

"We have lost a couple of packages, two to be precise, and need them to be located in Europe."

"Okay," Sergey said. "Just send the details through the latest route."

"Okay, thank you," Martinez said.

Bill—London/Geneva, Friday

Bill called a few of his contacts in the reinsurance market; he had got a sniff of a few things which didn't seem to add up in the corporate life insurance market. He arranged to meet one of the key underwriters in Geneva to discuss this issue.

He managed to get on a flight in the next few hours out of London City Airport and would make Geneva by three thirty in the afternoon; he had a meeting for a few hours and then would return to London, hopefully with a new mandate to explore further his initial findings.

Check-in was a few minutes at City, and he had a forty-minute wait before boarding. He grabbed a beer at the airport bar and guzzled it back, whilst dabbing away at his BlackBerry, then another beer just for good measure.

Bill had booked a meeting room in one of the hotels adjacent to Geneva's airport. Here he was to meet his insurance contact, an ex-colleague that now worked in the large re-insurance markets and managed several contracts.

Guy, the reinsurance contact, had relocated to Switzerland some years ago; he saw Bill at the hotel bar. *Bloody typical*, he thought. Guy was forty-four, six feet two inches tall, full head of blond hair, green eyes, wearing Armani black-rimmed glasses.

"Hi, Bill, what gives?" Guy said as he picked out Bill's open hand, shaking it, in fact nearly crushing it. Bill grimaced, whilst hugging him at the same time with his free arm.

"Hi Guy; good to see you. Beer?" said Bill.

"Sure, I'll have one of whatever you're drinking," Guy responded, looking Bill up and down at the same time.

Bill looked well enough: clear eyes, slight tan. The suit had seen better days, a little shiny on the thighs and jacket elbows, which enhanced an overall shabby demeanour of his old friend and colleague.

"How's your family?" Bill asked, handing Guy a glass of ice-cold beer.

"They're all good," Guy said, raising his glass in Bill's direction. "Cheers."

They clinked glasses, and Bill responded, "Cheers, prost, nostrovia, bottoms-up, salute, konbe, down the hatch, or whatever it is you say in Switzerland."

"Proscht, but prost will do," said Guy.

They both took a good gulp of the sweet nectar and smiled.

"Good to hear," Bill said. "I am pleased to hear all is well on the family front."

Guy warily asked, "How about you?" knowing much of the past history.

"Same old, same old," Bill said in a weary and nonchalant way.

The two men caught up on more family, friends, colleagues, and the insurance market and enjoyed a few more beers while chatting.

Guy was keen to find out more about why the need for this urgent meeting, and Bill suggested they move onto the room he had booked.

"All cloak and dagger, getting a room?" Guy enquired.

"Just wanted to be able to chat through a few things out of earshot," Bill replied. "Nothing untoward."

Coffee had been laid on in the room, and Bill poured them both a cup, wishing he had brought a beer along with him.

"Guy, I have been following up on this statistical anomaly," Bill said. "There have been two accidental deaths in the same bank group in a matter of days, plus another is now missing, in the same management tier, all in the last couple of weeks. One death in Belgium, one in the UK, and a missing guy in the US. Coincidence it may be, but the odds are millions to one that this would happen in such a finite time period in this age group and in the same company."

"Yes, would strike me as strange," Guy said, "but maybe it is just that: a coincidence, after all, it's two people, wrong place, wrong time, and you say accidents; also, nothing confirmed on the missing guy. Why are you telling me?"

"All of the bankers are part of an executive keyman insurance policy, a life insurance plan that pays out in the event of death, covering key employees in organisations to recompense the company for the loss of the employee; this is arranged by the bank, underwritten, and sold by one of the bank's minor subsidiaries, based in the Caribbean, and with the policies then re-insured by larger insurance underwriters in London and Switzerland. Your company is one of the insurers," Bill added.

"The cover is exceptionally large at five million to ten million dollars per employee, but the amounts are parcelled up into smaller reinsurance amounts and spread out amongst the reinsurers, thus the claims look small until they all end up back at the issuing insurance company."

Bill stopped and stared at Guy, who had snapped out of his beer-infused state of mind and was beginning to wonder if this was indeed some deeper conspiracy.

Bill went on, "Obviously, the bank's captive insurance company has sold down the risk to other insurers, thus the policy payouts will show as net profit in their accounts."

"I agree the amounts seem large," Guy said, "but this is a large bank, and from what you've told me, these executives were big earners."

"But they worked in the same division of four hundred and sixty employees, not spread across the bank as a whole," Bill shot back.

This was astounding; now the pool was much smaller, and the probabilities seemed fantastic.

"Bill, this is still all conjecture, and who really gets any benefit, but I am listening as maybe someone has a grudge against the bank. This isn't something I can take through the line until I have more information.

"These are accidents," Guy added, "not murders, after all, as strange as it may seem, and probably with the third, you have some stressed-out manager in the US who has taken some time out or absconded with a load of money."

"Well, that's what I thought you would say and why I flew over here to see you face-to-face. I'd like to spend some time in the States; if this third banker turns up dead somewhere, then I will have a head start. I have all the information on the other deaths coming through but need to see if anything ties them together." Bill smiled as he slid his contract across the table.

"Bill, we'll pick up ten days of your time and expenses; if no links and certainly if the US guy turns up, then we're finished with this, okay?"

"Sure," he said.

Guy looked more sombre and asked, "Which bank is it?"

"I'd rather not say at the moment."

"I just remember seeing a claim for a bank client based in California cross my desk," Guy said. "There you have me at this conspiracy theory now."

The two adjourned to the bar, sank another few beers, and Bill headed back to catch his flight. Guy decided to go straight home.

David and Melissa—Sunday

It was now a week since David and Melissa had fled the United States, It was late afternoon in Copenhagen as David pulled the car up to the entrance to the apartment building's car park; he flicked the window switch on his door, and the darkened glass sunk into the door in one swift movement. There was a light drizzle of rain outside; the wipers whirred a lethargic swing across the windscreen. The sky was grey. David's arm extended to the small metallic box, and he dabbed his index finger onto six of the numbers on the keypad. The metal, criss-crossed gate rattled into action and lifted up into the ceiling with a clatter.

The journey now behind them, Monte Carlo had been spectacular. They ate at the Cafe De Paris; David didn't have a tie and was handed one to wear as he walked in. Milan suffered more shopping; Geneva was tranquil and allowed David to sort the money transfers out; Munich a vibrant German city in the throes of an annual bier fest, or beer festival. Melissa had marvelled at the serving girls carrying eight to ten steins of lager to their drunken guests, followed by Hamburg, where supposedly, but still unclear, the hamburger was imported to the United States (the Germans have a lot to answer for); all flew past.

David drew the car into one of his two allocated spaces and, with a long sigh of relief that the journey was over, stepped out onto the concrete floor and stretched every muscle in his body.

Melissa was fatigued and was still absorbing all of the sights of Europe that she had seen and experienced in this whistle-stop of a drive.

He flipped open the rear window of the car, brought down the tailgate, and started unloading their luggage. He would come back down for the many shoeboxes and clothes carriers accumulated on the way.

Melissa yawned, smiled at David, and placed her handbag on one of the large wheeled black cases. David locked the car, and they headed over to a single elevator door at the end of the car parking area. The brushed steel doors opened immediately David had hit the button, and he placed the four large bags in up against the back wall. Making sure Melissa was in, he placed his key in the board and put his fingertip on the "P" for penthouse button, which lit up neon blue.

The apartment was very close to Copenhagen's old harbour, where boats lined up a narrow waterway that was the hub to many restaurants, bars, and a rainbow of old townhouses.

The elevator doors opened to a large square hall, some twenty-five by twenty-five feet. Melissa stepped out and held her hand over the door sensors. David spun the luggage around, and the wheels skirted across the teak floor as spotlights in the ceiling sprang automatically into action. The walls and ceilings were white; there were two mirrors on opposite walls, under which stood small black ebony wall tables.

"I should have carried the new Mrs Johansson over the threshold," David said.

"One day, perhaps, baby," Melissa said as she helped David with the cases.

"The apartment has three bedrooms," David said, "all en suite, and a main restroom, integrated lounge, kitchen, and dining area taking up one whole half of the floor space."

Melissa's heels clicked on the wooden floors as she explored.

The main lounge was enormous, with large cream rugs wrapped around a central fireplace, with a circular metal base that rose from the floor and glass chimney funnel that dropped from the ceiling. Once again, there were a number of small spotlights in the ceiling, plus a couple of black floor lamps. To the left was a black dining suite of eight chairs around a long rectangular table and beyond that a black marble top, supported and surrounded by diamond white kitchen units.

There were three, four-seater sofas, black leather with wooden frames, strewn with white cushions.

One half of the large rectangular room was an L shape of glass; floor-to-ceiling windows covered with white lace curtains, through which Melissa could see the lights of the city beyond. The opposite bottom of the L was the kitchen and the back wall a bare white, dominated by a large canvas depicting a yachting scene, painted purely in white and grey.

A large balcony wrapped around the penthouse, some twelve feet wide, to opaque glass partitions topped with steel runner handles. Melissa stepped out into the drizzle and took in the view of the harbour beyond.

David just stood there behind her, allowing her to take everything in.

"It's all very minimalistic," he said, "but I know you will be able to make it home; we can go shopping for furnishings and paintings. Do you like it?"

"Yes, it's lovely, the fireplace and terrace are exceptional. It does need some warmth, but we can give it that. Show me the bedroom." She smiled, despite her lethargy.

Hans—New York, Saturday/ Sunday/Monday

Hans and Cheryl had just returned to New York. They parted company at the airport. Cheryl had given Hans her personal number and genuinely had had a great time. Hans had enjoyed the few days but was keen to get onto LA and then home. Cheryl had been great in bed, but conversation had become mundane; she was bright but not worldly.

The hotel car was there to collect him, and the driver took his bag and opened his door. Soon they were pulling up outside the Pen, and Hans was taken up to his room; the hotel had managed to ensure he kept the same one. His other luggage left with the hotel was already there; suits and shirts had been cleaned and pressed as required and were hanging in the wardrobe.

Hans threw his jacket on the back of a chair, flicked his shoes into a corner, and laid out on the sofa with his iPad. Details of LA hit four were awaiting him.

Another guy, bank employee based in LA. Hans's PA had also arranged for a few meetings during his visit.

Sunday was a quiet day. Hans took in some more the sights, including the Empire State Building.

JJ—LA, Sunday

The local police were at a loss. No witnesses, no CCTV, and really very little motive. They had discovered that JJ's business was struggling, but there were no major disputes with creditors.

For all intents and purposes, they had a contract killing in an affluent area and nothing to go on. They looked into the wife, but she had little to gain. There had been no evidence of any affairs on either side. Any life insurance went to the bank under a policy assigned to them for $5 million.

Jenifer had arranged for a subtle yet elegant burial to be attended by family, close friends, and senior employees from the company.

The company's bankers had called in the loan facilities and had effectively replaced management with their own team.

The funeral service was faultless; the white coffin had been delivered to the chapel door and collected by six of JJ's closest friends and family: two brothers, a cousin, and two neighbours, and a business associate.

The overall air was one of disbelief, shock, and nothing made any sense.

There had been no developments from the police; their conclusion was that it may have been mistaken identity.

David and Melissa—Monday

Sergey had checked in with Martinez, Martinez with Sergey, and still nothing beyond Madrid. The Johanssons had checked out of their hotel, and no one there knew anything more.

- No taxi or hotel car transport. Nothing on flights.
- No passport updates. No contact with family.
- No credit card or known cell phone use. Just nothing.

David and Melissa had decided to pop out for lunch on the small harbour just across the street. The weather was brisk, but the sun was up in the clear blue sky, and the couple were well wrapped in padded blue jackets and jeans.

Last night, they enjoyed dinner out; Melissa had looked stunning in a little black dress, which was revealed when she took off her long shawl. David was matching in black Armani suit, pink shirt, and long black trench coat. Melissa had wound up his gold Breitling watch, which she loved, as all his watches had been kept in the wardrobe back at their apartment, and he had not worn this one since their night out in Madrid.

They decided to enjoy the clean air and chose a table out on the promenade, overlooking some of the colourful trawlers, matched by their building counterparts on either side of the water channel, moored along the walls.

There was a gas heater covering a number of tables, and this took the chill from the air.

David ordered a large glass of Pinot Grigio for Melissa, a bottle of sparkling water for them to share, and a large pilsner lager; he was speaking Swedish, and he and the waiter seemed to understand each other.

When she was introduced to Danish, Melissa had learned that the three Nordic languages of Denmark, Norway, and Sweden are of the dialect continuum; that is, similar but culturally different, with some pronunciation from different areas, making it more difficult to understand. She was also told that the Norwegians understand Swedish and Danish much better than the other way around, with Swedes and Danes sometimes struggling. Generally, the language construction is similar to English. That said, everyone seemed to speak very good English, but David was keen that they fitted in and were not conspicuous to outsiders as tourists.

The two perused the menu, which had a wealth of seafood, and both ordered lobster and fries.

The boats were some ten to fifteen feet below the cobbled walkways, which ran beside and over the deep but narrow waterway channel, resembling a wide canal lock. There were many people taking in the sights and looking at the menus of the many restaurants.

Today, they had been to the bank; David had set up an account for Melissa and transferred three hundred thousand

Euros into it, arranging to pay a further ten thousand Euros per month into her account going forward.

Yesterday and for the first time since they disposed of their cell phones, they purchased a couple of the new Samsung Galaxies on pay-as-you-go contracts.

Without David knowing, Melissa had called and spoken with her mother, but there wasn't anything to say; her mother was in a different world.

David was still wearing the Breitling and glanced down to see it was just gone one thirty.

The drinks arrived, and with the food ordered, the two began to discuss what they were going to do for the years to come. David had taken some advice from the bank with reference to investments, but he needed to be careful not to bring too much money into the country so as not to alert the authorities of possible money laundering. The reference he had given was sufficient to explain away circa one million Euros, but much more coming in from Switzerland would need to be explained. The Swiss bank had some schemes for buying residential properties for his own use and potential rental.

"Great night last night, darling," he said, keeping his voice down, as the tables were filled with myriad different nationalities.

"Yes, lovely food and great company," she answered, also softly. "So much has happened," she went on, "in such a short period of time that it is difficult to take it all in at the moment. Thank you for my money; as you know it makes me feel more secure knowing I have my own funds."

She leant over and kissed him.

They finished lunch and spent the night in the apartment, snuggled by the fire, and watched a movie.

The next day, David had a number of potential property investment deals he wanted to review; the papers had been sent over by his Swiss bank.

Bill—Heathrow, Monday

Bill sipped a beer at Heathrow in the British Airways lounge; the boozing had subsided, but there were occasional lapses, and a stream of air hostesses had kept his sex life going. "There's always two certainties in life," he reported to whomever would listen. "One's death, the other's an air stewardess or trolley dolly or tart with a cart," for variation on the theme. This thought crossed his mind in the lounge; he had once told this as a joke when on a business lunch. His client looked at him sternly and said, "My wife is an air hostess." Not so strangely, the relationship with the client was never quite the same again. He chuckled out loud as he went for a beer, much to the bewilderment of the other guests; it was only ten in the morning, after all, as he chuckled again.

He rustled through his briefcase and went through the post he had picked up from home before he had left. He had also printed out the coroner and police reports on the two accidental deaths and was now looking at them intently. He had had the Belgian report translated, although not really taking much in, and he found himself rereading the same statements several times over before anything sank in.

Bill was booked on a flight to New York to look into the disappearance of David Kettner, the banker, and would also visit his daughters. Monica had, strangely, also suggested that they meet up for lunch. He had also arranged to meet with an old chum in the New York Police Department.

He looked down at his crumpled suit and un-ironed shirt, an outfit he would probably be able to explain once in New York as being creased in the suit carrier. He hadn't managed to shave, but why bother, given that he would be on a flight for six or seven hours?

Bill grabbed another beer, picked up the same report again, and read the same paragraph again. Nothing was going in, so he took a newspaper and studied that instead.

The screen showed that the flight was now boarding; he had managed to retain a Silver Tier BA frequent flyer card that allowed him access to the lounge, but like all flights nowadays, he was flying economy, or cattle class, as he called it.

He headed off to the gate and would entice a few gin and tonics from the cabin crew and try to get some sleep. Even though he was tired, he just couldn't get off to sleep and started watching some newly released alien invasion film on the small screen in front of him.

Hans—LA, Monday

As Hans's car passed the international terminal at JFK, he thought he recognised the shabby guy from the London pub climbing into a cab.

The flight arrived at LAX in hazy sunshine. His office had arranged a hire car; he wanted to drive not be driven. It was a red Corvette, one US car that was truly inspired, as the majority of American cars all look the bloody same, boxes on wheels, in his opinion.

He strode purposely out of the airport building into the 88 degree heat; this reminded Hans of home, having left behind the cold drizzle in England and changeable New York weather. He looked for the hire car company coach that would take him to collect his car.

He picked up the Corvette, threw his bags into the trunk, and familiarised himself with the car's controls. The engine sprang into life and set off the car alarm on the car parked next it. He revved again and pulled out of the car park, handed in documents as he left, and dropped the roof.

His first meeting on Tuesday was in San Diego. Hans had arranged to stay in La Jolla on the West Coast and drove down Interstate 5; he eventually found his way, as the directions given were hopeless, and trying to make sense from the road signs was a non-starter. He managed to get some directions from a Mexican doorman at a local supermarket and headed south, towards San Diego. This state-of-the-art assassin was at a loss trying to find his way and could not understand why the road signs had road names rather than the damn town names.

He finally managed to find La Jolla and drove down the main road, parking outside his hotel, the La Valencia, a beautiful Spanish hacienda. His car was immediately unloaded and whisked away by the hotel staff.

Hans walked into the superb reception area, complete with waterfall and natural foliage.

He checked in and adjourned to his room; he stripped and took a cold shower in his suite overlooking the ocean.

He called down for his car and drove through town and towards San Diego; he pulled off at Sea World and went straight in and sat waiting in anticipation for Shamu the Killer Whale's performance. He had long since had an affinity, an admiration, for these majestic, beautiful creatures. So large, so powerful, so graceful, and yet so lethal. In the wild, they would position themselves in the surf, half-on and half-off the beach, still, silent, and ready for the first opportunity to snap up an unsuspecting seal.

These cunning free spirits travelled hundreds if not thousands of miles weekly; he adored watching these great animals, albeit in this frustrating and confined environment.

The killer whale began swimming round and then drenching the screaming crowds with gallons of water, with the kids pinned up against the glass walls squealing in delight, covered in water from head to foot.

The sheer power of the whales was awe-inspiring, the mass of muscle gleaming in the morning light, a beauty to behold.

Hans smiled, as he looked back at the whale at the end of the show and then left.

Back at the hotel, he slipped into tan slacks and a blue shirt and strolled down to the terrace bar, overlooking the pool and the bay.

He sat still, flicking the ice in his Manhattan with his fingers as he enjoyed the sun which was beginning to sink towards the ocean. He called his wife and children from his cell phone and said that he had arrived safely and missed all of them.

He sauntered out of the hotel onto the main street and headed for the aptly named Crab Catcher Restaurant, where he devoured Alaskan snow crab legs, moist and slightly salty, dipped into melted butter with a touch of lemon juice; the accompanying mashed potato was left. No more alcohol, either, just iced water.

Tammy, his waitress, had been extra attentive and was rewarded with a large tip.

Hans made his way back to the hotel, peering into myriad art shops on the way, making a mental note to make some purchases before he left town.

He sat down in his hotel suite and began to decipher briefing note number four; this detailed general information and routines came through in an uncoded message but had no reference to anything else, no location and no name, until this was called through, again in code, at eleven. Photos would also follow.

Target four was very fit and enjoyed marathon running; *a challenge*, Hans thought.

Hans's Breitling clicked on at eleven that evening, and the cell phone rang: name, address, work, and so on. The name meant nothing, but the employer was the same bank as target one. *This bank has pissed someone off,* he thought.

John—NYPD, Monday

John's New York Police Department was bustling; yet another murder. Detective John Duke was now in his tenth year in homicide; the hours and stress had taken their toll on his pragmatic mind. John, however, remained tremendously committed to the job; it was all he had left. The job had left his marriage and family life in second place, and Mary, his ex-wife, and John Jnr had been out of his life for three years now.

John was just over six feet tall, black, with cropped hair; he took pride in his fitness and worked out every morning, murders permitting. He was wearing a crisp white shirt, sent out to the local Chinese laundry, grey tie, and black suit with sturdy black, laced plain shoes. John had celebrated his forty-fourth birthday two weeks previously.

Bill had contacted him a few days ago, saying his was in New York and that they should catch up. Great idea, John had thought, and responded likewise.

He had first met Bill about nine years ago; Bill had been looking into a large life insurance claim and had worked alongside the police to convict the wife of her husband's murder. They had found a common theme in their commitment to work and the enjoyment of alpha male company over beers.

Life was different then; both had "happy": their illusions, marriages, kids to talk about, but never really involved with as they should have been, and a zest to climb the slippery ladder of their respective organisations.

They had met when John was relatively new to the department, having moved through from narcotics to homicide. Bill had been investigating a supposed suicide, which, if it was the case, would result in a large payout to the victim's wife. There had been a suicide note typed and left on the computer; nothing handwritten. The husband had apparently discovered the wife's affair with a work colleague and, rather than killing the wife, had taken himself off to the garage and placed a hose from the car's exhaust to the compartment, started the engine, and apparently killed himself. There had been a high level of sleeping pills and booze found in his system, not unusual, as this was all considered part of making sure he killed himself.

The police didn't expect much more than that, but Bill had had the wife followed and phone calls monitored. There had been little to go on, and the wife had reacted a little nervous and had not made much eye contact during their couple of meetings; slightly strange but just enough to give Bill an inkling that all was not as it seemed.

Bill started to look into the affair and had the cell phone records of the other guy looked into. There had been a number of calls during the previous day of the suicide, and then also at six the following morning; she had apparently discovered the body at seven in the morning. She said she had assumed her husband had headed off to work earlier than usual, so perhaps she could have taken a call at that time. Bill was then able to determine that the lover's cell phone had been in the area that evening; he lived some twenty-two miles away. Bill then checked the surrounding area to the house to where the cell had been located and collated CCTV from the local shopping mall car parking lot, just a five-minute walk away, and had discovered the lover's car had been parked there in the early morning of the suicide.

Bill had sent blood samples off to specialist laboratories for analysis, and they had worked through the level of sleeping tablet dosage and general absorption of this, together with the carbon monoxide, and had concluded that the suicide victim must have been in a comatose state an hour before he was in the car. On checking the effects of the victim, Bill's team had discovered scrape marks on the back of the suicide's shoe heels, indicating that he had been dragged along, probably from under his shoulders. On further investigation of the clothing, they had found a DNA sample, probably a sweat droplet that didn't match the wife or the victim, but in the end turned out to match the wife's lover's DNA.

All of this was put to John; the couple were arrested, and in a classic pincer movement under police interrogation, they had blamed each other in the murder. Job done for Bill, and John had been given a commendation for solving a murder.

The two had become firm friends, and although Bill had a significant network of investigators, who could glean information outside of the law, they shared certain mutually beneficial information from time to time.

John had not taken a holiday since the split from his wife, who had moved to Idaho with her new boyfriend and John Jnr. He had been denied any custody on the basis of Mary saying that he had physically abused her, a lie supported by Mary's mother, who had never got on with John.

The years had seen John move from relationship to relationship, but nothing had worked.

The contact with Bill these days was generally the odd email, maybe a chance beer when Bill was in town, and a rare telephone call to discuss a potential case.

Bill had actually called this time and asked John to look into a missing person's case before they met, a guy called David Kettner, a senior banking employee.

The report had been filed by David's landlord, on the basis that the apartment had been trashed, and they had been unable to contact David. The discovery of the damage to the apartment had been reported by an estate agent, engaged by the landlord, who had been told by David that he was leaving at the end of the term; they had been given a set of keys to market the place. She had gone there during the day, having agreed with David that she could call anytime during work hours, with a potential lessee and found the place in disarray.

She had called the landlord, and in turn he had called the police, not being able to get hold of David.

The police met the landlord at the apartment, which had been systematically and completely done over: cushions and mattresses slashed, floor and skirting boards lifted. It seemed strange to the police that items of value, such as some of the electrical goods, had not been taken, unless of course they had found cash or jewellery of significant value, as personal effects seemed light, just clothes in the wardrobe and drawers. That said, the police felt that the place had been searched, looking for something as yet to be identified.

The police checked credit cards and his passport, discovering that David had flown to Mexico; his mobile phone wasn't picking up, but maybe he had turned it off, given getting away from work. As such, there no longer seemed to be a missing person case to follow in respect of David, either a disgruntled tenant, wrecking the place before he left, or a burglary that would need looking into when he returned. It was a little strange when the police spoke to the bank where David worked, where they seemed unclear as to whether he was on leave or not, but the police had more pressing cases to deal with.

John had checked phone records and found a link to Melissa, who had also been on the same flight to Mexico. Just to make sure, he had checked the CCTV at the airport to the passport photos, and yes, they were both on that flight.

All of this had happened in a space of days. David had left for Mexico on Sunday, the apartment damage had been first reported late on Tuesday and followed up on Wednesday morning. Bill had called on Friday; how did he know what was going on thousands of miles away? But nothing surprised John where Bill was concerned.

Bill had also suggested John find anything out he could concerning the bank that David worked for. This had brought about some interesting information from John's network.

John looked at the clock on the wall; twenty minutes to go and an opportune time to pack up and make a move. He was already late.

Bill had suggested that they meet in the Irish bar that had been a frequent haunt in their earlier escapades, once he had checked into his hotel. Bill had arranged to stay at the Hilton on Avenue of the Americas; one of the insurance companies he was representing had a corporate rate there. He walked into the very large and bustling reception and headed for the check-in desk on the left. He registered and handed over his credit card details.

He headed up to his room, threw his bag on the bed, stripped, and headed for the bathroom, wash bag, laptop, and cell phone in hand. He ran a bath, lowered his weary body into the warm bubbles, and soaked away the flight.

Bill stared into space; he was thinking about his daughters, and about meeting up with Monica tomorrow, about the strange parameters of this bank insurance case, and about catching up with John later. For some reason, he felt panicked, trapped in a nonsense world where he yearned for something more rather than this insincere rat race that he himself had strived for, only to find out that there is no gold at the end of the rainbow, just another treadmill.

Bill changed into jeans, brown suede shoes, white tee shirt, and jumper and loaded himself into a camel-coloured overcoat. He put his laptop on charge and checked he had money, wallet, and cell.

Stepping out onto the covered drop-off and pickup area, he joined the queue for a cab; positioning himself under one of the halogen heaters, he checked his cell for messages. He had left a message for Monica but had heard nothing back.

New York was, as always, very busy, lots of noise, although car horns were few and far between, given the fines now applied. People were shuffling past, umbrellas raised against the rain.

About ten minutes later, the rain stopped, and Bill grew tired of waiting and decided to head to O'Brien's by foot. It was some ten blocks, but Bill had woken up and felt the walk would do him some good and also make him feel less guilty about the numerous pints of Guinness that were about to be consumed. That's what he told himself, anyway, not believing a word of it.

He strode out onto the street and headed straight up, away from Central Park behind him, past Rockefeller Centre to his left and up to West Forty-Sixth Street. As he turned the corner, he could see the Irish flag waving about in the wind and the white sign with "O'Brien's" scrawled across it. He neared the pub, with its gold writing on a green background, and entered the long bar and headed for a couple of empty bar stools.

John had just texted to say he was running late. *No surprise there*, thought Bill. John was always spot-on for anything work-related, but anything social, he was never on time.

"Good evening there, sir," the barman said. "What would you like?"

"Hi there, a pint of Guinness please," said Bill.

"Coming right up."

Bill looked around the busy bar as he tentatively perched himself on the bar stool, pulling the adjacent stool a little way along the floor by his feet, to keep it for John's arrival.

Bill clasped his pint and sunk a large mouthful, savouring the excellent taste and flavour. He licked the cream from his top lip.

He looked down the length of the bar as this large black guy with wide grin stalked towards him. Bill rose, and the two hugged each other like long-lost brothers.

"Hey, great to see you," John said.

"Let me get you a beer," Bill said as he beckoned the barman over and ordered two more pints.

The two saddled themselves onto the stools and went about catching up.

"So, who you shagging, John?" Bill asked, with a grin.

"I'm seeing a girl from Traffic," John said enthusiastically. "She's beautiful, twenty-eight, Puerto Rican, and better than J-Lo. And you won't believe me, but she's called Jenifer."

"Great," Bill said. "Any photos?"

"Hey, yeh, here she is, fully clothed," John said, passing over his cell.

"Wow, you are batting above your weight with that one. She is lovely."

"So how about you, Bill?" John probed.

"Must admit, I have been on very good behaviour and nothing for the last six months," said Bill.

John stepped off his stool and stared at Bill; he placed his hand on his forehead.

"We'd better get you to the doctor's pronto, and if they can't find anything, straight to a mental institution," John said, laughing.

Bill smiled. "Hey, I'm reviewing life. I still enjoy a few beers," he said, rubbing his stomach. "But I want a bit more out of this life."

"This isn't about Monica again, is it?" asked John.

"Well, we have been communicating a lot better," Bill replied, "and I have been getting on so well with the girls."

"Wow, she's married to some multimillionaire, and I thought you were done with her, given all that's transpired," said John.

"Hey, look, it's nothing like that. I am just taking some time off," said Bill. "Anyway, let's get some beers!"

They continued to catch up and talked more about Jenifer over a number of pints.

Finally, John asked, "Well, Bill, what is it with David Kettner?"

"Let's sit down at the end table," Bill said, "and have a chat."

They ordered another couple of beers and huddled themselves together on one of the far tables, out of earshot.

"Well, this is all speculation," Bill said, "but two European members of the same bank and division have met accidents over the last couple of weeks, and I had a thought that this David guy might just end up being found dead somewhere."

"Where in Europe?" asked John.

"Hey, you guys think the United Kingdom is an Arabic nation; what the fuck does that matter?" Bill threw back smiling.

"Humour me," said John, suddenly serious.

"Just outside of London, that's in England, and Brussels ... "

Midway through, John interrupted Bill: "In Belgium."

"Wow, very clever," Bill said, laughing.

"Listen to me on this one, Bill. During my enquiries on this, I spoke to a few friends I have in the FBI and the Fed, you know, the bank regulator? They have also spoken to their contacts."

"Go on," Bill said, suddenly interested and sobering up.

"This can't go any further." He waited for Bill to nod in agreement before carrying on. "The FBI and the Fed have a joint operation looking at this particular bank. I won't say why, but they picked up on a few detailed messages leaving the New York office detailing itinerary movements of some senior guys in the bank, one based in London and one in Brussels.

"This wasn't of any interest to them or me at the time, as I was looking into anything to do with David Kettner. Let me see if I can find out the names of the individuals in Europe."

John stopped and waited for Bill to speak.

"Jesus, that's a bit of a curveball," Bill said. "What about itineraries?"

"The FBI seemed to think it was laying out diary and meeting details for someone to meet them. But if they ended up dead, perhaps you need to look into this a bit more," John warned.

"Well, this is a great conspiracy theory we are cooking up, and given a big helping hand by the beers," Bill joked.

"You have a nose for this type of thing, Bill; anything you're not telling me?" John asked.

"Not at all," Bill said reassuringly. "You have what I have: a couple of accidents in Europe that are paying out on insurance policies to the bank, this guy David, and now what I've heard from you."

"Okay, I'll continue to dig around. It may be a good idea if you stick around for a while."

"Not going anywhere. There's smoke here, but early days, David K seems to be a coincidence but it would be helpful if we can look at anything and everything to do with this bank. More beer?" Bill smiled, after all, he was on expenses and intended to make the best use of the insurer's chequebook.

The conversation entered the realms of complete drivel.

The two carried on and ended up in a titty bar, completely unaware of time or place.

David and Melissa—
Copenhagen, Tuesday 3

David and Melissa rose early and enjoyed a continental breakfast, overlooking a very grey-looking city beyond the windows.

Melissa had been a little distant over the last couple of days. David had asked whether she was okay, and she had just fobbed him off with "Yes, I'm fine, just still trying to settle."

David had been concerned that conversation between them had dried up, and Melissa seemed to be constantly cleaning and wiping things down.

The two had been living in each other's pockets for some time now, so Melissa said she would go out shopping and then to her language class. David would spend the day on the properties, and the two would catch up for dinner later.

David gave her a peck on the cheek as she headed off to the elevator. The weather was overcast and raining, but Melissa was well wrapped in a Barbour quilted jacket, jeans, and knee-high boots. She would take the car in any event, as the forecast was likely to see heavy rain later on in the day.

Melissa descended in the elevator and felt a chill as she stepped into the car park. She climbed up into the comfort of the Range Rover, engaged the engine, turned on the driver's heated seat, and twisted the heating to full. She sat waiting for the gate to rise, feeling trepidation. As she pulled up the ramp, two white, shaven-headed men, both in black leather jackets and black jeans, stepped in front of the car. She could just make out tattoos on their necks.

Monica—New York, Tuesday

Monica had awoken to see Joe Jnr off to school in the morning. Joe Snr had already left, leaving her sleeping. Hannah had prepared breakfast and was ready to drive Joe Jnr to school. Monica kissed Joe and said her goodbyes. The girls were at boarding school but would be over for a weekend soon.

Monica sipped fresh orange juice and read the paper whilst listening to the news on the television in the large dining kitchen. She was balanced on a stool pushed up against the polished granite counter. She occasionally picked at a bowl of chopped fruits and berries in front of her.

She had told her husband that she was to do some shopping in town; no, she couldn't fit in lunch and would be off to the local Women's' Institute meeting straight after.

Monica had met Joe about eight years ago when she had been thirty-one. She had left her husband, with whom she had had two beautiful daughters, over sheer frustration with his work commitment and the fact that they were based in Europe, not near her family, who were all centred in the US. There was also a feeling of having reached her thirties and not really knowing where things were going.

She had been pretty hard on her ex, blaming him for all of the woes in their relationship. However, she had mellowed over the years and had gradually allowed him back into her and the kids' lives. Joe had been a kickback from all of this. He had known her family, was wealthy, and had been totally charming. Monica had been starting afresh as an architect, and Joe had been her first (and effectively last) client. He had been a breath of fresh air, so attentive, so understanding, and so supportive. There was an air of authority and confidence about him that had drawn her in, when she was at her most vulnerable. Her family had also pushed her in this direction.

It wasn't long before the engagement had been announced, a date set, and she had become pregnant with Joe Jnr whilst on their honeymoon in the US Virgin Islands, where Joe had hired an enormous beachfront mansion.

All had seemed so good then; she felt she had moved on, but within a year, the true side of Joe had begun to come out: the controlling, the flirty glances between some of his female staff at functions, the secretive business meetings held at the house, the strange whispered telephone calls. Their relationship had gradually died, and Monica had begun to wonder if she had been the issue. She had begun talking a lot more to Bill recently, her former husband, in the ways that they used to talk when they were young and carefree; he had been her friend, her confidant, and this spark had come back. Perhaps it had never left; she realised that the hurt she had wanted to cause him was to gain attention, to force him to do something about it, but he had continuously ignored the warning signs, and when it came to it, he just didn't have the emotional backbone to step up.

Now, however, he seemed more mature and aware; perhaps he had realised what he had lost.

With Bill, she had been young, too young to commit to a family life, away from home, from her family and friends. With Joe, it had been the mature, powerful side, but now it had come up wanting; she had seen the other side to this monster. Monica was now a lot more conscious of her own needs; she knew herself and now was getting to a period in her life where she had never felt as confident about what she wanted and how to go about getting it.

Bill had collapsed into his little cave, started drinking a lot more, and pushed away instinctively to protect his own feelings. More recently, he had seemed to have grown up, opened up; he had changed his perspective on work, and she looked forward to catching up with him more and more.

Monica had arranged to see Bill today for a light Italian lunch in Greenwich Village; no chance of bumping into any of Joe's cronies there, and his family would all be working. Monica loaded her dishes into the dishwasher and headed upstairs to her private study, where she caught up on a few emails, dropped a few messages to the girls, and asked them what they wanted to do when they visited, outside of the family commitments already arranged.

After finalising some paperwork, Monica headed to her changing room, hung up her dressing gown, and went into the bathroom. She brushed her teeth and turned the shower on, and once warm enough, climbed in and washed her long hair.

She felt quite excited about catching up with Bill. She finished up and turned the shower off, grasped a large bath towel, and wrapped her hair in a smaller one; she then finished drying herself off and admired what was quite a spectacular body in the full-length mirror. She had had a boob job four years ago, nothing too big, but the shape and firmness were superb. She dabbled with Botox from time to time and looked a good mid-twenties, as opposed to her thirty-nine. But there was always something that she wasn't happy with; today, she thought her thighs could be slimmer.

Monica dried her hair, put on some light make-up and pink sparkling lipstick, and sprayed some perfume from her large collection.

"Oh, what to wear," she wondered to herself.

She walked into her wardrobe room and headed for a long line of casual trouser suits, pulling out a dark silver-grey suit. "No," she said to herself out loud.

Jeans, she thought, and chose a pair of Armani's which stuck to her and accentuated her svelte figure, showed off her beautiful tight backside, and held in her thighs.

No bra today, but she put on a black tee shirt and covered this with a black Armani wrap-around shirt. She took a black neck scarf and black Armani overcoat. Shoes were simple Prada loafers, and she took a small clutch bag, moving money, cards, and keys from her dressing table into the bag, plus a small phial of perfume.

Fernando, one of the staff, would drive her into Greenwich Village, drop her off at shops, and return when she called.

Monica called out to Fernando to bring the car around. She checked herself again in the mirror, ensured that she had everything she needed, and shouted a goodbye to Hannah. She crunched through the gravel and into the back of the black Cadillac Escalade, sliding across the black leather seat as Fernando closed the door behind her.

The drive into town was comfortable; Monica spent much of the time of her iPhone.

Fernando pulled up to the kerb, and Monica thanked him and said she would call later, as she stepped out.

Fernando pulled off and went to find somewhere to park.

Monica was about twenty-five minutes early and decided to do a little window shopping before strolling in the direction of the restaurant.

Bill—New York, Tuesday

Bill woke with a start. "Ouch, ouch, ouch," he said out loud as his head pounded from the night before. He staggered across the room and into the bathroom; these two red pools stared back from the wall mirror. He cleaned his teeth (his mouth tasted like what he thought a Turkish wrestler's jockstrap would taste like) and pulled a Diet Coke from the fridge, which he sipped slowly as the bubbles kicked back in his throat.

He had been woken by a text from John, just saying, "Ha, ha, ha, trust you okay, it's 8 a.m., and I'm at my desk, drinking copious amounts of tar-like coffee. Speak later."

"Shit, what the fuck happened?" Bill said to himself. He lay back down on the bed, keyed in an alarm in his cell for ten fifteen and tried to get some more sleep.

The alarm began its steady climb to a crescendo, not so Bill, who hit the snooze button and gradually clawed his way up. He did feel better, and his eyes were nearly normal. He once again cleaned his teeth, shaved, and ran a bath.

Bill lowered himself tentatively into the warm water, laid back, and stared at the ceiling; he was now beginning to feel relatively human and started to think about his meeting with Monica later. Things had improved a great deal over

310

the last six months. A lot of that old spark had returned, and conversations were good, not yet great, but they seemed to be able to relate so much better than before. This was probably a return to their early days and a better balance in their lives and priorities. Bill even felt a stir in his loins as he thought about the great sex they used to have, and *Wow*, he thought, *she did look good.*

He soaked for forty-five minutes and decided he had better iron a crumpled shirt from his case, to wear under a sports jacket with his jeans. He peered out of the window and gazed out onto the street; the weather looked good, and he decided on a tee shirt under his shirt and jacket. No need for a coat today.

Bill put on some antiperspirant, splashed on aftershave, and got dressed. He headed out of his room, took the Do Not Disturb sign off the door, and placed it back in the room.

He moved out from under the canopy and motioned to the hotel doorman for a cab straight away, asking for the Village. The driver was from Zagreb but had been the city for fourteen years. They shared a few stories about European soccer teams, which calmed Bill down; he was beginning to have that nervous little frisson of excitement bouncing around just above his stomach.

Bill made a habit of always being on time; now, he hated to think of Monica waiting alone in the restaurant, looking like someone's mistress, or worst still, getting all the unwanted attention of other men. Strange he never thought or worried about keeping her waiting before; work priorities were always more important. That said, he had tried to juggle things back then to keep everybody happy and ended up pissing off the many.

The cab went up and down the one-way streets, avoiding the beginning of lunchtime traffic, and he dropped Bill off at the restaurant ten minutes early. He paid the driver and wished Dynamo Zagreb the best of luck at the weekend, which was reciprocated for Manchester United, and strode into the restaurant. He was immediately greeted by an attractive young hostess; he surmised from his travels that she was probably Polish but didn't want to embarrass either her or him.

"Good afternoon," she said, smiling.

He said that he had a reservation for two under the name of Davis; his hotel concierge had called through the booking yesterday.

"My guest should be here in a few more moments," Bill said.

The hostess picked up a couple of menus, and he followed her firm little buttocks at the top of long athletic legs, encased in black jeans, to a white marble-topped table nicely placed in a quiet corner, with cushioned bench seating to the back wall and a chair to the other side of the table.

"I'll get someone over for your drinks order," the hostess said, whilst again smiling intently at Bill. Sure enough, a waiter was at the table in seconds with iced water, and Bill ordered a Heineken. He said his guest should be there shortly.

"Heineken coming straight up," the waiter said "and not a problem; take all the time you like. I'll be straight over when your guest arrives. Would you like a bowl of olives while you're waiting?"

"Yes, please," Bill said as he tore open a bread stick packet.

The service in the US was always exceptional, he thought, *unlike the surliness in many parts of Europe. But they were working for their tip.*

The restaurant was beginning to fill up behind Bill, and he looked attentively at the entrance, doing a little people-watching at the same time.

He once again looked up at the door, and there she was. *Christ, she looked good.* She smiled across at him, and he beckoned her over as he stood to greet her. "Wow, you look good enough to eat," Bill said as they exchanged double cheek kisses.

"That type of flattery will get you anything you want, Bill," Monica said. "You don't look so bad yourself. I see you have a hair of the dog already"; she knew he had been out with John the night before.

"Was a little of a heavy night, but good to see John," he said, blushing slightly that she knew him so well.

The waiter appeared at the table and asked if Monica would like to leave her coat and order a drink.

"A large glass of Chardonnay," Monica said, "and you had better bring another beer please. And yes, please take my coat."

After the waiter left, she asked, "How is John?"

"Very good form, and new girlfriend to boot," Bill said, going on to tell Monica about John's beautiful Puerto Rican.

"You sound quite smitten yourself," Monica teased.

Her glass of wine arrived with another beer. "Cheers," she said as the two clinked glass and bottle.

The beer felt good as Bill took another large swig and emptied the first bottle and swiftly moved on to the new addition.

"Good to see you," he said. "You look like you are keeping well; how are the girls?"

"Thanks," she replied. "Yes, the girls are the girls. They are back for a weekend soon; if you are still here, I could see if I can sneak them out for a few hours."

"Great, hopefully I will be," he said. "Can I confirm later?"

"Yes, okay," she answered. "There's no urgency. It would be such a nice surprise for them."

The girls were eleven, going on eighteen, and had started boarding at seven. Joe had been keen to get them packed off, Monica thought, and there had been nothing yet planned for Joe Jnr, who was studying in a private day school.

The waiter was back. "How's everything going?" he asked. "Would you like to order?"

Bill suddenly realised he hadn't even looked at the menu. "Give us a few more minutes," he said.

"Sure, just give me a nod when you are ready," and the waiter was gone again.

Both of them perused the menus.

"What are you going to have?" Monica asked.

"I think I'll go for the spaghetti Bolognaise and a side of fries," Bill said.

"Sounds good," Monica said, smiling. "I'll do the same but share a few of your fries."

"Would you like some garlic bread with that?" asked the waiter.

"Yes, please."

Bill and Monica continued catching up for another five minutes or so.

"Would you like another wine?" Bill asked as he beckoned the waiter back over to their table.

"Please," she said. "May as well try and catch you up."

Bill placed the order.

The two huddled intimately into each other across the table and carried on chatting until the food arrived.

They finished up with coffees. Bill picked up the check and held Monica's coat as she slipped her arms into the sleeves.

They stepped out onto the sidewalk; Monica turned round and kissed Bill passionately on the lips, catching him completely by surprise.

"Thanks for lunch," she said. "Let me know about the weekend, and have a good finish to the week." She winked, spun round, and was gone.

John—NYPD, Tuesday

John had arranged to meet his FBI contact, a five-foot, eight-inch-tall Rottweiler of a man called Brandon; he would rather have a quick chat face-to-face as opposed to over the phone.

They had chosen an Italian diner, just off Times Square; meetings at the office might be frowned upon, and they didn't want to be fielding questions about why an FBI agent was meeting with a homicide detective without any case on the books.

It was three thirty, a good time to meet, as the busy lunch hour had finished, and the early diners would still be an hour or so away.

John decided to walk the thirty-five minutes; as always, the New York sidewalks were busy but he made good headway, with suited businessmen taking a wide berth of the muscle-bound detective and a number of admiring glances from some of the passing women (and a few young men).

The sky was clear above and the temperature in the low sixties. John took a cross section gradually drifting towards Times Square; with the grid system in New York, it should be impossible to get lost. For the myriad foreign cab drivers, all they needed to know is what street crossed which;

high-numbered streets cut through Madison, Avenue of the Americas, Fifth Avenue, and other main thoroughfares. John was based on West Fifty-Fourth Street off Eighth Avenue. He strolled out and cut across Eighth Avenue and onto Seventh and walked the twelve blocks to Times Square.

He headed into the bustling square, illuminated advertising boards in front of him, Toys "R" Us to the left as he manoeuvred off to the right and saw the canopy for Mario's less than a block down. He was five minutes early and felt warm in his suit and coat; there was the bright green lettering of Mario's curved in an arc across the diner window, underscored in red. He walked through the green door; to his right was a steel bar counter with a green faux leather bumper along its length and single poled stools, topped with green, equally spaced like soldiers on parade, at the counter. To the end of the bar was a large pizza oven. To John's left were a number of segmented tables, square booths in the centre of the floor area, and to the far left, six curved booths all facing the bar.

The air was thick with the smell of garlic and herbs that were unfamiliar to John, but the combination was good.

There were eleven people in all: two at the counter, a tourist couple having a coffee and amaretto biscuits, a family of four, two young kids and their parents, at one of the centre tables digging into pizza, a young couple in one of the booths, two office guys at the far end in the centre, and a lone man, reading a book at a table for two on the other side of the centre. Cops noticed these things.

Behind the counter was a forty-plus-year-old guy in a green and white striped shirt, good pasta gut overhang, black moustache and hair, chef's hat, and a big grin. *Must be Mario*, John thought. To the end of the counter area and next to the oven was a twenty-something guy, same outfit but skinny as a rake, toiling over a white marble countertop, flipping pizza bases waiting for the evening invasion.

There was a solitary waitress, black hair, olive skin, Italian no doubt. Mario's daughter, John assumed, with similar blouse and black skirt; she eyed John up and down.

"You can take any free table," she said. "We won't be busy until five."

John nodded an acknowledgement. He stepped through the central walkway and headed for the booth farthest away from the young couple and nearest to the window. He slid into the curved green seating, around a semi-circular laminate-topped table, ignored by the other customers. The kids were making quite a lot of noise, and the parents were getting more exasperated with their off-springs' unruly behaviour. An early night for those two, John thought.

The waitress followed him around to the table.

"Can I get you a drink?" she asked. "How many menus would you like?"

"Large Diet Coke," he said. "I am expecting a friend; we'll have a look at the menu when he arrives. Thanks."

"Sure, would you like some garlic bread while you wait?" she asked, smiling.

John's mouth watered; he was sold.

"Good idea, garlic with cheese, thanks," he said.

He took a double-take of the two fighting puppies above her black pencil skirt and then turned to see Mario's eyes boring into him. "Oops," he said quietly.

John took his BlackBerry out and started to look at imaginary messages.

The door opened, and John looked up expecting to see Brandon, but no, it was another young couple, who waved at the resident couple in the booth and headed over to greet them.

The soda arrived and, within minutes, the garlic bread with melted cheese, the size of a medium pizza; these had been lined up on the marble behind the counter by the skinny chef.

It was now ten to four, and John was beginning to fidget. The screaming kids had now gone, lucky for them, he thought; after all, he was toying with his gun and was considering flashing his badge for causing an absolute nuisance (just a fantasy thought).

Just before four, Brandon marched into the diner, black slick hair, bleached blonde at the sides (natural, he always said), hence Rottweiler, black suit, dark blue silk tie, white shirt, and the darkest shades John had ever seen. *Jesus*, John thought, *it's a combination of* Men in Black *and* The Ego Has Landed (playing on the eagle). John stuck his lips together, ensuring he didn't blurt this welcome out loud.

The waitress and Mario thought they were being invaded by the Environmental Health Office, and Mario looked quite flustered, but they both eased into normality when Brandon waved at John and said loudly, "Sorry, I'm late; got caught on the phone."

"Phone or throne?" John whacked back to the blushing face behind the sunglasses.

There was no retort, just Brandon's five feet eight inches, both height and width, heading through the narrow corridor to get to the table. *Was this truly SpongeBob Squarepants?* John lit up his sarcastic brain with.

A pudgy hand shot out from the black suit jacket and shook John's hand tightly.

"Good to see you, fella," Brandon said.

"You too," John said. "Took your fucking time."

"Yeh, yeh, think you have made your point," Brandon responded.

"Would you like a drink, sir?" the waitress asked.

"A latte would be great," Brandon said.

"Another?" she asked, looking at John.

"I'll have a latte as well, thanks," John said.

Brandon looked down at the four out of six slices of garlic bread still left, snatched the largest slice, and stuffed it into his mouth, grease pouring down either side of his lips and onto his chin. He grabbed a paper napkin to stop the waterfall heading any further south and slid into the booth seat opposite John.

The coffee machine was snorting in the background.

"So why the need to meet on this one?" Brandon asked, "although always good to see your ugly mug anytime."

"You too," John replied. "I don't know, just thought a better idea. Things just don't seem right on this, and I thought it would be better if we could chew the cud and confirm I'm wrong."

He mentioned the bank investigation and the earlier discussions they had about David Kettner. Brandon had known John for a long time, and there was solid mutual trust between them. There wasn't the typical macho thing going on between competing departments; they realised they were both on the same side.

Brandon explained that the FBI and the Fed were looking into money-laundering activities but they had crossed an investigation being undertaken by the SEC on insider-dealing.

It was the SEC that then had told them about covert calls and email traffic. They had monitored a call and some email traffic going on between Joe's secret phone and email accounts and the third party, although nothing was clear on why this information was being shared.

Joe had been under investigation by the SEC for potential insider dealing for some time, and although they had nothing concrete, they had been monitoring a number of his accounts, cell phones, and email accounts. They had picked up some strange traffic with a consultant regarding movements of some key worldwide employees, but this had just been filed as irrelevant, albeit strange, but it came up when they were sharing information.

Their coffees arrived, and they declined the offer of more food.

After John had called Brandon, he had recalled the SEC dialogue. He now had the names of the employees concerned in Europe.

"It was James Buchanan and Jack Ashurst," he said.

"Okay, thanks," John said, writing these names down in his notebook. "Time for a beer?"

"Yeh, why not? It's nearly five o'clock," Brandon said, digging into what was left of the now cold garlic pizza bread.

On the way to the bar, John took a call.

"Hi John, it's George. I've just taken a call from Interpol. David Kettner has just been found in Denmark, floating next to the Little Mermaid in the sea, with a slit throat. He had been tortured, few fingers missing, and a crushed testicle."

"Shit," was all John could muster. He stabbed at his phone and called Bill, saying, "Meet me at the pub."

"Not more," Bill said. "I haven't quite recovered from last night."

"This is important," John snapped.

"Okay, see you there."

After a little while, Bill arrived at the bar. John told him the news about David.

The three stood in silence, not moving for several minutes, toying with their drinks, considering what could possibly be going on.

"Fuck, this doesn't make sense," Bill said. "They are getting messy if they are just cutting people's throats now."

"We are waiting on further details from Interpol," said Brandon. "I will also step up our monitoring on the bank officials, but all has been quiet recently. I think phones have been changed. Also, Joe sweeps his bank office for bugs on a regular basis."

Peter—New York, Tuesday

Peter had received a message to call Martinez.

"Hello, it's Peter; you wanted me?"

"Hello, Peter," Martinez said. "I just wanted to let you know we found David. He won't be returning to work."

"So you have the money back?" Peter asked quickly, his banking background taking over before he realised who he was talking to.

"No," Martinez said, and the phone fell silent.

Well, Peter would never know whether they had the money or not, but he would bet on them having retrieved the cash, and now they would double it with the commission forgiveness.

Peter went and told Joe.

"Yes, I know," Joe said. "I have stopped Todd, but we move on to LA."

"M said he didn't have the money back," Peter said, anticipating Joe and wondering how he knew about David.

Joe said nothing and returned his gaze to the computer screen.

The bank's auditors were still in at Joe's division, more finalising and assisting in the sale process than anything untoward. An online file with numerous documents on the division, client details, loans, financial performance, employee details, and other assets was being used by many potential bidders for the business to put together a shopping list of information required and also to assist in the final questions they would have for Joe and his senior management team.

The bidders, not unusual in large acquisitions in the financial sphere, would not be allowed much more than three days on-site at the company they were seeking to acquire.

Obviously, the data room information was immaculately put together by Joe's team. Everything had been checked several times; they had practice sessions of who would answer which questions, and there would be no contradiction on what anybody said. This was all perfectly stage-managed. Without spending months on the accounts, it would be impossible to determine exactly where the income streams were coming from.

This particular month would see record profitability, with the benefit of $12 million of insurance monies flowing into the accounts of the division. It had been carefully set up through a complex web of holdings of insurance companies in the Caribbean. Joe's division was a shareholder in these companies but not a majority, although he had effective control of the companies via overriding contractual structures. That way, he did not have to report them in the consolidation of his own division's accounts but could exercise management of the companies. They had brokered the keyman insurance policies and then sold the risk to a number of insurance syndicates (these were specialist companies that took direct investments from investors and underwrote specific risks), so when the claims were processed, the monies were paid back into the broker and then at Joe's behest distributed to his division as income, profit from broking operations.

The next few days would be very busy; tomorrow, bidders were expected to finalise their bids, and if they were considered sufficient, they would be allowed the three days on-site to meet management. If one bid was significantly bigger than others, they may be offered an exclusive period to formalise their final offer, at a cost. So following this initial bidding, Joe and his team would be on call to meet and answer ongoing questions from the bidders.

The loss of some senior managers in Europe had been glazed over. Joe was the lynchpin, as other people were not essential and could be replaced. David Kettner was not on anyone's radar.

Hans—La Jolla, Tuesday

Hans rose early on Tuesday; it was six thirty, time for a quick splash and into his training kit. The gym was empty, and he warmed up slowly on the treadmill, gradually building to a bristling pace for thirty minutes. He slowed down again and then began fifty crunches and fifty press-ups.

He showered and dressed in jeans, loafers, and a shirt; after a small fruit breakfast, he felt good. The San Diego meeting was still sometime away, so he took time to read a few of the newspapers.

The next hit was John Schroder, an executive vice president at the bank's regional office in LA. Hans had studied the photos and dossier. John went for a run early each morning in the hills behind his mansion, and this is where Hans would strike. The hills were apparently pretty deserted; John regularly went off the beaten track to take in the more scenic route close to several cliff edges.

John was young and athletic, so Hans would need to ensure that things happened quickly, as getting into any type of fight would make it difficult to ensure investigators saw nothing but another tragic accident.

Hans lay down on the bed; all of a sudden, he began experiencing a panic attack. He was struggling for breath, gasping, and clawing for air. He had experienced this twice before; the first time was when he was twelve. His father had come back to the family home after drinking all day and was up for an argument.

Dinner had been set by his mother, Dawn. She had prepared an avocado appetiser, to be followed by fried chicken. Klaus stumbled into the room and poured a bourbon partly onto the cabinet top and partly into his glass. He swung round and sat down at the table, staring at Hans. Hans had not liked the avocado, and Klaus picked up the small dish and launched it through the window, snarling, "I pay for this, and you fucking waste it. Fucking get out of my sight."

Hans disappeared to his bedroom, shaken and crying. He then heard the clatter and shouting as Klaus laid into Dawn, both verbally and physically. Hans had frozen, overcome by nausea and sheer panic. He so wanted to help his mother but felt unable to move. He vowed then to become strong, learn martial arts, and exact revenge.

The second time was in his first real combat environment, when he froze with panic and was gulping at the air as rocket fire burned through the sky above his head. His friend Tim had stepped out of the ditch to move forward, shouting for Hans to follow, but then Tim's decapitated body fell backwards.

Hans snapped out of the inertia and charged through the debris-strewn street to kill the three terrorists who had ambushed his squad.

Why now? he thought. Was it because of the anti-climax of St Lucia or the recurring fear of being caught and letting down his family? He began to weep and drew in the needed oxygen as he calmed down. He had to make that meeting in San Diego.

John Schroder—LA, Tuesday

John Schroder had been with the bank for many years and covered its Los Angeles region. He was six feet one inch tall and was very muscular, working out and running eight miles daily; running had been a commitment since college, where he had played football. He had swept-back blond hair, with a few touches of grey to each side, blue eyes, and a handsome, square-jawed face.

He had married his beautiful wife, Lucy, eleven years previously.

John's day today revolved around seeing a couple of clients, another local bank looking to do some business together, and a credit committee call with New York, which had been set for two in the afternoon.

John had read and agreed to the new business submission, a local retailer which wanted to borrow $25 million.

The client meetings went well, and it was time for John to meet the banker for lunch. His secretary had booked a local Italian restaurant (Joe was always keen on his team supporting Italian businesses) just a few minutes' walk from the bank.

Bruce was new in town, having come down from Wells Fargo's San Francisco office. He was keen to do some larger syndicated transactions, where the banks share risk on bigger lends. John had looked Bruce up on Linked-In and memorised a few facts: Stanford educated, the photograph of a man in his late thirties, brown hair and long face, which sported some ferocious-looking teeth.

The sun was shining, and John enjoyed the short stroll down to the restaurant with the warmth of the midday beating down on his back and easing his muscles, which were a little tense, as they always were before a credit committee with New York. That said, he was determined to have a relaxed lunch.

John turned into the restaurant; his PA had booked a table on the terrace, and he was a few minutes early. One of the waiters, Doug, recognised John and immediately glided over.

"Hello, Mr Schroder," he said. "Welcome back. I see you have a table for two, and you are the first to arrive."

"Hi, Doug," John replied. "Good to be back."

"Would you like a drink at the bar or go directly to your table?" Doug asked.

"I think straight to the table, please. Need to be gone by one forty."

"No problem," he said. "Please follow me."

Doug moved off to a quiet table in the corner of the canopied terrace. About two-thirds of the tables were empty, but John knew from experience that the restaurant would be full by noon, with a mix of business diners and "ladies who lunch."

John settled down at the table, next to the glass wind break, on the timber decking, which was also interspersed with tubs of baby bamboo shoots, which gave a cosier and segregated impression to the crisp white linen-covered tables. The wine and water glasses sparkled in the sun, which was creeping through gaps in the overhead canopies, keeping the diners covered from the harsher rays.

"I'll get you some iced water," Doug said. "Would you like anything else to drink?"

"An iced tea, please," John replied.

"Sure. Would you like a menu now, or wait for your fellow diner?" Doug was beginning to warm to his ongoing performance on this stage.

"I'll wait for my guest, thanks," responded John.

He looked out beyond the terrace and subconsciously found himself staring at the passing number of silicon babes, believing himself an expert on "has she or hasn't she?"

Doug returned with a jug of iced water; he poured John a glass and placed down a long glass of iced tea, burgeoning with lemon slices and basil leaves.

John mumbled a thank you. He then spied a set of teeth coming onto the terrace. *That's Bruce,* he said to himself as he rose and waved a Rolex-clad arm at Bruce, who smiled and walked over to the table. The two said their hellos, shook hands, and sat down. Doug was upon them like a leopard dropping from the trees onto prey.

"Good afternoon, sir. What would you like to drink?"

"A diet soda, please," said Bruce.

"Be right back," and Doug was gone.

The two men chatted generally about the weather and then Bruce's move to LA; they shared a few stories on people they both knew in the finance business, particularly at Wells Fargo, where John had worked previously.

Doug came back with the diet soda and menus. He asked the gentlemen if he could run through the specials, and both nodded in unison.

Lunch finished up with both men agreeing to work on some deals in the very near term and to keep their respective head offices in the loop.

It was one thirty, and John picked up the bill and headed back to the office for the credit meeting.

Joe—New York, Tuesday

Joe sat in the large boardroom at the New York office, attended by sixteen of his senior executives: thirteen credit board members and three from the Boston office, who had flown into New York to present the $75 million lending proposal.

Joe seemed preoccupied, and the meeting had not gone well this afternoon. There had been a lot of shouting (from Joe) about why he was running a fucking charity and no one seemed to give a shit about earning fees and fleecing clients. He had already loaded some substantial charges on clients that had missed certain financial covenants, and the client managers had left the room one by one, red-faced and very quiet.

New business opportunities were now being discussed, and these too were getting a very rough time on structure and pricing. There was just no arguing the case; Joe had seemed to have made up his mind that all the deals were utter shit.

The Boston trio left the room deflated; although they had an approval, it was on the basis of substantial changes that they would have to sell to the prospective client, who had the expectation that all major negotiations had been finalised and the credit committee sign-off would be a rubber stamp.

The conference telephone was on; they flipped around the country from office to office, discussing transactions that had been sent over and distributed a few days earlier.

John Schroder—LA, Tuesday

John sat down in his office with his local senior vice president and vice president of sales and marketing to present the retail transaction to Joe's credit committee meeting.

At two o'clock, the conference phone rang, Steve pressed the answer button, and before he could say a word, on they came:

"New York here; who do we have in LA?" asked Stan at the other end. No one quite knew what Stan did, other than call the offices and ensure Joe wasn't interrupted when in mid-tirade.

"Hi, everyone, it's Steve, Gary, and John here," John said.

"Hi guys," Joe said, very warmly (for once). "How's your weather over there? Raining buckets here."

"Sun is shining," said John.

Stan asked Steve, the vice president responsible for the deal, to present the transaction.

Steve began the usual monologue, explaining the transaction, the numbers, and why the office thought they should do the deal. There were the usual to-ing and fro-ing and checking numbers from the underwriters in New York. Usually these things took a few hours, but Joe stopped everyone dead at fifty minutes and said, "Approved, good job." Everyone was aghast, but they knew not to utter a further word in New York.

There was a chorus of "Thank you, Joe," from the Los Angles team.

The phone clicked to an empty whir of dial tone.

The trio looked in shock at each other, then John said, "Bloody hell, either it's his birthday or he's just had a blow job, a birthday blow job. Well done, Steve and Gary, get a term sheet ready for signature, and let's tell the client and their introducer the good news before Joe changes his mind. Well done again."

John busied himself with reading a few files that he thought he would be taking home and arranged to leave at five; he'd get to see his wife a lot earlier than usual.

Hans—LA, Tuesday

Hans had headed out of San Diego after his meeting and back towards Los Angeles; he had been invited to a football game by one of his clients at the Rose Bowl, where UCLA Bruins were hosting a special midweek game. The journey was about one hundred and thirty miles to his hotel at the Westin Pasadena; he had checked out of his La Jolla hotel earlier.

Hans checked into the Westin and went to his room. He looked for any cameras on the way, and there were none in the halls or elevators. He slipped on a curly black wig and brown contact lenses. He strapped a false pouch around his waist to add a few pounds and headed out dressed in jeans, tee shirt, and pumps with a small bag.

About two blocks from the hotel, a car had been left for him to pick up in a car parking lot. He pulled on gloves and, having checked that no one seemed to be paying much attention, slid the keys off the rear offside tyre and pressed the door release. He drove the car off in the direction of the Sierra Madre Mountains and parked up in Arcadia. He slipped out of his jeans, revealing shorts, and exited the car wearing sunglasses, heading off in the direction of the Sierra Madre at a jog: an overweight guy trying to shed a few pounds. A few miles later, he entered the Sierra Madre area, jogging from local streets into a spectacular rugged terrain, and ran the route he knew John Schroder would be taking tomorrow morning.

The trails narrowed and climbed up into a wilderness of canyon walls; John would be out very early the next morning, and Hans wanted to get a better feel for the place.

He traversed the steep, rocky paths and went off some of the more well-beaten tracks to the older, washed-out pathways that narrowed to a couple of feet in places, with sheer drops to the side.

After making himself comfortable with the area, Hans jogged to his car and drove back to the parking lot; he alighted and walked casually back to his hotel, where he returned to his room, removed the disguise, showered, and got ready for the game. He had made all of his calls home on his way back from San Diego.

He had been told that they would pick him up from the hotel, park up at the game, and enjoy a barbeque and some beers before the game.

Hans enjoyed the evening and adjourned after a few more beers in the hotel bar.

Helen—England, Wednesday

Helen, James's ex-wife, arrived at the inquest with her new husband, Steve, a tanned and tattooed gym instructor: an Adonis in Helen's eyes and eleven years her junior. She was thirty-seven, slim, and well-honed; Steve ensured they worked out together daily, not just in the bedroom. Helen had pounced on the gyrating Steve in a nightclub, and the sex was awesome. She had him rigid for days, all that sucking in and out; Helen was an expert. Steve had not known what hit him.

The verdict, as already known on James's death, was determined as an accident, a stumble or knocked over accidentally by the dog; Betsy was now living back with Helen but barked non-stop at Steve.

James hadn't changed his will, and Helen became very wealthy. Steve was thrilled.

"Thank you, James," Helen said under her breath, "all those boring nights were worth it after all."

Steve cuddled into her side, nuzzling her hair with his nose; he licked his lips and thought about the new car she had promised him.

Ah, a wealthy, dirty woman, he thought. *What else could a man ask for? Of course, the twenty-year-old aerobics instructress I've been screwing a couple of times per week, as well.*

The two walked out of the hearing as on air, hand in hand swinging along as they skipped to the Porsche. Steve grabbed Helen in the car and immediately stuck his tongue down her throat as she swivelled round in her seat to feel his hands all over her. His left hand lifted her jumper and undid her bra, and he squeezed her silicon breasts and headed down to feel out those huge, erect nipples with his tongue.

Helen loved every minute until she realised that they had an audience of two old-aged pensioners enjoying the show; they had been out walking their dogs.

"Let's go before we give these gents a heart attack," she said pulling her top down.

"Think they would prefer a stroke," Steve said, grinning.

"There's a secluded car park on the edge of the woods a mile down the road. I want to take care of that bulge in your jeans." She licked her lips and started the engine, pulled off, and waved at the geriatrics, who both looked very disappointed.

The Porsche roared off down the country lane; a mile or so down, Helen pulled the car onto a small one-lane track, with passing places on either side every twenty feet or so. The Porsche struggled with the bumpy terrain, which had been laid with gravel but had seen better days, heading to a woodland park.

"I used to walk the dog here from time to time," she said as the track widened into a large parking area. There were a couple of four-by-fours and a camper van. Helen pulled the car over to the farthest point away from the entrance to the woods. She leant over and unzipped Steve's jeans.

"Pull them down," she ordered, grinning.

Steve was more than a willing participant and pulled his jeans down to beneath his knees. He wasn't wearing any underwear, and his cock stood to attention. Helen got to work on it with her tongue.

Steve was groaning in under a minute. "Not so fast, you," Helen said.

She lowered Steve's seat, moved over, and straddled him, pulling her G-string to one side. She felt that extreme hardness enter her and started grinding away until she had a delicious orgasm. She finished Steve off with a blow job that lasted less than a minute.

The windows were steamed up; Helen started the car and hit the demister button as she adjusted herself.

Steve just leant back in the seat, jeans round his ankles, eyes closed, and a huge smile on his face.

"I'll take you for a pub lunch," Helen said. "I think you might need your jeans on for that."

She pulled the Porsche around, rear wheels spewing gravel and dirt in all directions, and headed off to a country pub that she knew.

Once at the end of the lane, she headed the car left; the road was embraced by dirt banks of about four to five feet high on either side, lifting up into the woods and the trees that umbrellaed the lane with their autumn leaves of bronze and gold, dimming their path so much so that the car automatically turned its headlights on.

"I still think it's strange that James would take such a tumble," Steve mused. "He was hardly the most athletic person, and to break your neck like that doesn't make a lot of sense to me."

"Well, the police seem satisfied," Helen said. "Remember the dog was there, as well; maybe she bowled him over. Wouldn't have been the first time. Betsy running at full pelt had lifted both of us off our feet on occasions."

Helen turned down a smaller lane to the left; she didn't need to indicate, as they hadn't seen a car on the road since they left the town.

The lane narrowed to a large car's width and descended down at a steep angle. The overhanging trees had literally blacked out all light until the road flattened as they approached an old wooden bridge perched above a bubbling stream. There was also a passing place to the right of the bridge, allowing more sensible vehicles to wade through the water, not an exercise to undertake in a sports car. Helen dropped the revs and took the bridge in sedate fashion, rumbling over the boards. On the other side, some ten feet above them to the left, was an old country pub, a coach house that probably had stood there for four centuries.

The building was three stories high, whitewashed walls and black, timbered beams and window frames, interspersed with bubbled glass and bullseye panes. There was smoke rising from both chimneys and a large sign that identified the pub as the Old River's Edge. A board outside proclaimed "Open all day for good wholesome, home-made food and fine ales."

To the end of the public house was a steep turn on the left into the car park. Helen pulled the car to a stop; there were five other cars stacked into the small area; Helen suggested Steve exit the car so she could park his side close up to one of the trees, encroaching on the parking space that she had identified. He jumped out and took in a deep breath of the crisp autumn air, realising that he had only a tee shirt on.

Helen drew into the space, leaving little room on the passenger side, and stepped out of the car, clicking the auto lock button as she walked towards the pub's large, black wooden door.

Steve opened the door for Helen, cranking the iron handle, which probably had stood the test of time over hundreds of years. The black paint hid the studded three-inch-thick oak, and even Steve, muscles bulging, struggled to push it open enough for Helen to pass.

She thanked him as she stepped through the doorway.

There was a small corridor that passed the restrooms to the right and into the main bar. The uneven stone floor was well trodden. The bar was straight ahead, laden with large brass and black ceramic beer pulls. This was a real-ale pub, serving eight varying bitters, warm British beer, and two lagers, one an Australian cooking lager, low in alcohol, and the other a 5.5 per cent beast from the Czech Republic. That said, one of the bitters, Owd Roger, was in at just under 8 per cent alcohol to volume.

The pub itself was split into four main rooms on the ground floor; a formal dining area was laid out with small two- and four-seater tables, covered with dark pink linen and candles. A snug was off a stone spiral staircase and led to a small wood-panelled room, with wall bench seating all the way round, and a centre oak table, a saloon bar with carpet, and the main bar, in which they now stood.

There were open fireplaces in the main bar and formal dining area, and the air was infused with the smell of burning logs.

The snug was taken by two young couples. There were four elderly gentlemen precariously perched on bar stools at the main bar; the formal dining area had one couple, and at the saloon bar, six or seven locals were enjoying a catch-up.

The landlord, they both assumed, dominated the bar, a bear of a man, whose head was brushing the low cream ceiling. He had to duck in order to avoid the hop-covered beams.

"Hello," he boomed at the pair. The four at the bar stopped their conversation and stared intently at the couple.

As Helen moved closer, she took in the landlord's huge overhang of belly, a ruddy-looking face, split veins across a bulbous nose, wired reading glasses perched on the end of it, receding grey tufts of hair, and a beard that swamped his chubby face.

"What would you like?" Helen asked Steve.

"The Czech Pilsner, please," he said. Steve enjoyed a few beers, especially after (and indeed before) sex.

The walrus behind the bar snorted. *Another lager ponce at the bar*, he thought; he clutched a long- curved pint glass from under the bar, in huge dough fingers, and started pouring the amber liquid.

"And what would you like, my love," he said, peering over his glasses at Helen's nipples, which still hadn't calmed down.

"Half a Guinness and black currant," Helen replied, "heavy on the black currant, please."

The four vultures on their stools were still agape at her bust, tidy little figure, and bare legs.

"Here you go," the landlord said, handing over the lager, followed by the Guinness after it had settled from the second pour.

"Do you have a menu?" Helen asked.

"We do, this is the formal menu," he said, handing over two red leather-bound folders. "The bar snack menu and specials are on the blackboard above the fire mantle."

"Thank you," Helen said and headed over to a small circular table next to the fire, where Steve had taken their drinks.

Helen took a look around the room: dark stone floor, cream walls and ceiling, all intersectioned by wooden beams, a solid stone fireplace surround, blackened on all angles, with several large logs spitting away. The blackboard above the stone mantle listed all manner of bar snacks and specials; a number of local village and woodland scene paintings were on the walls, a few caricature pencil works of the landlord, the aforementioned dried hops ranging from a light lime to deep lemon in colour, a large selection of ceramic Toby jugs, brass and pewter tankards on shelves close to the ceiling, horseshoes, and brasses nailed onto the beams or hanging from leather straps.

The two took a sip of their drinks (well, Steve more of a large mouthful intake) and looked silently at the blackboard.

Steve felt his mouth watering and was suddenly very hungry.

The options were extensive, covering all tastes, and a number of items caught their eye:

- Homemade chicken liver pate with toasted homemade granary bread and caramelised onion marmalade
- Seared hand-dived scallops on a bed of pureed celeriac
- King prawns, shell off, baked in garlic butter
- Marinated anchovy fillets

For mains:
- Ten-ounce Aberdeen Angus burger with hand-cut step chips.
- Beer-battered whole tail scampi.
- Entrecote, Béarnaise sauce, and fries.

Helen went for the scampi tails, Steve the garlic prawns, on negotiation with Helen that she would also share the garlic, followed by the burger, to be cooked rare.

A young waitress/barmaid took their order. She was obviously Polish; even here in rural England, the hard-working Poles had infiltrated. Steve's eyes stayed on the waitress for a little longer than Helen liked, and she pinched his arm.

"Ouch, what was that for?" he pleaded in total innocence.

"You know, bastard," she said.

"Get the beers in," he said.

Helen stepped up to the bar and ordered another pilsner.

James's name never entered the conversation.

Joe and John Duke—
New York, Wednesday

John Duke from the New York Police Department sat looking at the two relics, Joe and the desk, silently waiting for Joe to finish what he was doing so he could talk through details concerning David Kettner. John had contacted Interpol and the Danish police to offer his assistance in their investigation.

Joe was still busying himself checking share movements on the screen. He peered over at John and wondered what the dollar buyoff amount was for this man. He could be bought, just like everybody else; it all came down to price.

There was a buzz and a light flickered on Joe's desk phone. He stabbed the flashing button, and his PA announced that Monica was on the phone.

"She says it's urgent, Joe," Linda said.

"God damn it," he muttered to himself.

Joe motioned John to leave the room and thanked him, saying it won't take a minute.

John took a seat just outside of Joe's office and pondered if Linda was related to his Jenifer.

Joe slugged the button. "Hi, it's me."

"Hi, darling," she oozed.

Jesus, what is she on? Joe mused to himself. "Where the fuck are you?"

"On the beach in the Virgin Islands" (she was actually in Bermuda but didn't want Joe to know that), "spending your money, darling."

Why had he given her all of those platinum cards? he thought. Then he realised what she had just said and snapped, "What do you mean in the God damn Virgin Islands spending my money?"

"Just check your bank accounts, darling," she said as the phone clicked off.

Joe frantically keyed in his account details and one by one saw that accounts had been closed, shares sold, and money transferred: London, the Caribbean, Lichtenstein, Switzerland, and Luxembourg, all empty. Monica had effectively cleared 50 per cent of his net worth.

Joe whelped liked a wounded hyena and his head hit the desk with a thump.

John and Linda rushed into the room, John lifting Joe's head from the table; Joe's face was contorted, as if he had been terrified to death. His heart had exploded, and he died on the spot.

John stole a quick look at the computer screen; just a screensaver. *What had that phone call been about?* he thought.

He stabbed at the phone and called 911 for an ambulance. He shouted out for help to the outside office: "Get some medical help. I called an ambulance." He rolled Joe onto the floor and started CPR. Linda just stood there, shaking, tears rolling down her reddened cheeks.

Monica—Bermuda, Wednesday

Monica toyed with the straw in her drink; she had no idea that Joe had dropped dead on the spot and she had just inherited his estate, but her half was already gone and hidden. The forensic experts would have no idea who had withdrawn the money, nor where it had ended up.

She had taken the girls out of school for a few days; they were playing on the pink sands of the beach in front of her. She didn't think Joe would dare come after her; the information she had gathered would ensure she and the girls were protected. She planned to leave it for a while before making Joe perfectly aware what information would be released to the authorities, if anything happened to her. She made sure to leave her registered cell phone at home.

She sipped at a strawberry daiquiri cocktail.

John Schroder—LA, Wednesday

The next morning, John rose early for his daily run and headed off into the Sierra Madre Mountains.

There were few others about, and he enjoyed this time of day to get his head together and think about the previous day at work, thus negating being distant at home with his wife.

The sun was just up, and John powered into the shrubbery wilderness that had become his home almost every morning for the last four years.

John noticed a burley, black-haired guy a little way down the trail but thought nothing of it.

A few minutes later, he was surprised that this overweight guy was just a few paces behind him on the narrow trail. John pulled over and said good morning as the man passed; he smiled and said good morning back. John couldn't place the accent.

John reengaged and put his head down, but as he came round the corner, he was felled with a karate chop that broke his collarbone; within seconds, he dropped like a stone two hundred and twenty feet to his death. He didn't have time to scream.

The guy with the black curly hair carried on down and was gone.

Melissa—Saturday

The sun was hot; Melissa stepped out of the large black Range Rover, her long yet-to-be tanned legs headed out first, led by patent red leather strapless heels, bought in Madrid. Her small white skirt flapped in the light breeze, and she pulled down her red, ruffled strapless top, exposing both her shoulders and midriff. Gone was the cool air con of the car, and the heat immediately took her breath away. The driver was busily collecting her luggage.

A tanned athlete of a man glided towards her, all smiles and arms extended. Melissa dropped her sunglasses into her bag and extended her arms; the two embraced and enjoyed a lingering kiss.

"I have missed you, my darling," Martinez oozed charmingly, his eyes searching into hers.

"Me you too," she said. "Copenhagen was so dour."

"I thought we had lost you," Martinez said, looking at her suspiciously.

"Never. It was so difficult to get away to a phone. David was there all of the time. I did make him wear his watch in Madrid and called my mother to let you know we were in Madrid, but I had no cell and was only able to get away once. David made sure I didn't keep any of the numbers on my old phone, and no, I hadn't memorised your cell phone number because it changes so many times a month."

"You could have called before you left," he said, his eyes narrowing.

"He didn't tell me anything," she lied. "I thought it was a short holiday."

Melissa had wanted to make sure she had the money, and perhaps Martinez was right; at that time, she wasn't too sure what else she wanted.

"Yes, yes, of course, it must have been difficult for you," Martinez replied, seeming to agree.

"Then I called my mother from Copenhagen, knowing that you would be listening again. That way, you knew we were in Denmark, and I once again made David wear his watch.

"I had no idea what was happening or how else to contact you," she added, "but I left the apartment, and there were two Russians outside, so I used my key to let them in via the elevator."

Melissa had known Martinez since she was eighteen. Life had been difficult, and she had turned a few tricks for wealthy clients in New York to supplement her income. On one of these occasions, she had been taken to a party in the Hamptons, just wealthy men and a load of hookers. Martinez had been the guest of honour and had taken her under his wing (as well as under the bed sheets).

When David had been turned, Martinez had ensured that the two would meet, and Melissa was tasked with keeping an eye on him. David was always a worry to Martinez, as he was so flaky and a major risk to their operation. Melissa had calmed him, but perhaps she had been the catalyst in his decision to abscond.

The Breitling watch David had been given carried a transmitter, but it was charged by the watch mechanism movement, and when he decided not to wear it, no signals were given out. It was also relatively short range, so the tracking device had to be within twenty-five miles. They had been unable to react to Madrid, but Melissa knew that and had been waiting for David to give her the money he had promised so many times. She could have called many times but waited until the day before the visit to the bank.

She was now wealthy in her own right, with an additional ten thousand Euros per month flowing from Switzerland for many years to come. David had only given Sergey his own Danske bank details.

Once Martinez knew where they were, he told Sergey, and his men tracked David through the signal emitted by the watch.

"Come, let's have some champagne and catch up," Martinez said, taking Melissa's hand in his.

Melissa smiled a nervous smile; there had been moments when she thought about staying with David and vanishing, but she knew in her heart of hearts that it would only be a matter of time before Martinez tracked them down. She also realised her mother and David's parents would be tortured and killed in the process.

"I have arranged a welcome-home party on the yacht for you later," he said.

Martinez had named his boat after Melissa, the *Assilem*; he had said at the time it was a true reflection of her: beautiful, sleek, perfectly proportioned, and powerful in spirit. Maybe he did care; Melissa loved him in her own way, and perhaps they could have a family life.

Hans—Saturday

Hans was heading home at last; he sat back into his first-class seat and sipped champagne as he laughed out loud, nearly uncontrollably. What a way to end the year; another $3.5 million in the bank, all expenses paid, and what fun. *But this is it,* he said to himself. *Time to get on with my life. I need to get back to being a human being. I cannot do this anymore.*

The 747 was taking him home, via Switzerland (he wanted to count his money, well, go through the necessary investment advice; he never invested in life insurance), and then on to JoBurg. He had missed his wife and boys; they were all named after one of the respective hits that Hans had completed just before their conception. A fitting epitaph, he thought; he laughed again and began to think which one of the names he was going to give to the next. Perhaps they would have triplets.

The stewardess looked at this gorgeous hunk chuckling to himself as the jet started its long haul across the Atlantic.

An hour into the flight the aircraft hit some severe turbulence, and the captain switched on the fasten seat belt sign. The whole experience was like being on a hurtling roller coaster, up and then dumped down, shunted side-by-side, passengers being driven out of their seats but saved by their restraints. Hans was gripping his hand rest; there was a woman crying somewhere in the back, and he was sure he heard someone praying.

The captain came on: "Hello, ladies and gentleman, there is a considerable storm brewing up ahead, and we will be seeking to divert around it, but in the meantime, please remain seated."

Some minutes later, the plane settled; the tumult of the last ten minutes faded, and the seat belt lights pinged off.

"Hello, it's the Captain again; we have rerouted and should now miss most of the unpleasantness caused by the weather."

A further hour into the flight, there was a loud bang, like a shotgun going off next to Hans's ears, followed by an explosive decompression as the air was sucked from the passenger compartment. There was nothing that could be done; the aircraft was lost. As the jet dipped, Hans suddenly realised that his bag must have been damaged in the hold during the turbulence; the chemicals must now have come together and caused an explosion, ripping a hole in the side of the fuselage.

The stewardess staggered across the cabin, and Hans jerked from his seat as the jet plummeted down into its death dive. Six minutes later, it left the radar screens.

NYPD/FBI/Fed

All of the departments and Bill had continued to work together tying up leads, calls, messages. They felt that they were just one step behind on everything again and again, but eventually, with the help of the bank's auditors, they discovered the insurance company set-ups, but Joe was dead, and there was not much more they could prove (not even the murders, given the accidental nature and circumstantial evidence).

With the help of Interpol, they had managed to get a list of people who had been in the same areas as the murdered bankers and were gradually interviewing as many people as they could. There were just too many, but Hans had been sidelined on the basis of his bona fide business trips.

Peter

Peter had made good money. The bank was abundantly aware that he had hidden and manipulated things, but they didn't want their shareholders to know this. Thus, he and Frank were just told to leave. Peter decided to retire and look after the kids and grandkids.

A year later, the division remained unsold, and the bank had provided for $427 million for losses.

Frank

Frank cashed in his shares and was wealthy, but Joe had taught him something: "You are never wealthy enough," and he now had a job as chief operating officer at one of America's huge car companies.

"Tell me," he asked of his new CEO, "what is the greatest challenge facing the company?"

"God damn pension costs," he replied, "and even worse are the rising costs of healthcare for our retired employees; they just seem to live longer and longer. It's the biggest cost allocation against every car that leaves our assembly lines. As bad as this sounds, if the average age of death fell by just one year, we would all make millions."

Frank smiled a contorted, wicked, yet knowing smile. "I'm really pleased to be on board," he said smugly. "I am sure I have the skill set required to drive down costs."

John Duke/Bill

John and Jenifer were out having dinner with Bill and Monica. Both were bronzed, having returned from a break in Cancun, Mexico. Having buried Joe, Monica had immediately set up home together with Bill. Joe Jnr was off to boarding school with the girls, enjoying the interaction with other kids and being captain of the tennis team.

John looked at Bill and Monica; what a beautiful sight. *They are in love*, he thought. Then it began to click into place; piece by piece, the puzzle unfolded. This is how Bill knew so much, so soon, and in so much detail. John smiled to himself and began a deep chuckle. Bill and Monica looked around and smiled knowingly.

Jenifer excused herself to head to the restroom.

"So tell me again, how was it that you found out about all of this?" John said asked.

"I don't think I ever did tell you," Bill replied, with a wry smile across his face. "Not sure I can quite recall now; just solid detective work. Happy to help you out with yours any time you like."

Monica had bugged Joe's home office, a sanctuary he always felt safe in, thinking he was taking calls from his mistress but had overheard plans for the terminations of Jack and James; regrettably, there was no other detail nor had there been any mention of the proposals for Todd and John Schroder. Even the recording of Joe, Peter, Frank, and Giuseppe discussing everything was deemed inconclusive evidence. Any defence would just say that Joe was discussing dismissing people for non-performance; no surnames or locations were detailed. It was Monica and Bill who had started to put two and two together. She also had the computers set up with tracking software and had been able to discover bank accounts and security passwords. She then had set up her own secret email account and had been sending Bill regular updates on her pay-as-you go BlackBerry.

Sergey

"We have a margin call on our fucking reinsurance company investment in Switzerland," reported Sergey's money man, who was standing next to one of their external financial advisors.

"What?" Sergey snapped. "You told me investing money in insurance was a no-brainer and would always make us fucking money; how much?"

The money man pushed the financial advisor forward. "You tell him," he growled.

"We invested in a specialist syndicate underwriting keyman insurance of professionals. All of the historic data was reviewed by our actuaries, and there's been a huge blip. We need another ten million dollars," he finished off shakily.

"Fucking keyman, actuaries, blip ... whoops," Sergey said as he pulled his gun and shot the advisor through the left eye, brain tissue and blood spraying up Sergey's arm and over the face of the money man.

Ironically, Sergey's execution of David, Martinez's killing JJ at Joe's request, and Hans's handiwork would cost him millions of dollars.

Hans

Upon notification of Hans's death, his lawyers informed Sabrina of the codes to access his Swiss bank accounts; no explanation other than a note from Hans:

"My darling Sabrina,

"I am so sorry that I can no longer be with you and my gorgeous family. You are my soul mate, and I hope to be with you in our next life. You have been the greatest wife and mother, and I have loved you with all my heart.

"There is money in Switzerland; it is hidden from the authorities.

"Until we meet again, my love. My love to the boys.

"Hans x"

There had been other notes to be released dependent on the nature of his death, explaining different scenarios.

If he had been exposed and Sabrina in danger, there were detailed instructions on how to disappear and protect the kids.

If killed by police while on a job, there was a note to explain (or try to explain) his darker side.

Luckily, Sabrina didn't need to know; the money would never replace Hans, and she thought it was just tax avoidance money, but wow, it was such a lot.

The lawyers also released files to the FBI and Interpol about the latest hits; these could not be traced back but implicated the agent who had passed on the details.

Hans always had these fail-safes in place just in case he was next on another hit man's list. However, no one knew who he was. The agent disappeared, and Joe was now dead but seemed complicit in the deaths because of the itinerary details sent to the agent. The insurance companies ended up doing a compromise deal with the bank; although they had details of the hits, there was no more backup. The note proved little but added more conjecture. There were no other details; the fingered agent had disappeared, and neither the insurance groups nor the bank wanted the negative publicity.

SEC/Fed

The SEC proved some insider trading on Joe's account and seized several million dollars from his estate, but that was that.

The Fed secured a fine against the bank for money laundering but only on a small scale. David, now dead, was blamed; no other individuals were indicted.

The Scattinis

There was little to implicate the main family in anything; historic paperwork had disappeared. Giuseppe, though, continued to be under investigation but ran a thriving perfume retail business in California, although he was seeking new banking facilities with some urgency.

Printed in the United States
By Bookmasters